EXPRESS DELIVERY

Esther Popkin-Clurman

To Irene, Dan and Gail

*Anyone who has a reason for living
endures almost any mode of life.*

—Nietzsche

PART ONE

1

February 2006

When one is young, a fall is just a fall, Edith Martin thought, as she watched a girl pick herself up and continue running. Edith moved from the large windows of the Co-op over to the bulletin board. Amid the jumble of notices posted, one stood out. The card was white, the block letters in red: EXPRESS DELIVERY. Edith stood looking at the card for several minutes, impressed by the neatness and design. The card had been carefully planned. She liked that; it showed a desire to make good, to provide a service. After a long hesitation, she took a small notebook from her purse and wrote the name and phone number. Quigley Biggs, an unusual name.

It was late February, 2006. Outside, the snow still piled up in front of curbs, blocking crossings. The pristine white first snowfalls had turned to an indeterminate brown, heavy with sand and gravel and whatever else the fumes of the cars contributed.

The Co-op was crowded–young people, old people, children, hippies beyond their youth from the Slocan Valley. She watched a small boy grab an orange from a fruit stand. The mother, dressed in long skirt, large wool scarf and sandals, took the fruit from his hand, and, in a soft voice, explained her action. The child lay down on the floor and began kicking the air and screaming at the top of his lungs. The mother lifted him, still screaming, and went to the checkout.

Edith shook her head. A good slap on his backside would get better results. She called a cab hoping that this driver would be nice, not one of the snarly ones.

Edith Martin's Victorian house was on a hill. It was not one of the classic gingerbread houses with extravagant ornamental structures—elaborate turrets, porticos, cupolas and gables—but the windows on the sloping roof, set within decorated dormers, and the small turret-like structure at the top gave a feeling of that time. The wrap-around porch, too, was a concession to function and a desire to evoke the past.

Edith sighed gratefully. Just seeing the house dispelled her fatigue. How she loved it. The house had always been her domain. Her kingdom. The long winding staircase would be waiting for her; the dining room with its large mahogany table and velvet drapes, the kitchen with its cupboards, counters, cutting boards. They were all worn, had lost their gleam and polish, the drapes faded but, thought Edith, like old friends, they are here for me. She smiled to herself again. The house understood that she, too, was old and worn. The house knew she could no longer keep it as spotless as before. Everyone had left. James had died, Tim, her only child, was somewhere in Africa, and Matthew, her grandson (Skye, he now called himself) meandered here and there and hardly knew her. But the house remained, faithful. The house would always be here for her. She liked to think the house greeted her as she entered. "Hello, you're back. I've missed you."

This time the cab driver was helpful, took the groceries into the house. Edith debated a moment, then gave him a tip, more than she had intended. She put the groceries away slowly—the carrots, onions, broccoli in the fridge, the special spelt bread in the freezer section. As she put the gelato—coffee this time—way back in the freezer, she held onto the counter for balance.

The phone rang as she was sitting down to dinner—homemade vegetable soup, a slice of the spelt bread, and yes, just a bit of that gelato. As she picked up the receiver, she remembered she hadn't had a chance to get the new Ekhart Tolle book from the library. Too many errands.

"Edith, I wonder if there's anything I can get you when I do my big shopping?" Adelaide McPherson asked.

"Thank you, Adelaide, but I have already been and gotten what I need." She could hardly tell Adelaide to change her shopping habits. Adelaide meant well but still kept to the foods she had loved as a child in Scotland—kippers and oatcakes and not a vegetable in the lot. Another thing, Adelaide was always thinking about ways to increase her meager pension, and would be sure to buy a lottery ticket. And, of course, she'll buy one for me too, Edith told herself, and I'll have to give her the five dollars, and that's money ill spent.

Mr. Godfrey was another kind person she had met at the senior centre before she stopped going. He was hail and hardy but hard of hearing, and, even if she wrote the items down, he was sure to lose the shopping list.

She decided to go to bed early. She'd had a long day and her arthritis was bothering her. She put her cane carefully in its special place. After she got into her nightgown, she let down her hair. Brushing it, seeing its greyness, her strong features softened as she reflected: seventy-eight and not in too bad a shape. The arthritis made getting around a nuisance–no doubt about that. Time she made things easier for herself. This Quigley Biggs–she'd written his number down. I'll all him tomorrow.

She thought of calling her dear friend, Leo. Leo, who raked the leaves, cleaned the gutters, did the house repairs. Leo, who loved the house too—as much as she did. She smiled. Her face looked different, her eyes charged with an odd luminosity as she thought of Leo. But then she remembered that he was very busy these days.

That night as she lay in bed, sleepless, her thoughts drifted back to when she had first met Leo.

"But where did you learn to put a splint on?" she had asked Leo. "And on a crow, of all things. It was as though you were a veterinarian."

"I went to medical school for a couple of years."

"Why did you stop?"

"I didn't want to dissect. After a while I was treating the digestive system, the heart; not the whole person. It was all memorizing, more and more, finding symptoms. And there never seemed to be the time to deal with the whole person"

Edith had become thoughtful. "You made a decision and stuck to it. I'm not good at that. I guess it's worked out OK for me but I wonder what I would do if I had to make a really shattering decision."

"I am sure you'd make the right decision, Edith." She had thought he was joking but strangely, Leo gave her that kind of confidence.

She shifted position in bed. She remembered saying to him, "You don't seem like a handyman." She had smiled. "Were you always fixing things around the house for your mother?"

Leo considered. "Not exactly," he had said after awhile, "it's more that I was taking care of her."

"Was she sick?"

"No, not really. Just that her life wasn't too easy. I guess that's why she got carried away by some of the old Hebraic legends."

Edith recalled that she had been curious. "What legends?" she had asked. A shaft of moonlight lit the wall and Edith could almost see Leo's face then—like a small boy caught unaware by a difficult question.

"Well, one legend especially," he had said after awhile, "An ancient Hebraic legend that says the world could not continue to live unless there are thirty-six men willing to take on its pain and suffering, they're called the *Lamed-Vov—the Just Men.*" He shook his head and smiled. "My mother was convinced I was one of the thirty-six."

"And are you, Leo?"

"Oh, come now, Edith," he had grinned. "It's all a myth anyway.'

"But my father didn't believe in legends. The Ten Commandments was enough for him. Of course, one might say that's a myth as well."

"And what do you believe, Leo?"

"I suppose I believe in individual conscience," Leo finally had said. "What about you, Edith?"

She remembered frowning. "All my life I've gone to the Anglican Church, sang the hymns, celebrated the birth of Jesus and never wondered about anything. But now I wonder, if Jesus was the Saviour, why is the world in such a terrible state—conflict and violence and...?"

She recalled that after that, they had discussed jobs to be done—the garden, the plantings along the driveway, the landing that led to the turret. But before he had left she said, "Tell me about The Just Men, who are they?"

"The Lam-ed Vov," Leo carefully pronounced each syllable.

4

"It's only a legend, Edith."

"But who are they?"

"They can be anyone. It's even possible a Just Man doesn't know he has been designated by God."

"Poor God," she said, "even He finds it hard to get good help."

Edith moved uneasily in her bed. Before drifting off to sleep, she recalled that Leo had said, jokingly, as he was leaving, "You know, Edith, my mother took that legend with her when she died." Leo had smiled tenderly. "'Never forget who you are, my son,'" she whispered at the end.

As her eyes closed, all she could think of was her own mother saying "Sit up straight, Edith."

* * *

A new client today. Quigley Biggs considered his appearance before he started on his day's work. His usually long and scraggly hair was presentable; he'd had it cut. Neat, he told himself although the color was still red.

He looked down. His jeans were okay–not worn or torn. He'd spent some time picking them out at the Salvation Army. His polo shirt was all right too—blue, the color of his jacket. His runners were not all beat-up and filthy. A streak of luck–the man bringing them in, didn't fit. And just when he needed them. Quigley nodded to himself; sure would be nice if he could change his appearance like that; big guys didn't have to work so hard for their money.

He sighed. He could tidy his hair, speak politely, pay strict attention to his clients' requests–two-percent milk, a liter not the big one; free-range eggs, not the other kind. He could provide satisfaction–Express Delivery–but he could not change his short height, his slight figure–as though a puff of wind might blow him away.

His father, a strapping man, his laugh more a blow, had called him Tiny Tim, but in a harsh voice that demanded how he could have begotten such a son. "But Quigley's a good worker. He's good at everything," his mother, who had given him his smallness and lightness, had said. And even though she'd died when he was a child, he could still hear her soft voice beseeching.

It was a toss of the coin—being born, Quigley thought, inheriting his mother's frail body instead of the big hardy body of his father. As though God was saying, "That's what I'm going to give you. Take it from there."

With a glance, he swept his small apartment—lights out, stove clear, everything in place. The hide-a-bed was neatly folded away. The sofa sagged, but he had gotten it cheap. He'd saved on the coffee table too—crates stacked together. Yet again he thought how good it would be to have a really nice place with nice furniture.

There were a few crumbs on the tiny kitchen floor. He picked them up and dropped them into the refuse bag. He closed the door and took out his list: Mrs. Norman first, pick up prescription at Excel Pharmacy; Mrs. Livingston, groceries at Safeway; Mrs. Martin was the last.

He went into the street, got into his little white Fiat, braced himself for the day. Satisfaction guaranteed. On time. Having to be polite, having to be calm when you didn't want to be, having to do what you didn't feel like doing. Money. Real money. You could do what you wanted when you had big money. You could do anything at all. You didn't have to bow and scrape.

He turned on the ignition. Express deliveries this time, he went on to himself, but it had always been some kind of service—Quigley's Handyman—Quigley's Repairs—Quigley's Pet Care.

* * *

The night before going to the bank, Edith talked to Teddy. Teddy was a plain old-fashioned bear with a button in its ear, made of mohair and quite worn. Every time she looked at the bear, she thought of Leo. He had found Teddy at a garage sale, given it to Edith as a present; he knew how much she'd liked Winnie the Pooh when Tim was a child.

Edith had started talking to the bear shortly after James had died when silence and loneliness, had gotten to her. Of course, the house was a friend and she often talked to the house itself, but more and more lately, the bear had become a companion.

"What do you think, Ted?" she asked. "It's such a chore to go to the bank. All the things I have to take—the safe deposit key, the bank card—and then to go early to get a parking place right there in

6

front. It's too hard."

Teddy gazed at her, deeply attentive. "Yes," he surely acquiesced. "This getting around is much too hard. Still, things have to be attended to."

"Well, food, shoes to be repaired–someone else can do those kinds of things."

"But not the bank." Teddy regarded her knowingly. She nodded in agreement, then put him back on his shelf. She'd get up early. She went over the steps again: key to the safe deposit, bank card in one pocket of her jacket; house and car keys in the other; all zipped up tight. No handbags. Old ladies with handbags were an easy target for the drug addicts.

Early the next morning, Edith parked her old Packard in the fifteen-minute space right in front of West Kootenay Bank. It was eight-thirty; the bank opened at nine-thirty. From this space she could round the corner, get off Baker street and onto Vernon where there was less traffic. She sat in her car and opened her book. *The Power of Now* by Ekhart Tolle. When the bank opened, Edith Martin was first in line.

Wondering if she shouldn't perhaps add the money from her husband's pension check and her old age check to the cash in the safe deposit box, she finally decided, not this time. Too bad she'd brought the key. Endorsing the checks, she dropped her cane. Mr. Filmore from Customer Service ran out of his office, picked it up and handed it to her. "We're going to be doing some renovations pretty soon," he said, "just to let you know." Then kidding around, "I guess banks, like us old people, need some repairing after a while."

The next morning Edith woke up drenched in perspiration, yet fearfully cold. She must have thrashed about because she wasn't as stiff as she usually was on awakening.

In the nightmare there had been–not a party–but some kind of gathering; people coming and going–many of them. Her son, Tim, was there too, to say farewell. She was to take a trip–an important journey.

She needed help, suggestions on what to take, arrangements for tickets. Go by plane? By ship? By rail?

Someone said, "internet. Get on the internet!" Another cried out, "Excelsior Voyages, that's your best site." Still another shouted,

"Top Notch Trips, that's the one I use." She tried to find her son, but he seemed to have disappeared. She was threading through the crowd looking for him, when suddenly—"Hi, mom," he said, coming up to her. "Tim," she said, "thank God you're here."

"I was looking at the film in the other room, about the worsening AIDS situation in Africa. You should see it, mom."

"I haven't time." She put her hand on his arm. She had to keep him there. "I need you to tell me, Tim; no one seems to know—where can I get the tickets? What do I pack? Clothing for cold weather? For hot? And how long does it take to get there?"

"I don't have that information," he said. "Listen, mom, it's all on the internet. You should have taken that course for seniors."

It was then Edith woke up.

* * *

Quigley Biggs parked his Fiat in front of Al's Auto Leasing on Front Street. Al was there, for which he was grateful; Jock, his assistant, was inclined to be moody, hard to deal with on his bad days.

"Hi, Wiggley," Al said. Ever since Quigley had let slip about his father calling him Wiggley, Al liked to tease him. "Hi, Al," he said, wishing, but not daring, to tell him to cut it out. He came to the point—Al didn't like beating around the bush—"I've got a favor to ask. A couple of my steady clients are away for the month so can I just hold off this payment?"

"No problem, Wiggley. You've always paid up. How's that new client of yours, Mrs. Martin? Her son used to lease from me—years ago—before he went to Africa on that AIDS program."

"She's a nice lady."

"A little off." Al touched a finger to his head in a good-natured way.

Quigley hesitated. For some reason of which he was unaware, he felt it necessary to correct Al. "Lonely. She's just lonely."

"See you, Wiggley."

Quigley nodded as he closed the door, careful to smile back. After all, he needed Al.

The weather was bright and sunny, not a typical March day. An azure sky capped Elephant Mountain. Below, the lake sparkled and glistened. The air felt fresh and new.

If only a person could start life all over–the way the sun comes up each day and the buds come out after the long dark winter. Not have to deal with teasers or cranks. He leaned his elbow on the steering wheel, sank his head into his hand: if only he could have another chance.

"I'm calling from Safeway, Mrs. Martin, to ask if halibut would be all right. It's just come in fresh and there's a sale on it. The sole doesn't look that good."

"Halibut is fine, Quigley. Not too big a piece." She was about to hang up, but didn't. "Thank you, Quigley," she added.

When Edith hung up, she had to sit down. The bank statement was on the table and she still hadn't decided whether she had too much money in the account; a safe deposit box was more secure, after all. But somehow her mind started to give way to a warm and wonderful feeling she couldn't quite understand.

She took Teddy down from his shelf and placed him beside her on the couch. "But Ted, all Quigley asked was if halibut would be all right."

Teddy's eyes looked deep into hers, reminding her: "But then, didn't he stop by at the library to pick up that book they were reserving?"

"So it's not just the service, Ted—he cares about me?"

She sat gazing at Teddy for confirmation and was rewarded. He was nodding his head.

* * *

During March fierce winds blew; Elephant Mountain was often covered by fog and the lake was grey. Edith longed for spring, for bright colors, for the dreary days to lighten. She kept thinking about the coming of Easter. Families would get together; there would be delicious aromas all through the house–turkey or ham, sweet potatoes, sprouts, a pie or two.

Living alone all these years, she had gotten out of the habit of cooking. A slice of toast, a bit of cheese, tea, sometimes an egg or a can of soup. She told herself old people did not need much food.

"They have lemon meringue pie on special," Quigley phoned

9

from Save-On Foods. "I know you like lemon, seeing how you have them on your list a lot."

"Oh, but Quigley, what would I do with a whole pie?"

"Perhaps you can have a friend to tea."

A friend to tea? Of course, Leo would be glad to come. But he had phoned only yesterday to say he had a big job in Balfour. Nonetheless, she found herself saying, "Do get the pie, Quigley."

When the doorbell rang, she was sitting down to tea–Red Rose this time, a tea bag–no sense in getting the pot down for one–and a slice of what was left of that old tea cake. Eating alone so many years, she had forgotten the taste of food. She got up, opened the door and there was Quigley with the groceries.

"Let me put this down for you, Mrs. Martin," he said, taking the bag of groceries and putting it on the counter, his small body moving quickly. "Oh, I'll get the lemon meringue. It's on the table outside."

She was about to tell him to take off his shoes, but she didn't.

As usual, as he was ready to leave, he doffed his cap. "Have I got everything on your list?"

"I don't have to check, Quigley." Then, more as an afterthought, "And please, you can call me Edith." She coughed–a slight cough.

"That cough–Edith–you should take care of it."

"Oh, just a bit of that old tea cake caught in my throat."

He turned to go. "I hope you and your friend enjoy the lemon meringue."

She tried not to cough again; it might worry him. She looked at his slight figure walking down to the street. Soon he would be getting into his car.

"Quigley," she called out. "Could you come to tea Sunday? We could have the lemon meringue."

He turned around. "I'd really like that." Even from the street, he could see her outstretched arm.

2

"Thank you so much for having me to tea, Mrs. Mar–Edith," Quigley said. "I thought you might like the paper." He handed her the Nelson Daily News, all rolled up.

"Just put it on that old recliner in the corner. I used to get it delivered, but no more. Nothing but bad news these days–the Middle East–terrorist attacks everywhere–Korea building nuclear... Come in, Quigley, and sit down. The table is all set. But what's this?"

A squat little animal with rabbit ears, short paws and curlicue tail was about to follow Quigley inside.

"Oh, that's Duck. He kept following me, so I finally took him home." He waved a hand at the dog. "Sit outside and wait for me."

"But—Duck?"

"He waddles." As Quigley spoke, Duck started out the door, his body swaying from side to side, tail spiraling down.

It was chilly. "Would you like me to start the fireplace?" Quigley asked. He had dressed for the occasion–nicely creased trousers, a new Salvation Army shirt.

"That would be nice. I haven't used the fireplace since Tim went to Africa."

They were sitting at the table, the lemon meringue on a china plate, a silver pie server beside it.

"I made a pot of Earl Grey; James, my husband, liked it best. I'm afraid it's only tea bags now."

Quigley wished she wouldn't apologize so much. He kept looking around. On the mantle were a couple of photos–an older man, with a rather stern expression. The other was a man about fifty or so, his own age, curly-headed and smiling. She followed his gaze. "My husband and my son. Of course those photos were taken a

11

while back. My husband's dead, and my son was younger then. He's fifty-one now."

"My age."

"I wouldn't have thought..." He seemed more like a sprightly elf, she told herself.

They ate silently, each feeling a little awkward. Edith enjoyed watching Quigley. He ate delicately. Good manners, she thought. James, her husband, had barely taken one bite before he took the next. Tim had been a hearty eater, but she didn't like to think about him; it just upset her, his being at the other end of the world.

The fire was going nicely, when they heard a plaintive "Woof, oooh woof" from outside the door.

"Duck probably wants some water," Quigley said, getting up.

This time from outside the door, Duck spoke again, but more urgently, like the beating of a drum–"Woof ah, woof ah, woof ah..."

Edith deliberated a moment. "It seems Duck would like to join us."

"That's very kind of you."

"You'll have to wipe his paws."

"Of course."

Quigley opened the door. Duck came in, scanned the room, then waddled purposefully to the Nelson Daily News which lay, still rolled up, on the old recliner. The dog surveyed the newspaper from all sides, measured its distance from the floor with slide-rule eyes, then waddled to the sofa. With one front paw, then the other, he probed the pillows. Finally satisfied, he took a couple of plump cushions in his mouth, one after the other, and dropped them in front of the recliner. With his two front paws he went up and down the pillows several times, then, with an extraordinary leap, seized the rolled-up paper in his mouth and laid it at Edith's feet.

"Duck only brings things to a friend," Quigley remarked.

All this time Edith had been observing Duck. She could not make out the dog. Strange, like his owner, she thought. Nothing like her old faithful dog, Rover, who had died years back.

Duck tapped the newspaper briskly with a paw.

"He wants you to read it."

She picked up the paper and unrolled it. "Another school massacre in the States," she said, shaking her head. "LOCAL WOMAN SUCCUMBS AFTER SCAM." Her eyes raced down the column. "Why, it's Adelaide McPherson!" she cried.

"Do you know her? What do they say?"

"Story continued on page three." Quickly, she thumbed through the pages. "One of those scams. A Ponzi Scam. A friend had talked her into investing. Adelaide lost her savings." She dropped the paper and sighed deeply. "I only talked to her a week or two ago. And now she's dead. It was too much for her. She had a heart attack."

Dusk was coming on as Quigley left. "Come on, Duck," he said. The dog was gazing at Edith with swimming eyes. "Duck's really taken to you," he went on, then, "I suppose your son will be having Easter with you. You mentioned he might possibly get to Canada for some holiday time with you."

"I'm hoping he can. It's been a few years since he's managed to get back to Canada. Africa is so far away and the AIDS crisis keeps getting worse and worse."

Quigley opened the door. "Well, you have a Happy Easter, Mrs.–that is, Edith. Let's go, Duck."

That night Edith couldn't fall asleep. The suicide bombings and bloody conflicts round the world were terrible but they were far away. Adelaide McPherson was right here in Nelson, someone she knew, and Adelaide had been the victim of a scam. Although Edith was critical of get-rich-quick schemes, now she found herself forgiving Adelaide for falling for the scam: after all, she was only trying to increase her tiny pension.

"Money," she told Teddy, as she took him down from his shelf, "that's what made her fall for that scam. And who can blame her, Ted? What else do you have if you're old and alone in a world gone mad?"

Outside the dark windows, a steady drizzle. Inside, all was quiet. Her fingers sought the pad of his paw. She kneaded it, stroked it, trying to find comfort in its velvety softness, but now, with chilling revelation, she understood what she had been able to deny before.

"You're only a stuffed animal." Her words came slowly, her heart dragging them down. She felt herself encased in a block of ice, like a fly trapped inside a lucite cube–cocktail novelties in the fifties.

If Tim were here, everything would be different. Tim, big and strong. He had been gone a long time. Too long. The image of her son stayed–tall, powerful, like the figurehead on the prow of a ship. Tim could protect her, as her husband had protected her. He'd written some time ago–a note really–*Maybe I can get back for Easter, but it's doubtful.* He would be going to a small village–no phones, primitive, isolated–in one of those African countries. He would be caring for orphans whose parents had died of AIDS. Edith tried not to think about the letter, but the thought wouldn't go away.

Other thoughts kept coming. By the time dawn lightened the window, a stony determination had chased away her loneliness. She'd see about her will. Tim was her son, but what kind of son was he– caring for everyone but his mother. To give him a last chance, she made a wager with herself: if he calls, if he gets back, even for a bit, I'll leave the will as it is–for Tim. But if he doesn't, I'll call Alfred. She could see the letters on the office door: *A. Seaman, Attorney At Law.* Different than her husband in certain ways: James had tended to a nice dark suit, a waistcoat, a proper tie, but Alfred had always been a regular Beau Brummell with his silk foulards and custom-made suits. She went on to herself: he likes things too–Alfred does, always did– Jaguars and such. She wondered about that, as she had wondered about the trips he and her husband had taken together. "Why can't I go?" she had asked James, but, "It's business," he had said. Well, James is dead, she reminded herself. She had to rely on Alfred. "A good friend and a good lawyer," James had said.

3

Quigley delivered the ham and two more cartons of Breyer's ice cream to Mrs. Livingwell. He had delivered a turkey and a carton of ice cream only a couple of days before. The long driveway to her house worried him; everything seemed to worry him these days. Al was being downright nasty: "Business is business, Wiggley." The problem was there was no business —or very little. He had the feeling of just about everything starting to close in on him. He made an effort to arrange his face in a smile when Mrs. Livingwell came to the door.

"You have a lot of people for Easter," he said.

"Oh, my sister and her brood decided to come at the last minute, and they prefer ham, and her kids (spoiled brats) all want different flavors of ice-cream."

It was his last delivery of the day. He hadn't had a chance to eat. He'd grab a bite at the mall. He got into the Fiat. "Let's go, Duck," he said, pushing him over from the driver's seat. Duck didn't budge. Finally, Quigley took him up and put the dog in the passenger seat.

At the mall, he left Duck outside, beside a small carton where he placed a few of his toys and some doggie treats. "Look," he said, "I can't take you inside, but I'll try not to be long, so just amuse yourself as best you can." Duck stood on his hind legs and saluted.

Inside the mall, Quigley decided his hunger would have to wait. The damn faucets in his kitchen were leaking again; he'd have to get new washers. And the windows—never had shut right–he'd have to get some weather stripping. His less-than movie star jaw tightened: apartment falling apart, the whole damn house falling apart. He got what he needed at Wal-Mart and started down the mall for A&W at the other end.

Coles Books had a few display tables outside: *Chicken Soup for the Christian Soul–for the Teenage Soul–for the Mother's Soul.* Mother's Day; May. Next month. Vaguely, almost as in a dream, Quigley saw himself, a tiny boy, clutching a bouquet, handing it to the frail woman who was his mother.

He passed by the next table: *Philosophy for Dummies–Computers for Dummies–Real Estate for Dummies.* He was about to go on, when he saw a crowd standing before a large table. He made his way through the crowd. The table was filled with hardcover books, all bearing the same title: *The Secret.* He picked one up and opened it at random. Something about a law of attraction. You think real hard about what you want to attract. And then, you put it out.

He closed the book, his face set in determination: "I'm putting it out to you," he said, "whoever you are. Money. I want to attract money!" He must have said it aloud, for a couple of people next to him edged cautiously away.

Really hungry now, he walked rapidly down the mall, passed Healthy Living, the Body Shop, F.B. Insurance, Shopper's Drugs, Victoria's Secrets, Mariposa. A couple of stores had closed. At the other end of the mall, Save-On Foods was having a case lot sale. He made his way through a couple dozen cartons: cans of tomato soup, packages of noodles, boxes of macaroni and cheese…

There were several people in line at A&W: a special on Papa burgers. He ordered one and the large root beer then looked for a table. One near the window, where he could look out. As he ate, he thought about eating here Easter Day. They'd be open, they always were, and it was cheap.

But he didn't want to be here. Not in this place. Not at Easter. There'd be some people sitting around–old usually–lonely, with no families waiting for them, with no money to go anywhere but their lonely rooms.

He took another bite of the Papa burger, a long sip of root beer. He looked out the window. A shiny Cadillac and a rusty pick-up were trying to get into the same parking spot. He watched as, with one deft turn, the Cadillac swung into the spot. He waited for something to happen. A fight, maybe. But the pick-up was moving away looking for another spot. That Cadillac, he told himself, must cost forty, fifty thousand. There it was. Money. If you had it, you could get away with anything.

A strange sound that he couldn't make out. When he looked

up he saw why: a woman–not young but not old either–was eating and crying at the same time. He watched her take a bite of her Mama burger, start chewing, then crying, and finally begin to choke. She did the same thing with the fries–dipping one into the gravy, chewing, crying, then choking.

Finally, Quigley got up and went over to her. "Are you okay?"

She looked up. Her brassy hair was tangled about her round face, which had gravy and catsup all over, so that it looked like one of the paint-yourself jobs children did at fairs. On her left cheek a dimple began to appear, as she tried to smile: "Yeah, I'm all right." But then, "No, I'm not, I'm miserable," she went on, and the dimple retreated.

He had no idea what to do. He couldn't tell her to be happy when clearly she was not. She was looking at him intently. "You're the guy does those express deliveries," she said after a while. "I've seen you around. Are you on a break?" He told her he was through for the day. "Can you listen? If I can't talk, I'll keep on eating," she said and took another bite.

He sat down. Now that he could see her close up, he was aware of lines around her eyes, which were an innocent blue. She was in her forties, he figured, though these days you never knew.

"Talk away," he said, and thought, better than going back to that crummy apartment. "I'm Quigley Biggs."

"Me, I'm Sidonia Grout. Pleased to meetcha." She laughed. "Some names we got." She took one of the fries, was about to dip it into the gravy but put it down. Her dimple went flat: "It's Leopold; we've broken up. We were near the top of Pulpit Rock and you know how it's all rocky, and like–I was really wiped out, so I said we should go back. And Leopold–his name was Leonardo but he changed it to Leopold on account of all the Prussian Generals were called 'Leopold this' or 'Leopold that'–he said he'd had it with me, that if I wasn't so fat, I wouldn't be such a spoil sport."

She stopped and drew herself up. Quigley realized for the first time that she was rather plump. She took another bite of her Mama burger. "You know, they don't make these burgers the way they used to, like, they skimp on everything, that's how it is these days."

"What did you do?"

"I climbed down."

"By yourself?"

"Yeah."

She lowered her eyes. When she looked up they were full of tears–"Like, I called him later to say maybe we could be friends, but he said we couldn't. He said I wasn't what he wanted–like that time I said I didn't like my name, and he said all I had to do was change it. 'You can make it Sylvia Swan,' he said, but then he said no, I couldn't 'cause I'd have to look like a Sylvia Swan and I didn't."

Quigley waited. After a long moment, Sidonia went on. "Well, ya live an' ya learn. He said he'd really miss me, though–like, in bed, you know, I wasn't like all those other prissy women." Her face brightened; the dimple re-appeared. "I think I'll have a chocolate malt." She leaned forward giggling: "When I came in there was this little dog lapping up a chocolate malt a little girl was feeding him."

"Oh my gosh, that's my dog! Please don't go, Sidonia, I'll be right back." He raced out, seeking the place he had left Duck. The dog was standing on his hind paws, his front paws kneading the air. In front of him stood a line of children. As Quigley approached, a small boy was putting a large chunk of popcorn chicken into Duck's open mouth. The girl next in line was holding a half-eaten burger, and the one after, a bag of fries. In the carton beside Duck was a hodgepodge of pretzels, peanuts, trail mix…

Quigley picked Duck up, raced to the Fiat and put him inside leaving the windows half-open. "I can just imagine what your b.m.'s are going to be like. You stay here." Running all the way, he raced back to A&W. Would Sidonia still be there?

"I'm sorry I was so long. Thanks for waiting."

"I couldn't leave. Here I've been talkin' 'bout myself and, like, I know nothing 'bout you but your name. Are you married by chance?" He said he wasn't. Almost, he could have said, but it hadn't worked out. Violet had been her name. But their romance had wilted as fast as it had blossomed, like her flowery name.

"Nothing much to tell. Been doing this and that trying to get by. This Express Delivery was going pretty good but it has kind of slowed down. One of my regulars, though, is real nice. I feel kind of sorry for her all alone in that old house, son off in Africa helping those AIDS kids." He wondered if her son would be coming home for Easter. "Look," he said impetuously, "are you doing anything for

Easter? Maybe we could have dinner together."

"Gosh, Quigley, I'd love to but I have to go up to Nova Scotia. My sister is having another kid, her fifth, and I have to help. But hey, look, maybe I'll give you a call when I get back, maybe I'll need an express delivery, you never know."

As he put the new washers in the leaky faucets that night, he realized he didn't have Sidonia's phone number. Would she be in the phone book? Then he decided it was just as well; he had given up that kind of thing–ever since Violet. People said you couldn't, that it was nature–a man needing a woman–but he knew you could. After all, he'd met Violet when he was twenty-five…and after that, relationships were on and off…but mostly off.

* * *

"Do you need something delivered?" Quigley asked. It was four in the afternoon and he was on his way home when his cell phone rang.

"It's just that I'm going to Nova Scotia like I told you in a couple of days, and, like, I want to see you again before I leave, so can you come over this evening, so we can, like, talk some more, 'cause I feel so good talking to you?" She went on: she'd come to his place–wherever that was–only there was the packing and all that stuff to do before she left.

The rain was pouring down when Quigley got to her basement room. He wasn't sure why he was there. Maybe because in all his life he'd never met anyone quite like Sidonia. There was always some reason why he had to be on guard–keep up with the latest scores for hockey or soccer was one. It was different with women. A careless motion, a chance remark, anything, might show him up for a lack of manliness–as his father had called his small boy's tears.

When Quigley walked down the steps to Sidonia's apartment, he was thinking, with astonishment, of how she'd asked him to come: "'Cause I feel so good talking to you." He could not remember anyone saying that to him. Certainly not Violet. "Let's not talk about it," she'd said time and again, widening the space between them, until there was no way to span the distance.

He knocked on the door. "It's you," Sidonia said. Quigley had that feeling of happiness again. She was glad to see him. It was the

19

way she said it, her whole body saying it too—the dimple coming out of hiding, her round face glowing.

The basement apartment was more like a room. It had one small window, a ragged window shade hanging halfway down. There was a bed with clothes on it, a chest of drawers, all opened, a lamp with a faded shade. Sidonia was in baggy pants and a T-shirt. She had been packing.

"Do you believe in God?" she asked. He said he never thought about stuff like that. "Well I do," she said. "Like you turning up when I needed someone so bad. I think God's saying, 'Hang on there, Sid'—He calls me that—'it's all going to come out roses for you.'"

She sat down on the bed, brushing aside some clothes, and made a place for him. She turned to him. The little creases around her eyes were deeper than they'd been in A&W. "Things have been tough for you," he said, "Leopold…" She said Leopold was only the last. "What do you mean—the last?" He wasn't sure he wanted to know.

She sighed: "I just want things to be, like, you know, nice. That's all I ever wanted, but things kept going wrong. My father died when I was a kid, and my mother, like, she got a tenant. I guess she needed the money, and then he became her boyfriend. I'm not blaming her, she had a couple of kids to bring up. And she got a job too—in a factory, three nights a week—'cause the boyfriend worked days in some kind of factory too. This boyfriend would come to me nights when she was working. He'd put his finger on my lips and, you know…"

"Where was your sister?" Because his sense of outrage was so fierce, the only thing Quigley could do was to take her hand.

"She was only a little kid—she was fast asleep. I tried to tell my mother but she didn't believe me."

Outside, a teeming rain was splashing the small window and hammering the refuse cans. The light went out. Sidonia rested her head against Quigley's side, as though the effort to talk was too much for her. He waited, feeling bad for her

"So I left the moment I could. Went off with Bobby, and then there were the others…" in the dark, her voice was faint, "…and always the same, nice to me at first, and then…Leopold was the last. You know about him."

20

"But why—why keep on with these men who hurt you?" He found himself cradling her head.

"I don't know. Maybe I got in the habit of being hurt. But I don't want it anymore, I'm tired of all that. You would never hurt me, would you, Quigley? Oh, I'm talking too much. Tell me about yourself."

"Not much to tell."

"Everyone's got something to tell. You've done things for people—all those services."

"Little services. My father didn't think I would amount to much. I guess he was right. My mother, she tried—but then, she died when I was so young. It's like you said—you get in the habit of being a certain way; you forget the person you could have been."

"Yeah, that's how it is, and you worry 'bout getting along and you scramble and scramble to keep goin', like that fly there—in that bowl—look at it—poor thing."

He looked. The fly was going round and round trying to get out. Trapped, he thought—the way we are, the two of us. Her hand still lay lightly on his. He enclosed it, felt its warmth. "Quiggy," she said, looking up at him, "I feel so safe with you." He could feel the roll of fat round her belly as she pressed close to him. Then, she raised her lips to his.

Outside, the rain had turned into a storm and was falling in torrents. In the turgid sky, lightning flashed through the black swollen clouds. The lone tree on the street shook and quivered under the driving wind.

Quigley and Sidonia made love through it all, clothes strewn about them, pillows fallen to the floor, the suitcase overturned. For a long while afterwards, they lay silently side by side.

Then Quigley said, "Did it matter?"

"Did what matter?"

"My being—you know—small—inside you." In his history with women, and especially with Violet, it had mattered, and trying to make up for this deficit had called for ever-new ways and devices on his part, including a plain brown parcel—Fantastic Toys on the return address—containing the French ticklers. And even those hadn't worked for Violet.

But Sidonia was saying that kinda thing didn't matter to her. "You and me—we were great. You knew that, didn't you?"

"Yeah, I knew." He felt happy in a way he couldn't remember feeling for a long long time. They were friends, they could tell each other everything–without the need for caution, without pretending.

"Don't you hate it–the world hangin' over you like some kind of monster?" Her eye had returned to the bowl with the fly. "It's not there. It must have given up; probably lying on the bottom, dead."

He kissed her hair. "We're not flies."

"I don' know. Sometimes I think we're–not flies but like–just going round and round getting nowhere. Wouldn't it be wonderful if we could go away together–you and me–and not have to think about anything but being happy?"

The storm had stopped. The light came on. "I better get going," Quigley said, "you have to be up early." He began putting on his pants. "Anyway, you can't live on happiness."

She sat up, leaned on her elbow, gazed at him. "I keep tryin' to figure things out, but there's always something missing."

He was dressed now. He bent down to put on his shoes, and an extraordinary sensation came over him: he felt himself taller.

"Money," he said. "Real money, not bits and pieces of it, not scrounging for it like rats. Like you're dying of thirst, and then you get all this water and you can drink and drink and drink."

She got out of bed and kissed him: "You're not going to play the lottery?" He shook his head. "Good," she said. "It's just another scam. I'll see you after Easter." She stood there, looking like a Kewpie doll. My friend, he thought, and the warm feeling softened his tiredness.

Duck had been sleeping. He jumped off the bed when Quigley got home, got his leash and brought it over. That's when it hit Quigley. Still another problem. He had to be away after Easter–a delivery in Trail–just a couple of days but he couldn't take Duck. He wanted to get back, get to sleep, but Duck had to lift a leg at every hydrant, every tree, every trashcan. Still, when he was in bed, Quigley couldn't sleep. There was talk of this old house being demolished to make way for a condominium, and then, what would he do? Rents were sky high. His business had fallen off with the coming of spring; people getting around more.

It wasn't only himself he had to think about—Sidonia needed his protection. It was near dawn when he finally fell asleep.

Duck was sleeping beside him, when the phone wakened him. Ten o'clock! He picked up the receiver.

"Quigley, can you come to Easter dinner?" Edith Martin asked. She sounded eager. "I'll give you a list of what to get."

"Thank you, Edith. I'd like very much to come." He tried not to let his excitement show, to say the words politely, but that son of hers isn't coming back for Easter, he thought, and somehow—he wasn't sure why—he liked the idea of her being alone.

4

The mahogany dining table was covered with a white embroidered cloth. "I did it myself," Edith said, "the embroidery. Still do it, keeps me going. Sit down, Quigley."

He sat down. He had dressed carefully–pants pressed, shirt instead of a polo, his hair cut and smoothed with Tio's Hair Tamer.

On the table was half a ham, a casserole of sweet potatoes, another of brussel sprouts and squash, a pitcher of apple cider. Quigley thought of A&W and how it would look today. Bleak, forlorn, like the losers sitting around, dragging out their hamburger and fries, getting another cup of coffee.

"Holidays..." Edith began, then stopped. "Help yourself, Quigley," she said instead. "I like to watch a man eat." She was dressed in her holiday dress–a blue shiny material with a detachable lace collar she had made herself. Her hair was in a chignon. He could see she'd put some powder on her cheeks, some rouge too. Just a touch, but old ladies shouldn't wear make-up, he thought.

He was careful not to eat too much and was glad he hadn't for she said, even as they ate, "It's nice to have leftovers. I..." He thought she was going to say she couldn't do much cooking anymore, but she said, "I don't do much cooking these days."

They ate in silence, each unsure of what to say. He wondered what Sidonia was doing up in Nova Scotia. Sidonia, he thought softly.

"We could have the radio," Edith said, after a while. "My husband used to like some music while he ate. But these days, it's more noise than music. There's that nice station–plays all those old time songs–but you have to have cable to get it." Her mouth tightened. "Everywhere you go, they're out for your money." Quickly, she added, "And I've little enough of that."

Tight, that's what she is, Quigley thought. Indicating the china cabinet, he said, "That's a nice piece of furniture."

24

"My husband found it. He had an eye for good furniture. Of course I don't use all that," nodding toward the sets of china, platters, glassware of every description, dusty with time. "But I like to keep it." She paused. "For memories." She followed Quigley's eyes to the large bookcase whose shelves were filled with vintage books. Fronting the books on the shelves were miniatures of every kind of classic car.

"Quigley, would you mind getting my scarf, it's in the bedroom." He went up the stairs. "The first right at the top of the stairs," she called out. The scarf was laid on top of the large bed. There were two massive mahogany chests, their tops littered with a variety of creams and lotions. Surreptitiously, he opened one drawer after another. They were jam-packed with old underwear, socks, pajamas, shirts and other men's garments.

"Ah, have you found the scarf, Quigley?" she called.

"Coming." But, before leaving the room, he looked quickly in the big closet. It was a massive disarray, cluttered with hat boxes, shoe boxes and a small chest. In between the boxes on the shelves and floor hung a number of out-dated men's suits and several georgette and muslin de soie evening gowns. As he raced down the stairs, his thoughts raced with him: endless places to hide things in this old house. Money—old people hid money away. But she keeps it in a safe deposit, he went on to himself, against his will. How could he even think like that. They're just thoughts now, Sidonia would say.

He placed the cashmere scarf around her shoulders, careful not to disturb the Medi-Alert button around her neck. She lifted her eyes to his. "Thank you, Quigley," she said, then, "what took you so long?" He said, apologetically, he'd had to use the bathroom, and was that all right. She found herself saying that was just fine.

When they finished dinner, Edith brought out the apple pie. "My treat," Quigley had told her. She said, "Ah, Quigley, I used to make these myself, once upon a time."

"Okay, Duck, you can come out from under the table now," he said. Duck waddled out. Edith looked under the tablecloth. "Clean as a whistle," she said. "He's eaten everything we dropped." Quigley wondered—she sounded pleased. "Is it all right?" he asked. "I mean—Duck being so naughty." But Edith seemed to be back in time: "How Rover would have liked Duck," she murmured, "Rover, my old dog. What a pair they would have made—Rover being so serious and cautious, and this little rascal Duck with all his tricks and pranks."

Quigley couldn't help a feeling of respect. Some old people would never put up with Duck. "I admire this old house, they don't build them like this anymore. They keep renovating these heritage houses. And your house has been so well-maintained."

"My Widow's Pension and Old Age Pension can no longer sustain the house," Edith said. "Quigley, have you heard anything about the mix-up at the bank?"

"You mean when they were renovating?" She nodded yes. "The computers are okay again, but there's some mix-up with the vaults."

"The vaults!"

"You know—the safe deposit boxes."

"What kind of mix-up?"

"Don't know, it's Easter and the banks are closed but they're working on it."

Edith told herself not to get all excited, there was nothing she could do today. As soon as she could, though, she'd get to the bank. She had to.

"Are you going so soon, Quigley?"

"Have to pick up a delivery at Greyhound and it closes in an hour. Thanks, Edith. Thanks for the dinner."

"It made my Easter, you being here." They were at the door. She gazed into his face intently. "You make me think of Tim."

"Your son? But I don't look like him, do I?"

"No, big and strapping—that's Tim, like his father. You're fifty-one, aren't you?" Quigley nodded. And not much to show for it, he thought. "Yes, that's it, I guess." Then, as though she knew what Quigley was wondering, "He's in Africa, you know, doing work with those AIDS people, Planet Health."

"You must be proud of him."

"Oh yes," she said without conviction.

Duck was waiting at the door. Quigley turned to Edith.

"Would you mind having Duck here just while I get the package from Greyhound?" he asked. She looks different, he thought, and then he knew why. It was the mix-up at the bank, that stuff about the vaults. The lines seemed to drag down her face. She's upset.

He had no sooner closed the door when the phone rang. It's

26

Tim, she told herself, somehow he's managed to get to a phone; full of hope, she picked up the receiver.

"Uneedit Marketing is conducting a research poll, Mrs. Martin. We would like to ask you a few—"

With all the strength she could muster, Edith slammed down the receiver. It was not Tim. He would not phone, even now, at Easter. She would do it. Tomorrow—no, not tomorrow, Alfred was away on one of his gambling jaunts. He'd be back in a couple of days. She'd go to his office. I'll tell him I want to change my will again. Not Tim. Tim had had his chance. She thought wildly –those poor little animals, cast away, unwanted–they had a right to life too.

The phone rang again. She couldn't get to the phone quick enough: It *is* Tim. He's managed to call his mother after all. She picked up the receiver. "How dare you hang up on me!" came the voice of that market research woman. Holding onto the counter–her arthritis was bothering her–Edith said she was sorry and proceeded to answer a list of questions. Pearly Whites Toothpaste. Tastefree N'Ice Cream. In a hurry to get rid of the woman, Edith said she would buy them all.

Shaking, she turned to go to the kitchen. She must give Duck some water. She put her foot out and, knowing what was about to happen, seeing her body twist for lack of balance, she could do nothing about it–and fell. Her whole right side hurt. She could not get up. "Duck," she called feebly, but Duck was already at her side, his nose nudging her, his paws all over her, and, in his frantic attempt to stir her into motion, stepping upon her Medi-Alert button.

* * *

Quigley was on his way back from the Greyhound depot to pick up Duck, when he heard the siren. He pulled over. After the ambulance passed, he drove on. Only when he turned onto Latimer did he realize where the ambulance was headed. To Edith Martin's house.

5

After Edith's fall, Quigley's days changed. There was no next of kin–or at least none available—so the social worker at the hospital called Quigley. That was what Edith told him; he was inclined to think that it was she who had given his name. It was a curious coincidence. It seemed to him that just when things were going from bad to worse for him in every way–Express Delivery business practically non-existent since the spring weather; the notice that his apartment had to be vacated; the building was to be demolished to make way for a condominium–Edith Martin had a pressing need for his services.

So he took her home from the hospital. It wasn't easy maneuvering her into his Fiat, but she didn't complain. She seemed, he thought, very quiet, as though she were hatching some plan. "Are you okay?" he asked, when, painstakingly, he managed to get her up the steps to her house. Her right dislocated shoulder had been fixed, but the arm was still in a sling. As for the internal bruising of her right knee, it would just take time, according to the doctor.

"I want to pay you for your services," she said, and, reaching into a drawer in the kitchen, she took out a twenty-dollar bill and handed it to him. He remarked the way she managed, using her left hand to open the drawer, while she leaned against the counter. When she went into the living room, she frowned in concentration as she put her weight on the foot without the badly bruised knee, even as she held the cane in her left hand.

Determined, he told himself; the way she was using her left hand and leg–when she was a righty. He took the twenty, thinking it was damn little for all he'd done. She knew it too, of course. A taxi and all the help he'd given would cost her four times the amount. Well, still, she was going to need help. He thanked her and decided not to say anything.

"Will you be all right?" he asked.

"Of course I'll be all right." Her angular face tightened; she almost glared at him. Then, remembering something, she changed her tone and her face attempted a smile. "There's an errand I need to do tomorrow." She sat down on the couch in the living room, the cane beside her. She said the words casually, but her hand was nervously fingering the cushion beside her.

"I'm seeing my girlfriend tomorrow. We've got to look for some work."

"Work? What do you mean—work? You've got a delivery service."

"I used to have. Not too many clients these days, not since the good weather; in fact, only a few."

She was looking down at her feet. Her right leg was carefully extended. "Girlfriend? What's her name?" Sidonia Grout, he told her. She shook her head: "What does she do?" He said that right now she was in the kitchen of Bottom's Bar washing dishes.

Then, before he could think about it, "You're going to need help," he said. "We could be a couple–Sidonia in the kitchen and housework–stuff like that–and I could take you where you need to go and be your handyman—"

At that last word, Edith flinched. Right when she had fallen, she had thought of calling Leo, handyman to everyone but a dear friend to her, first and foremost. But Leo was in Creston on a special job that meant a lot to him and she certainly didn't want to make him feel he would have to leave it. She looked at Quigley. "Live here? Is that what you're saying? Free rent and food too, maybe?"

He said they'd want to be paid, but of course, if they could have maybe that little room and bath upstairs and use the kitchen, well, they would take that into consideration. It could be worked out, he added. Even then, an idea was forming. She was old and not well, and what with the fall, she couldn't go on forever. It would mean some compromises, adjustments, but it was better than nothing, and right now, nothing was what he and Sidonia had.

"I don't know." Edith got up, dismissing with a wave of her hand Quigley's offer. "I'm tired. I think I'll get ready for bed."

"I'll make you a sandwich. There's the cheese and bread I got before I went to the hospital to take you home."

"Just leave it on the counter." She was walking toward the

kitchen. "Tomorrow, then, tell your girlfriend you've got something to do tomorrow. Early–nine-thirty—when it opens."

"What opens?"

"The bank."

"Nine-thirty."

"You won't bring Duck. Where is he, anyway? Silly animal."

"He's with my girlfriend."

In the end, it always came down to that–people being nice, then everything coming apart, Quigley thought as he lay in bed. Like now.

This change in her–paranoid–that's what she's getting to be. He put it down to the shock of the fall. No, the fall had only scared her more; it was that mix-up at the bank, the bank manager telling her that her vault had been closed, and she, fainting. That had only been for a minute, he remembered. Then, she'd drawn herself up, like some dragon–he almost expected to see smoke coming out her nostrils. She'd shown her key and asked for the President of the bank. She'd had everyone at her feet, and, in the end, she'd made them find her vault. "Nothing's safe anymore," she had said. "Nothing."

He knew what she was going to do at the bank tomorrow. All that money, he told himself resentfully; no damn family—and she can't give Sid and me a little help. And not really help, for wouldn't they be helping her?

* * *

Bottom's Bar was a few blocks from the Orange Bridge. Quigley parked the Fiat in front, wondering when he'd finally have to just give it up. Al was being real nasty. "There's a limit to being nice, Wiggley. Business is business. I can't carry you forever."

It wasn't forever–although, he thought as he pushed open the door and entered the darkness, if things didn't change...

"Haven't seen you in a while," said Bottom. "Business keeping you busy?" Quigley said, "What business?" He sat down at the bar and ordered a double scotch. He hadn't been in a bar for months. Maybe it was Sidonia working in the kitchen–yeah, that was the reason he was sitting there, having a double scotch.

But he knew that wasn't the reason. He was doing what he'd said he wasn't going to do—not ever again. He was sitting in a bar, having a double, because life was getting to him. The bar had been different with Violet—shining brass rail, different people. Not like here. He looked around. There were a few guys slumped over their drinks, looking like they'd been that way for ages. At the end of the bar a well-dressed heavy-set man, about sixty or so, was having a margarita: "The way I like it," he told the barmaid. He kept looking down the long bar at Quigley.

Without interest, Quigley glanced at the headline of the Vancouver Sun lying on the bar: TWO MORE SUICIDE BOMBINGS IN IRAQ—ICE DISAPPEARING IN... Those times with Violet, it had been oppressive regimes and dictatorships...they never went away.

He was thinking how long Sidonia was working tonight, when suddenly, the man at the other end of the bar was standing next to him. "Doing anything later?" he asked. Without waiting for an answer, "I've got a big screen TV in my place. We could watch the Canucks playoffs."

Quigley didn't answer. This too had happened before. Did things never change? Was the same thing destined to happen again and again? "Go away."

"Forty. Forty dollars. Okay, fifty."

Quigley wasn't even annoyed. Not anymore. The first time he'd been approached, he'd been furious, but the terrible thing was that now he wasn't; he had almost been about to say, okay. A quick and easy way to make fifty dollars. Why not? "Go away," he told the man again. He'd have to tell Sidonia and he wouldn't know how to explain it to her. Not to Sidonia, for whom something would always turn up...every cloud had a silver lining...

* * *

"You've had more than your usual one," she said.

"How'd you guess?" He didn't mean it to come out like that—kind of mocking.

It was after dusk. They were in Lakeside Park under a horse chestnut tree. On the picnic table, a pepperoni pizza, some bottles of Pepsi, paper plates and plastic cutlery.

"Did he do it again?" he asked. She didn't answer. "Did he? Did Bottom pinch you?"

"He doesn't mean any harm. Anyway, I don't mind."

"Doesn't mean any harm. Don't mind. I don't get it, Sid, don't you care? Don't you have any respect for yourself?"

"That's just it! The way some of them talk in that bar, bad words when they're loaded, and even when they're not—it's all, 'like, I do this, like, I go to the store'—and Quiggy, that's the way I talk—and if I stay there much longer, I'll never get out of the habit. I need to talk better. Maybe if Mrs. Martin could hear me talk like she talks, not exactly, but at least without all those 'I know's, I'd make a better impression on her. What's the matter, Quiggy?"

"Everything." He put down his slice of pizza. "Can you beat it! She's gone and gotten a housecleaning service. Come in for an hour, scrub the kitchen and bathroom floors, vacuum the living room—only the living room—leave. She's paying them—two sisters—thirty dollars for the hour. Hell, we could be getting it, Sid, you and I. All I've done for her, and she's got no appreciation. We could be living there even, there's a little ensuite on the top floor. Nobody using it, just getting dustier and dustier."

She shifted on the bench. "You gotta eat somethin', Quiggy. Maybe she wants her privacy. You know, like, she doesn't want anyone living in the house."

"It's not that. It's the money—she's got it hidden somewhere in that old house. She thinks I don't know she's got it in the house. I know. I went with her to the bank. She made me wait in back. Jesus! You should have seen her hobbling along hardly able to walk, but she wouldn't let me help her—she didn't want me to see her sign that card, go into her vault."

She put down her third piece of pizza, took a long drink of Pepsi. "She had a right, Quiggy."

He shook his head. "She had it hidden there—Jesus! Must be thousands—in that safe deposit. She's gone and taken it out. It was in that beat-up satchel she took in with her. She's got the money hidden in that old house. God knows where. There's so much clutter—closets—chests—dressers—cabinets..."

"So what? It's her house, it's her money, she can do what she likes—"

"If only things could be nice—that's what you said, Sid. And they could be nice. We could be a kind of family–you and me and her. We could take care of her. Her son's never coming back. She's cut him out, you know, cut him out of her will. I heard her talking to that lawyer–Seaman's his name. I mean, what's she going to do with her money? We need money and she's got it. I'm not saying she give it to us, but we could work, do things for her. She's just a mean old..." he stopped, out of breath.

Sidonia was looking at the broad leaves of the chestnut tree. "Been here for ages, poor old thing," she said. "She's scared, just like you and me."

"Poor old thing! Jesus! If I hear you say that one more time..." he stopped again.

It was dark now. The massed foliage of the chestnut tree that had been sheltering them now seemed to close them in. Glimmers of the pale moon filtered through the leaves. Quigley moved over to Sidonia, put his arms around her. "What are we going to do?" he muttered. "Tell me, what are we going to do?"

6

After Quigley took her home from the hospital, Edith felt herself returning to safety. In the hospital, white-clad figures had prodded and poked her, stuck needles into her, awakened her when she was asleep, and told her to sleep when she was wide awake. She bore it all with as much grace as she could muster. She was grateful too: her dislocated shoulder had been set right, her arm in a sling for purpose of stability; as for her badly bruised knee, it merely hurt, and Edith, accustomed to calculating pain in terms of relativity, told herself the knee was only a nuisance. The cane was no problem; after all, she had used it before; it was almost a part of her body. She was lucky, the nurses had remarked, no bones broken. Behind her back, they called her a tough old bird.

Once she was home, one thought dominated Edith's mind. *Your home is your castle.* How many times had she heard that. They had been mere words then because she had no need of a castle; she had been protected, secure. She had someone to shield her from the world outside, a world she did not know or understand. She had her husband. Now she had only herself.

Quigley had been standing there waiting. "Are you sure you'll be all right?" He was reluctant to leave.

"I'll be fine."

"Still..." he said. But she insisted. She had a plan, carefully devised during those few days in the hospital. For a moment she thought of confiding in him; they had become friends in a way. But the moment passed. She had confided in Tim, her son, but then he had married, and their cozy talks had stopped, and even when the marriage broke up, he'd gotten involved with the AIDS group and lost interest—in me, she told herself—*his mother.* He had asked her for money for that AIDS group—hard-earned money—for people at the other end of the world. Her thoughts raced on: and who will give me the money I need when I need it.

Money, it all came down to money. Where to put the money.

All the next day, she laboriously went about her daily routine—despite her injury. Where, where will the money be safe, she pondered. Surely not on the first floor, the place where she lived, where she had all she needed—the kitchen, the dining area, a bathroom, a small sewing room, the den that had been made into a bedroom after James died. Not on the third floor, which was hardly even a room, which she hadn't been into for years, didn't know if there was anything in it.

The second floor, she finally decided, yes, the closets filled to overflowing, the dressers with their drawers clogged to the brim. Her jaw set in grim determination, drawing upon a strength she had not known she possessed, Edith leaned against the polished banister as she dragged the heavy satchel up the stairs.

She approached one of the dressers, opened one drawer after another; they overflowed with every kind of underwear. She shook her head, it wouldn't do, too easy to pull them out and turn the drawer over. Then she opened one of the large closets, and she knew. The hodgepodge of James' old clothes—sweaters, shirts, pants—that she'd never got to bring to the Salvation Army—they were here for a reason; they were here for just this moment. It took a while for her to dismantle the pile enough so that the bag could fit at the bottom, then heap the clothes on top. But she didn't have to hurry—she had all the time in the world—no one needed her, not anymore.

For nights afterward, Edith lost herself in half-dreams, hardly knew if she was asleep or awake: James and her, just married; buying the house when his business expanded into mining; Tim, a toddler, taking his first steps; she, a grandmother, holding Tim's newborn son. She yearned for that world—known and safe—wanted to stay there forever.

She awakened one morning to the sharp ring of the phone—a foreign voice asking for a contribution to some charity she'd never heard of. Timidly, carefully, politely, she explained: she was poor, she would, if she could, give.

From where had this fear of offending come? She had not thought about this before. Agreeable, she'd been called, and then, tumbling after that word, others had followed–pleasant, not forever arguing as some of the young women did. Yet, surely there had been a time when she had been daring and brave.

Edith lay awake nights searching for clues to her–she wasn't sure what to call it–timidity, perhaps. Now that she was old, her childhood seemed almost a dream: a little girl neatly dressed, doing what she was told to do. Bold and courageous explorers ventured into undiscovered places filled with dangers–fierce tribes, crocodiles, pathless jungles, tempestuous seas... But they were always in books. In her childhood it had been *Moby Dick* and *20,000 Leagues Under the Sea* and *King Solomon's Mines*, which she had read, somewhat secretly, as though she herself had dared to venture beyond the safety of her parents' home into an unknown world.

One morning she awakened, unusually stiff. The difficulty in getting out of bed only made her more determined. "Stubborn," her parents had called her, when she questioned the teacher at Sunday school–something about Genesis and could God do everything in seven days? "Not a pretty trait for a girl," they had added.

Edith took Teddy from the shelf in the closet where he'd been sitting for many days. For who else could go with her on this adventure? Mad, they would say–the doctors, the health care professionals. She was going to do what she had not, could not do before. She would go on her adventure. She would brave not those danger-filled territories of her childhood explorers, but this house where she had lived so many years, and, where all she had once seen as safe and inviting–the handsome staircase, the parquet floors, the Persian carpet–now challenged, threatened, called for attention, for constant vigilance, for a daring she had never put to the test.

"There's no one going to tell me what to do anymore," she told the teddy bear, who, as was his manner, regarded her with attentive eyes. "It's you and me now, Ted."

As though Teddy knew what was in her mind, his gaze (or was he speaking?) asked, "But treasure–wasn't there always hidden treasure in those adventure books?" Edith felt a shiver of delight. It was as though they were already engaged in the journey–she and Teddy.

"It's all taken care of, Ted. Upstairs, beneath that pile of

James' clothes. Thousands of dollars. I've taken it all out of the bank; you can't trust them—them and their computers." She went on: "I've planned it all carefully. There's enough money in small bills to pay the tradesmen. They can bring the groceries to the door." A thought hit her. "As for Quigley, what do I really know about him. I thought I knew my own son but I didn't. Anyway, Quigley's got a girlfriend, and you know what that means."

She had to see about breakfast, go about the day. She was about to put Teddy back on the shelf but didn't. She propped him up on the table right next to the window. "This is our castle, Ted. We don't have a moat or drawbridge to keep those others out, but we've got ourselves. No one's coming in."

When Leo called, she would say she was unwell. She couldn't put her finger on it. She felt different. Of course, she was old now. Leo was sixty-six but certainly vigorous. She knew she was not only lacking in vigor but she was vulnerable. She did not want Leo to see her like this.

Teddy, sitting straight and stern, told her he understood.

7

The plotting and planning of how to do what she needed each day demanded an enormous effort from Edith. It was not only the need to be constantly aware of each step, each turn, but an unremitting attention to the smallest details–a scrap of paper on the floor, a bit of plastic wrap, an envelope–anything might cause her to fall. Her extension tool and her cane became her equipment.

She was lingering in bed one morning, finding pleasure in doing so, when the doorbell rang. Who could it be? Not a tradesman; she'd given strict instructions as to delivery times. And to Quigley too, the few times she had called him. Not letting him in, not resuming their former easier relationship, had taken determination but was necessary.

She looked at the clock on the night table. Only past eight. She thought of letting it ring, but curiosity changed her mind. Her arm, still tender, was no longer in the sling. The pain of her bruised knee had become mere background–something that must be tolerated–like someone's insistent nagging.

Slowly, she rolled herself from the bed. She put on her bathrobe over her nightgown and tied the sash in the same slow motion. Finally, she sat down on the bedroom chair and manipulated one foot, then the other, into the soft slippers.

She went into the kitchen, opened a drawer, and, caught up in her adventure, ready for any danger, she took out a knife. Never had she done such a thing. At the front door, she peered through the curtain. A youth eating what seemed to be peanuts from a bag stood there. A sleeping bag and backpack lay at his feet. She tried to fix him in her mind but couldn't. Finally it came to her: Matthew, yes, Matthew. She hadn't seen her grandson for months.

She hesitated. Her heart began to race, as if it were trying to run away. If he rings again, I won't open the door, she thought;

somehow the second ring would denote impatience and she was not going to put up with that. Not anymore. But he didn't ring again. He finished his peanuts and put the bag in his pocket. Then, he just stood there, waiting.

She put the knife in the drawer of the hall table. She opened the door.

"Hi, gram," he said, as though he had seen her only yesterday.

"It's you—" She was about to say Matthew but remembered, not Matthew—Skye was the name he went by, and like the wandering clouds, he had turned up again. When no one else will keep him any longer, she went on to herself with a spitefulness that surprised her. She would tell him to go away.

"I've come to stay with you a while, gram." Although he was taller, his youthful face filled out, his dark hair cut, instead of the ponytail, still he seemed not to have grown any older. His dark eyes regarded her with the same innocence as the first time—when he had left high school before finishing. "Can I come in?"

"A while? How long?" Her mind became a calculator: the first job—a fast food place—had lasted two months—a disagreement with a customer. The next job—some factory—he'd been late too often. How many times had he stayed with them? She lost count. The last time—James had died by then—the few days he was supposed to stay had turned into a month.

"Don't know."

"What about school?"

"What about it?" Then he said, "It's okay if you don't want me here." He picked up his backpack, was about to put it on.

"Where will you go?"

"I'll be fine."

She had only to look at him—unwanted, lonely, like that *Little Boy Lost* of Blake—to know he would not be fine. Unable to bear the look of him—like a child who has lost too many games and no longer wants to play—she turned and doing so, lost her balance. All her carefulness, her attention to each step, to every movement—of hand, arm, neck—could not help her now. In one moment of distress, she had forgotten to be careful. She could feel herself falling. A fall would mean the end of this adventure, the end to everything.

But her grandson's arms reached out and caught her. Then, as though she might break, he gently set her straight and handed her the cane.

"Are you okay?"

"Come in," she said.

"I'll sleep outdoors. I have my sleeping bag. Under the big oak." He showed no curiosity about the house. She was thankful for that. What if he should go up the stairs? But, in the way he had, surroundings didn't matter. "There's a lot of grandpa's things I'm still sorting out," she told him.

Looking at him across the table from her at dinner, she thought, this is all I ever want–someone to eat with, someone with whom I feel safe.

He said, "I could take care of the garden." She said she had no garden. "I could plant one," he told her. She said she didn't want a garden. He could be her chauffeur, he went on, take her places. She said she didn't want to go places.

She waited for him to make a move–a trade–some work that would insure his future. He got up late, went to bed at all hours.

They were having dinner–baked chicken, asparagus from Creston, a casserole of potatoes he had made–when she asked, "Where did you learn to cook?"

"Here and there."

"Perhaps you'd like to go to cooking school."

He said nothing.

"Or go to college, now that you've finished your high school requirements?" She must give him credit for managing that in between his itinerant life. She added, "You were interested in the environment: earth studies–there are all kinds of degrees. Or engineering–you used to like playing with the erector set grandpa gave you."

He did not look at her. He seemed to be considering some inner landscape. "Don't know what I want to do," he said after a while.

"You have to start somewhere, do something, you can't just go on..."

His eyes became distant, then turned to her: "Do you believe you can be walking down the street and you see someone, and you know, you just know, that that person loves you and you love that person?"

40

"I believed in love at first sight," she smiled, "but that was when I was very young. I don't anymore. Is there some girl...?" She thought, the right girl can make a difference.

He was shaking his head, impatiently: "No, not that–just loving everyone."

"That's for saints." She waited for him to say something, but he didn't. Silence could be good, but this lack of words or action–for he seemed to be sitting there, like a piece of furniture–made her uneasy. She felt there was something she should be saying, but she didn't know what.

Then, he left the room, quietly, unobtrusively. All the simple pleasant things she had done with him in his childhood–picture books, nature walks, the alphabet, *Aesop's Fables*, had been meant as a pathway into a certain kind of youth. Matthew would have said, politely, he had an errand to do–or something. But, Skye, she reminded herself, he calls himself Skye. She wanted to think about Matthew–the youth that little boy should have become–considerate, applying himself to some field of endeavor. Not Skye–she didn't want to think about that youth–getting up at all hours, going to bed at all hours, going off to meet, she didn't know who.

She found herself at the window. She stood watching the clouds, fleecy and white, float by in the pure blue sky. His well-being. That was what she wanted, more than her own, and carried by a surge of love, she decided not to simply send him away, but to do what was hard–what she had never done–confront him–give him a chance to make something of himself. She had no way of knowing that what constituted well-being for her might not for her grandson.

"I'm going out for a while," he said after dinner one evening.

She didn't bother to ask where. "I want to talk to you. Sit down."

He looked surprised.

"I'm giving you two hundred dollars," she said. "I want you to find a place for yourself, to get a job and keep it, or go back to school or learn a trade. Tomorrow, I want you to start tomorrow." She was amazed she had said all that.

"Okay." He got up. She tried to find in his face the one word–in anything about him–some hint of what he was thinking or feeling, but she couldn't. Then, in the same neutral tone, he said, "I'm going out now." She asked when he would be back. "When I'm back," he answered.

She waited up in a swelter of foreboding. The old familiar house whose creaks and crackles she had known for years now assailed her ears with strange noises. Phantom shapes peered from behind the curtains. Though the spring night was mild, the air around her was so close she had to loosen her blouse. The old recliner in which she tried to lie back–she had not gone to bed–became wet with perspiration. She had the frightening feeling that her ultimatum had been the passwords to a new and dangerous territory.

She could not sleep. Any sound–a distant horn, a dog's bark– caused her to start up from the chair, expecting him. The grandfather clock in the hall chimed four times when Skye came back, banging at the door, though he had the key. She groped for her cane. Leaning heavily on it, she wobbled to the door and opened it. He staggered in, the alcohol striking her like a blow, forcing her back, so that she had to grab the hall table to prevent herself from falling.

"I've got to lie down." He brushed by her and wove his way to the den where his sleeping bag lay.

"Mean," he called her the next day. "Just plain mean." Then he called her some names, bad names. But by that time all she could think was he'd spent the money she'd given him to begin a different life on drink for himself and his–not friends, but other creatures like him, without anchor, without aim. How many were there?

"I've apologized," he said. "Now you apologize. Apologize for what you just said."

He was examining his BlackBerry. He was doing something with it or to it–she had no idea–but she wondered if there was something she could do if she, too, had one–a button to perhaps make contact with him. But her head hurt and she was too tired to think anymore.

"Leave now and don't come back," she said again. Without another word, he took his backpack and sleeping bag and walked out the door. She watched him go down the road until he was out of sight. She felt faint, her energy drained, as though she had been on a long arduous journey.

She had to go to the second floor. She had to see if her

money was still intact. It took a while to climb the staircase. She did a step or two, then rested. The bad shoulder, which had eased up before the boy–she thought of him that way–had come, was acting up. Her bruised knee, which she had barely noticed, was painful again. The arthritis in her lower back made each step an agony. At the landing, she rested a long while. Then, she went into the master bedroom. An enormous undertaking awaited her.

Before the large closet, she took a deep breath. Then, one by one–she had time now–she dragged the old pants, shirts, undergarments of her dead husband from the mountainous heap. It took nearly two hours. Near the bottom lay the satchel. She opened it, sat down, and laboriously counted the bundles of hundred-dollar bills. She nodded to herself. She returned the bundles to the satchel, piled the clothing on top so slowly that to an outsider it might have been a parody of slow motion. But it was no parody. This rhythm had come about with time. At first, the slowness, the need to turn with care, had been annoying; the springiness of youth was still in her mind. When was it, she wondered–after seventy, perhaps later–when she had come to accept the change in the way she moved?

It was night when she finally went down the staircase, holding the banister, as though she were going down a minefield–probing each step with her foot, setting it down tentatively, before taking the step. When she arrived at the first floor it seemed to her she had taken a voyage. It came with surprise that she was hungry. During the encounter with Skye, she had felt she would never eat again.

In the kitchen, she heated some soup and set out some bread and cheese. She ate slowly; if she gulped her food she would start choking. When she finished, she washed the few dishes. She got into her nightgown, lay down in her bed, exhausted, but sleep did not come until after midnight, and brought with it a strange dream:

She was in a room again, a room she didn't know. Someone– a strange being who looked like one of those aliens from outer space–was introducing a young man to her.

"I've met you before," she said. "I'm sure I have."

But the young man shook his head. When he spoke, it was in words she couldn't understand. He opened his hand. A strange little device lay there. Touching it, he indicated she was to listen, but the music that came forth was unrecognizable.

"I..." She tried to tell the young man she was a visitor to his land, she was sorry she couldn't speak his language–perhaps he might teach her–but nothing she had learned or done in her life could help her make him understand.

A bird was trilling merrily outside her window. The sun shone through, announcing a fresh new day. Edith called her lawyer.

"What is it this time, Edith?" Alfred Seaman asked. He had had good luck in Vegas and was feeling on top of the world.

"I want to change my will, Alfred." He waited, looking around his handsomely furnished office, wondering where to take his new bimbo for dinner. The Caribbean, he decided–soft breezes, soft blue sky, soft (but insinuating) music–a good prelude...

"I want to take Skye out of my will."

"Skye?"

"Matthew. My grandson. He calls himself Skye."

"You've taken Tim off. And now Matthew. Who do you want to leave your money to if not your own flesh and blood? Are you sure you know what you're doing?" Poor Edith, that's what happened when you got old, Alfred thought—you went right off your rocker. He decided he was never going to get old. The gym. Plenty of sex. New studies verified what he'd known since puberty: nothing like sex to keep you young. Thinking of tonight–Bonnie, Bonnie Bum–he smiled: there was something pleasing in the way names sometimes meshed with their owners. Restaurante Carribe–all that decor–and then, champagne, truffles, one of those flaming desserts —appetizers for the main course.

"What I do with my money is my affair, not yours, just remember that, Alfred Seaman." Not *my* flesh and blood, that Skye, she silently told herself, and pictured him raining down money–her money–on anyone willing to drink with him. As for Tim–off in Africa with somebody else's flesh and blood.

"The Elephant Mountain Animal Shelter–that's my beneficiary." Poor unwanted creatures–she'd leave whatever she had left to them. She waited, giving him time to take this in. "And come by the house with the new will, please, it's not that easy for me to get around these days."

Edith hung up the phone, exhausted. All her feelings of the great adventure she had begun dissolved into what she had sworn never to allow–a flood of self-pity. She tried to talk the feeling over with Teddy, but Teddy was getting to be less and less satisfactory. It was hard, too hard, to be alone. Yet, she reminded herself, were not all explorers alone? Did they not face trials that threatened to kill them? Try as she might she could not get away from the knowledge that they had had followers, some, even a few, who were there for them.

8

"What took you so long, Quiggy?" Sidonia waved him over to the picnic table where she sat. Two others were sitting there. He murmured something about having a hard time getting away, annoyed that the others were there; it was to have been a picnic for just Sid and himself. He was eager to update her on Edith Martin's condition, her infirmities, the way she was trying–unsuccessfully, in his opinion—to manage the house and herself. It would have to wait. This obviously wasn't the time or place.

July 1st. Canada Day. It seemed that all of Nelson had gathered in Lakeside Park. The String of Pearls Band was playing, and the old time favorites–*Honeysuckle Rose*, *Song of India*, *Moonlight Serenade*–filled the air, along with the shouts of children, crying babies and the laughter of picnickers. The rage of the time was hula hoops, and all over the lawns hips and buttocks of men, woman, teenagers and children undulated up, down and around in varying degrees of showmanship and daring. On the beach below, sunbathers lay, greased, eyes covered by dark glasses. Toddlers splashed in the lake, mothers at hand. Farther out in the water, a couple of swimmers raced each other.

Quigley's mood didn't fit the holiday spirit. Why hadn't Sid told him there would be others here? Even now, she was introducing them. "This is Beau," she said, indicating the man who sat opposite her–the handsomest Quigley had ever seen–maybe fifty, but it was hard to know–some lines on his Grecian face that only made him seem more rugged, some grey in his thick dark hair that accentuated a certain self-confidence. "And this," she went on, "is Bright."

The woman was somewhere in her forties, Quigley guessed. The small mole on her cheek made her wavy hair seem more blonde and her flawless skin more smooth. "And this is Quigley," Sidonia smiled, putting her arm about him.

"Pleased to meet you." He meant to say hi, something like that, but he was in that state he always got into when he saw what was movie-star beauty.

He sat down next to Sidonia. "Did you ask Mrs. Martin again?" she said. He nodded. "What did she say?" she went on low. He said he would tell her what happened later, when they were alone. Mrs. Martin. And they had been on first name terms too. But now he couldn't think of the old woman by name. Stubborn, that's what she was, pretending she could walk okay when she couldn't and she couldn't see that good either. He took a slice of the pizza pie and a coke, then pulled a ten-dollar bill from his pocket and gave it to Bright: "Here's my share of the eats."

"I'll bet she haggled with you." Sidonia turned to the other two: "Quigley's been doing some work for this lady. Sad–the way some old people get–all suspicious and closed in. And she's got a lot of money. She could make life easier for herself."

Bright reflected, looked up. Her eyes became somber. "My mother was like that. Could hardly hear or see, wouldn't get a hearing aid, wouldn't change glasses she'd had forever. Wouldn't see a doctor. I'd try to help her–it's not easy taking time off from a job–but, after a few days of her going on and on about God knowing best, I couldn't hack it anymore. Anyway, she must have had something going–her faith, I guess–because she lived to be ninety-two and was pretty peaceful at the end. Said God was taking her and she was ready to go."

Beau laughed mockingly. He nodded at the sky. "Yeah, there He sits looking down, figuring out who's going to heaven and who's going to hell."

"C'mon Beau, no one believes in that God anymore." Bright turned to Quigley. "Beau's become an atheist. It's because of that priest who fondled him and—"

"Fondled, my eye! Anyway, the Virgin Mary, Jesus on the cross, they're all a bunch of stories–myths–put together for ignoramuses to swallow."

"You can't prove there's no God." Sidonia's voice, usually mild, had an urgent ring to it.

"Sure, and you can't prove there isn't a teapot flying around in outer space, either."

"Can it, Beau—you're upsetting Sid!" Bright reached out her

hand as if to stop him, and he suddenly did.

"Sid believes." Quigley had not meant to say anything. He felt uneasy. When people started talking about religion, he didn't know what to say. He had long ago decided it was better to kind of play it safe–not say anything. Anyway, he wasn't sure what he did or didn't believe. He hadn't thought about God. People were Catholics or Protestants, went to this church or that. There were also Jews, and it seemed the world had it in for them. These days Muslims were in the news all the time, but he didn't know any. Somehow, though, it seemed to him that the way Sidonia was–always finding excuses for people's bad behavior–had to do with the fact that she believed in God, although she didn't make a big deal of it. He said again, "Yeah, Sid's the big believer around here."

"I need Him, so I believe in Him." A belligerent tone entered into Sidonia's words. The others looked at her in surprise. Just as Quigley wondered how to get off the subject, a chanting that seemed to be coming from the entrance to the park started up. "Canada out of Afghanistan–bring our soldiers home..."

"Protesters," Beau said. "A lot of good it will do them. Harper's bent on peacekeeping–if you can call defending yourself against suicide bombers by that name."

Quigley shifted around on the bench, wishing he were someplace else. He had just about decided to make the best of things–after all, it was kind of peaceful here–the sky and lake like those blue lagoons in those old songs–but the protesters broke into all of that, reminded him of what he didn't want to be reminded. He had tried to go though he had not really wanted to go. The thought of defending himself against suicide bombers intent on blowing him up brought back memories of bullying at school. But he figured there were benefits. But they had rejected him. Another failed attempt. Like the bullies at school. Long ago but he never forgot. "Be a man and fight," his father had told him, and so he had–eleven or twelve he was–and one of them had hit him in the side with brass knuckles. He had landed in the hospital. "Lucky to be alive." He had said it aloud. Sidonia was looking at him in that way she had when annoyed. "Nice to have you back." As though she were joking. But he knew she didn't like his habit of daydreaming. It made him seem flaky–when he wasn't.

"We'd better get going," Beau said to Bright. He got up,

began putting various small articles into his knapsack. "We're off tree-planting tomorrow," he said to Quigley. "Ever been?"

He shook his head. It wasn't exactly a lie; you could hardly count five days as being there. He had tried, figured as so many of the others did on making a bundle with hard work. In the end, after exhausting himself with the baby trees–digging, placing, swathed from head to foot to defeat the sun–he had been defeated by some weird insect who had managed to get to his leg and bite him. He remembered reluctantly the swelling, the pain. It was after that August he had started his handyman service. A half-year then another failure.

Quigley watched Beau and Bright tossing stuff into their packs. It seemed to him the folding cups, the Swiss army knives, the suntan lotion went right into the packs–one, two, three. He always had mishaps–something falling, breaking, as though the inert things had wills of their own, kept thwarting his intention.

"Good luck with your planting," Sidonia waved.

Bright laughed. "Seven thousand dollars'-worth, that's what we usually make, but we're aiming for more. And we'll save on housing and all of that. We bought this classic '71 Chevy camper van. A steal–seven hundred–the guy was leaving for a monastery in Thailand. You forgot to buy mosquito repellent, Beau."

"No problem. We'll pick some up at Canadian Tire on the way."

Quigley managed a smile. "Hope you make..." he couldn't think of a figure–something astronomical–"whatever you're aiming for," he finally said.

"Oh, we will, we always do." Beau was starting toward the parking area. Quigley noticed his strides–long, even, purposeful.

When they were gone, Sidonia began clearing the picnic table. He tried to help her, but she waved him off. "Mrs. Martin is not taking us on," she said. "That's what you're going to tell me."

"Tomorrow, Sid, I'll tell you tomorrow night." She was working at the bar tonight, he knew, and he was running some errands for one of his few remaining clients.

"Yeah," she said, not sounding like her usual good-natured self. "You're going to tell me we didn't get the job."

"Hey, it's not that simple."

"It could be," she said.

49

That night Quigley dreamt he was driving the Fiat, looking for something–he didn't know what. Suddenly, he was in a field and he knew what he was looking for was hidden there. He drove round and round but there were only wild flowers, grasses of one kind and another, stones of many sizes and shapes. He got out of the car and looked and looked but found nothing else. He could make out a small cemetery farther away. He got back in the Fiat, drove to it and walked among the graves. When he came to a large ornamented tomb, he knew what he was looking for was inside. He opened the door of the tomb and saw a stone coffin. Opening the coffin, he saw thousands of hundred-dollar bills.

The next night he told Sidonia the dream.
"What did you do?"
"I woke up."
She sighed. "You always have dreams and you always wake up before you finish them. It's weird, though, because that sounds like a sarcophagus, that tomb, and we don't have them here. The Greeks and Romans had them. Anyway, it doesn't matter. You couldn't have taken the money–not from a tomb."
"Oh, I don't know."
They were lying in bed. Quigley was trying not to show his– he hardly knew what to call his feeling–resentment, he guessed. Sidonia sat up, shocked. "You'd take money from a tomb! It's like some kind of curse would come upon you."
"That's just superstitious bunk. You're even talking that way– like out of a book–*The Curse of the Mummy*. Anyway, when you're down and out you do almost anything." He sat up too. The lamp across from them was lit; they had not turned it off, as though they knew they wouldn't be able to sleep. On the brass fixture a small brown spider finished weaving the last circle of a silken web, then remained motionless outside it. They watched a moth hover on the wall, then fly straight to the lighted lamp. The spider caught it by the wing and drew it into its web.
"The spider will eat it," she said. "Do you suppose that moth knew it was committing suicide?" After a moment she said, "But all moths fly into light bulbs; they can't all be committing suicide."
"They think they're being guided by the sun–something like

50

that–I read it somewhere." He wondered what else he could talk about, but he couldn't think of a thing. She had not asked, she was waiting for him to tell her how the time with Edith Martin had gone, but of course she knew he had not succeeded. Again.

"You're in a mood."

"No I'm not."

"Whenever you don't want to talk about something, you get in a mood. What's the matter, Quiggy?"

"Why did you bring them–Beau and Bright?" He couldn't help adding, "The BB twins–bright and beautiful. We were supposed to have a picnic, just the two of us, we were supposed to discuss what we're going to do." He waited then supplied an answer. "To show me up, I suppose, to let me see the great B and B tree-planters, off to make ten thousand in two months."

"Don't exaggerate. Anyway, it was to fire you up, get you excited about what *you* can do. And don't say they had all the breaks. Beau's been through hell. I met him in that sexual abuse group. And Bright almost died when a doctor gave her the wrong antibiotic. I told you but you conveniently forget when you start feeling sorry for yourself. The way they've come through all their...stuff–that's what I wanted you to see."

"I'm not Beau." His long-time ability to pretend wasn't working. Sid seemed determined to do what he had always tried to avoid–get at his feelings–his real feelings. "I'm not feeling sorry for myself, I'm okay, I'm fine."

"Quiggy, everyone feels sorry for himself, herself, one time or another, it's no big deal."

"Maybe it's too late to talk, maybe we should just try to go to sleep," he persisted. But she shook her head and said that's what they were going to do–talk about their situation or she wouldn't be able to sleep. She was looking around. "Your place is just about as bad as mine," she said. "I think there's a mouse behind the walls. Something's scurrying around."

"They're going to tear this house down–all the tenants got notices–and put up a condominium so what's the difference if there's a mouse or a rat or a——"

"I'm going to make some sandwiches." Sidonia got up, went into the kitchen. The spider was now inside its web but there was no sign of the moth. She came back with a couple of cheese and tomato

51

sandwiches. "I've got the kettle on." She settled the plates on the bed, along with some napkins. "Okay, now let's get to it. Did you ask her again?"

"The old lady?"

"Of course the old lady. Only her name is Edith Martin. Did you?"

"Yes, I asked her. She said she wasn't interested in a couple working for her, that she just needed me for errands, that kind of thing. She got real mad when I talked about us moving in, being on hand. Said it was out of the question. So that's that."

"You said I'm a good cook and good cleaner and could help her with baths and you could do chauffeuring for her and handyman stuff and...?"

"Yeah, yeah, yeah."

"How did you ask her?"

"What is this? An inquisition?" Quigley watched her take a large bite of a sandwich. For some reason that made him angry. He tried to take a bite of the sandwich before him, then put it down. He wasn't hungry. "And I told her about our situation and how she would be getting good help, honest and hard-working, and all we'd ask was a room—she has all those empty rooms—and reasonable pay."

"And of course she refused." He said nothing. Rubbing it into me, he thought. Sidonia went on. "That's your problem, Quiggy, you let people walk all over you. Even expect it. You've gotten into the habit—like those stupid moths—flying into the light every time." He noted she had said, *your* problem. A couple of months ago, it would have been *our*. He wished she hadn't changed, that they could be the same as before, she looking to him for comfort and support, but even as he thought this, she was saying, "You just about bow down to people. Even now, you're looking away, you don't want to meet my eyes." Her dimple had disappeared entirely. Her sunny mouth was grim. "You don't want to hear the truth."

It was true. He had averted his eyes. He felt miserable, as though he were going down for the last time. Would it happen again? Would his relationship with Sidonia go the way of all the others—and all his puny little businesses too? Would this be his ultimate failure? She was leaning back on the pillows, her comfy nightdress loose around her. "What do you see in me, Sid?" he asked. "You say you love me. Why?"

Her eyes softened. "Because you're a good person. Quiggy, you're the kindest person I've ever known." She smiled at him and the dimple suddenly appeared.

"No, I'm not. I have bad thoughts. I don't know much about the Bible, but I remember this sermon the minister preached when I was a kid–about bad thoughts leading to bad actions."

"C'mon, you can decide for yourself. You think something, and then you say, it's only a thought—and that's the end of it."

Sometimes he was blown away by how smart Sidonia was. Behind her sweetness was a brain that knew how to really examine what you were saying and come up with something new. He had been thinking that Edith Martin was an old lady, hardly able to get around and had all this money hidden in the house–no question about that–and here we are, Sid and I, not young but not old, needing what she's got and not even using. Maybe thoughts were just thoughts; maybe you try to do the right thing, but then something you never expected comes along and you end up doing what you said you'd never do. "You're a good person," she had said. He wanted to remember those words.

Sidonia was deep in consideration too. "She asked you to come back, right?" Quigley nodded and said there were some errands she needed him to do. "I told her Express Delivery was just about finished. She said I could use her car." He waited. "Okay," she finally said, "she may be stubborn–old people can get that way–but she can't keep going like she is–not for long anyway. I mean–here's this old lady needing help bad–and here's this old house with just her in it – and here's you and me wanting to help her... It makes sense, it's the way things should be. Don't plead, Quiggy, we've got a lot to offer. And she likes you—you know she does. You can talk to her, make her realize we're a good couple of people to have there, helping her. You can do that, can't you?"

"I can do that." The way they had started the evening everything seemed doomed but now everything seemed possible. Suddenly, he remembered the state of Edith Martin's home–messy, bits of food on the carpets and floors, stains... And the old lady didn't seem to see any of it. What's more, she looked terrible. It wasn't only the wrinkles—it was new lines etched into her face, as though the strain of living was digging something out of her. "Listen, Sid, there's something queer about the old lady. She said she was on some kind of expedition—an adventure. I asked her what it was; after all, she doesn't budge from that house. She told me to never mind. She said a cloud had gotten in the way, but she had fought it off. She sure sounds a little off. People say that about her, you know."

"People say—people say... How many times have you been called a gnome or dwarf? How many guys called me Fatty? Stop calling her that old lady. She's got a name: Edith Martin. She's one of us, can't you see, Quiggy, one of us—not like the ones who have it all—beauty and everyone's admiration. Maybe being lonely and sad makes her say strange things." She stopped suddenly. "I feel safe with you, Quiggy. I know you're never going to hurt my feelings."

She looked to him for comfort and support. All of a sudden the image of the video at Coles Bookstore in the mall flashed before Quigley's eyes. *The Secret: Ask, Expect, Receive.* Edith Martin had changed her will. Twice. And she liked him. Quigley asked whoever was out there: "Please, let Sid and me get the job and let Mrs. Martin put me in her will." You had to have faith while you expected. He could have faith. He could do anything for Sidonia. Not that she wanted anything. But he knew secretly she longed for a lovely house, pretty things, children—a different kind of life.

"Duck," she said all of a sudden. "We've been so busy talking I forgot to ask if the animal shelter said they'd take good care of him."

"I didn't leave him there. They said he probably wouldn't be adopted—too funny-looking. They said dogs that weren't adopted after a couple of months were... So I took him along to Edith Martin's and she said he could stay with her."

"Duck—crazy-looking dog—he's one of us," Sidonia said. She was running her fingers through Quigley's tangly red hair. "Don't fall asleep," she whispered. "Not yet."

9

Edith prepared to move her money from beneath the pile of her dead husband's clothes on the second floor to the turret on the third floor. The July heat–thirty-six degrees Celsius–had been going on for two weeks–global warming–but the plumber had been up on the second floor for over an hour fixing a leak in the bathroom. She had checked on the money afterwards. That had been a terrible trip–going up the stairs, dismantling the pile of clothes, counting. It was all there. Still...

She knew she wasn't being reasonable, but as her physical state worsened and her isolation continued, the money became all-important. It was there for her to use when... She would not have known how to continue the sentence.

She would have tea before the arduous climb. She had not been feeling well these past weeks. In addition to the chronic arthritis and back pain, her feet were troublesome, hurting and inclined to sudden twists. She had to be very careful in walking, even with the cane. Her head throbbed constantly and her sinuses were clogged. Just eating–toasting a slice of bread, making a cup of tea–demanded new efforts. She was hard put to retrieve anything dropped.

She thought of going to the doctor. But she despaired of describing her infirmities. The list was too long: fragile bones, fading eyesight, decreased endurance; worst of all, the racking pain in her back that came when it wanted–an enemy attacking when least expected.

Duck came up to her with the ball in his mouth, his curl of a tail waving, eyes bright with play. She sat down in the comfortable easy chair in the living room and rolled the ball. The dog retrieved it–his squat little body working vigorously–then, gently he laid it at her feet. She rolled the ball a few more times–with her shoed foot–to avoid Duck's spittle touching her hand. "That's enough now, Duck," she said. "I have something to discuss with you."

She could talk to Duck. He would not betray her. With Duck she was safe. Teddy was, after all, only a stuffed animal, a toy. Now that she knew this she could not un-know it. Even now Duck was looking at her attentively, waiting for whatever she needed of him. Edith explained her dilemma: "I must move the money, Duck. It's not safe where it is. The plumber who fixed the bathroom leak on the second floor could have gone into the closet and seen the pile of James' clothes and..." But he didn't, she reminded herself. "Still," she went on, repeating the words wired into her head, "the money is not safe where it is–not safe."

She stopped to gauge the effect of this disclosure on Duck. The dog was not even glancing at the ball off in a corner. He was sitting quietly; his eyes, intent on hers, registered interest. She went on to explain the other part of her dilemma:

"We've got to go up to the turret, Duck. People think the turret is just an ornament–a little tower added on to make the house look more Victorian–but there's a room in it." She became animated. "That's where the money has to go." The next moment her voice fell. "But how can I possibly do it all by myself?—climb the two flights to the second floor; dismantle that heap of clothes to get the satchel with the money. And that's only the beginning. There's carrying the satchel up that last flight of stairs; there's the passageway to get to the turret..."

As she spoke, Edith could see the staircase looming, up up up. Questions kept forming in her head: Was there a key to the turret room? Would her bad leg act up? Her back? What shoes to wear? Heavy, sturdy–for stability–in spite of the debilitating heat. She wanted to cry but could not; she had lost the habit. "So you see, Duck, it's too much for me to do, it's like climbing a mountain–me, at my age. I can't—but I must." She stopped talking, as though she had delivered a summation to her jury of one. She waited for him to give her some sign of what she must do.

Duck rose, went to the hallway where his leash hung from a large hook. Taking the leash in his mouth, he wrestled it from the hook and dragged it over to her. After she took the dog out, Edith prepared for her mission. Alan Quartermain had his trusty companions, Captain John Good and Sir Henry Curtis, with him as they hacked their way through the African jungle, encountering warring tribes, seeking King Solomon's road that would lead them to the twin mountain peaks called Sheba's Breasts, behind which lay, entombed, King Solomon's diamonds.

Edith looked at the undeniably old woman in the mirror but saw herself as young and daring, about to start on a secret mission. And she would not be going alone. She would have her loyal companion with her–to carry the satchel. Duck understood. He was smiling at her. Three treacherous flights. But they would conquer the staircase, move the treasure to safety and descend in triumph.

Edith dragged herself up the stairs–one foot, then the other, holding onto the banister with one hand, her cane in the other. Why had she taken the cane? It was more of a nuisance than help. The force of habit, she supposed. Duck, his short legs stretching between steps, was ahead of her. "Duck," she called. When the dog turned, she pointed to the cane. He took it into his mouth, fumbling to hold it firmly, as though it were a long stick. It was only mid-morning but already the heat was intense. Perspiration dripped down her face onto her blouse. She tried to stay in the present, to place each foot carefully on the step, but the past kept flashing inside her head–Tim, as a child, running up and down this staircase–James mounting in the precise way he had–and Matthew, a small boy, before he became Skye, impishly playing hide-and-seek along the landings. Family.

When she reached the second floor landing, a sharp warning pain in her left leg chased away all random thoughts. The exultation with which she had begun the climb changed to fearful doubt. Perhaps it was best to abandon this foolish adventure. Her clothes clung to her. The pain in her leg would not abate. She could only lower herself by stages to lie down on the landing. All that still had to be done crowded in on her. "Too much–too much," she said weakly.

Duck lay down beside her, and now she realized he must be thirsty. Dogs needed more water in this kind of heat. She must try to make the pain go away. Cautiously, she worked the leg up and down, side to side, using her breath to help, until at last the pain went, and with this sense of freedom, her determination returned. What she had to do must be done today.

By degrees, she pulled herself up by turning on her good side, then using her knees and hands to raise herself further, until finally she was able to straighten by holding onto the hall table with both hands. "Come, Duck," she said, and took the cane from his mouth. For the hallway.

The master bedroom was even hotter than the landing. Quickly, she led Duck into the bathroom. James had insisted upon an adjoining bathroom. There was no bowl, no basin. She flushed the unused toilet twice and let the panting dog drink from it. How horrified she had been when Rover tried to drink from the toilet. How far away that time was.

The closet was hotter still. Edith took a chair from the room, sat down and began to lift the clothing, piece by piece–pants, shirts, pajamas... Duck lay by her side, panting. She had to stop and rest, stop and rest. It took a long time to get to the bottom. There it was– the satchel. She opened it. There lay the bills, wrapped in bundles.

Exhausted, still her mind kept working. What hard work dealing with money demanded. And now, Duck would have to carry the satchel up the last flight of stairs. He had grasped the handles with his mouth. "Good work, Duck." She patted the dog. Companion. Loyal companion. And the clothes lay in the same carefully haphazard jumble as though the money was still underneath. Deceiving. Duck's eyes followed hers; she was certain he was satisfied too. A renewed sense of excitement pulsed through her body; the agonizing pain in her leg seemed barely an ache. Dimly, in back of her mind, was the thought of another flight of stairs, then the turret, then descending, but she would not consider this. Not to continue on her mission–no, their mission, hers and Duck's–would be backing down, would mean defeat, cowardice. After all, the first vital stage had been successfully accomplished. Faintly, a telephone was ringing, but the sound was far off and seemed to belong to another world. "I could not have gotten this far without you, Duck," she told the dog, and she knew that he knew she was calling him a comrade, that they were united in purpose and concern for one another. Looking at Duck's squat little body, his short legs, she felt something within her stir, something once possessed then lost. She thought, he's not a nice-looking dog, not a dog someone would want or rescue. What would happen to him if I died? She would have Alfred change the will again. Not an anonymous animal shelter, no—she would name Duck as beneficiary with a caring person to attend to his needs.

The last flight of stairs loomed before Edith like what she imagined the final climb to a famous mountaintop might be–Everest.

She regarded the heavy satchel, which Duck had dragged along the hallway. The euphoria of minutes before left her. Somehow, he must get it to the top. Duck's eyes were on the satchel too. It seemed to her that he was pondering the same problem. What madness had possessed her to dare three flights of stairs in this unbearable July heat? Her back hurt terribly, her legs felt leaden, her head throbbed relentlessly. Perspiration dripped down her face into the hollow of her throat.

As she stood there–faintly, from that other world downstairs–the melodic chime of the doorbell. She had been surprised by James' insistence on the musical chime. How much of him I didn't really know, she thought. The chimes again, then no more. Perhaps a neighborhood child playing a prank. There was no time to consider.

The sun poured down from the skylight. She had forgotten her watch. About one o'clock, she thought, but it was hard to know. Duck had taken the straps of the satchel in his mouth and was dragging it up the stairs. "It's too heavy for you," she said, but was relieved when the dog continued; she could not do it herself. Dragging herself up inch by inch after the dog was draining away her energy. It took a long time to reach the third landing, but time didn't matter now; time was only a word.

Duck let the satchel drop from his mouth onto the landing. Was there a cut on his lips? She pulled and dragged and coaxed the satchel up the four steps that led to the passageway to the turret. Every move she made now, every step she took, seemed more than she could possibly do.

They went along the passageway until they came to the turret door. Was there a key? Vaguely, Edith recalled that once, long ago, there had been a key. But she had never used it. Indeed, she had never been interested in the turret and wondered what impulse had prompted James to have it built onto their house.

She opened the door and entered a steamy room. Thick dust lay over everything–a trunk, a chair, a small table over which a butterfly net hung. With a pang she remembered that Tim had liked to catch butterflies as a boy. He had come here sometimes–to play hide-and-seek. Long ago. But memories such as this were becoming enveloped in mist too difficult to penetrate. Lost, she could only think, my son and only child. And Skye who had once been little

Matthew–he was lost too.

Duck's attempt at a bark–as though to bring her back to the moment–caused her to sit down on the dust-laden chair in despair. Steeped in perspiration, she surveyed the small room. Duck lay on the floor, panting hard. He needed water, food, rest, and then a chance to run. They must descend. As one confidante to another, she asked the dog, "Where shall we hide the satchel?" He made a noise hard to describe–perhaps like the clearing of a throat. This difficulty in making himself heard touched a chord in Edith: This small creature is not so different from me. When the dog got up and went over to the trunk, she perceived this as an answer. She would put the satchel in the trunk. No one came to the turret room. She, herself, had not come here. James had come at times–to fix something or other.

The trunk was not locked. She opened it, expecting to find some old clothes, tools, she hardly knew what–but only bundles of yellowing envelopes with old stamps met her eye. They made her afraid. She wanted to think this was only a dream; she would awaken and the letters would vanish with the dream. But flickers of light that filtered through the window and cast strange shadows on the dusty walls dispelled the dream. Against her will, her arm reached out; her hand picked up one of the bundles; her fingers undid the string. The envelopes scattered.

She picked up an envelope and took out the letter. Words, unencumbered by starts or stops, sprawled across the page–an easy open hand: *Jocko darling–the last time–you lying there–your eyes...* She returned the letter to its envelope, took another, read it. Avid curiosity, stronger than fear, made her arm reach out for still another bundle, then another. When she finally had had enough, she had read some two dozen letters. They were much the same–love letters signed with an extravagant rose beside an even more extravagant *your Maddy.*

How could she not have known? That was the first question that came to her with the shock of this discovery. "Do you love me?" she had sometimes asked James. And he had answered, "You're my wife." She had asked no further. To venture beyond husband and wife was exploring uncharted territory, about which, she, safe in her familiar home, secure in her honored place, knew nothing.

Then, wildly, unpredictably, some hidden part of her started to scream to her husband who was dead, "But all the time I trusted you, as you trusted me. Oh, we didn't love each other–" she searched for the word, "passionately–but I took care of you and you took care of me–and it was all right–one doesn't need–" again she sought the words, "bells ringing, that kind of thing," she finally managed.

She had been slapping down one letter after another. She had read enough. What more was there to discover? But she could not stop screaming. There was no one to hear in this steamy little tower room. Only Duck. Words burst from her. "We had an arrangement!" A vein in her forehead began to pulse. Her eyes grew dark with fury. "You said, 'Edith, I couldn't do what I do without you.' And all the time, all the time... Do you hear me? I want you to hear!"

Her words bounced off the walls–*hear–hear–I want you to...* Suddenly she became aware of Duck inching away from her, his curl tail down, ears down, his eyes looking away from her. He's cowering, Edith thought, he's afraid of me—he thinks I'm angry with him.

Angry. Anger. So this is how anger feels, she told herself with surprise. She had not been able to put a name to her shouting and screaming upon finding the love letters. Recognizing the anger that had been buried within her, she now saw the endless small lies and deceits she had used to displace the too bold and headstrong feeling. That business trip James had made when Tim was a baby and very sick. Calling the hotel where James was staying, and he had not even registered. So where was he? And how much he had taken for granted her easy acceptance of his lies. Well, I suppose our marriage worked for both of us, Edith told herself.

Duck was still backing away from her. She leaned toward him. She began to croon to him: "I'm sorry, Duck, sorry. I wasn't angry with you." Her voice was full of entreaty. "Forgive me, Duck."

And now the dog moved toward her and allowed her hand to stroke his head. Softly she talked to him as she stroked, until his rough little tongue licked her hand and he held up a paw for her to take. She thought, Duck has seen my anger and he understands. Would James have understood? What would have happened if...?

Duck was walking to the door, eager to be out of the steamy room. She got up, put the letters back in the trunk and thought with shocked wonder that she had never fought a battle in her life, that she had never hacked her way through the jungle of her secret grievances and plaints but had taken the easier (or so it seemed at the time) road of small lies and deceits.

So much still to do. Too much. She must not think that way. After a moment she put the satchel in the trunk as well. Exhausted, head throbbing. But James did take care of me—here is the money to prove it, she thought—what does his amorous adventuring matter now? The trunk was not locked; there was no key. But no one came into the tower. And somehow, after all the day's work, she found herself thinking, and why did I move it anyway, it could have stayed where it was.

Duck followed her out of the room, down the four steps, along the passageway. At the landing, he stopped and waited. Edith was gazing down. The staircase seemed to have changed; the stairs were surely far deeper than they had been when she climbed them only this morning. This morning, she thought, but it seems like a long time ago. And the balustrade seemed less firm, the posts less able to support a clutching hand. The smoothly polished banister threatened. She felt terribly weak and shaky.

I must rest a while, she told herself. Slowly, as though unwinding a spool of something heavy and resistant, she lowered her tall and angular body onto the landing floor and lay there looking up at the softly hued skylight. She had always liked dusk, although with a certain awe and even fear: day was coming to an end; darkness would follow. But now it seemed to her this might be the way to die—enveloped in this stillness so profound and peaceful. Express Delivery, so to speak. But delivered into...? She had dismissed God too, as she had dismissed Tim and Skye. Out of sight, out of mind.

The melodic chimes of the doorbell sounded—but faintly, far away. Duck's ears went straight up. His curl of a tail stiffened. He nudged her to get up, but she was too tired. "I can't, Duck, I can't." The dog stood alert and listening. The deep stillness changed. It menaced. And now the heat, the long arduous day and exhaustion overcame Edith. Lying on the landing, she closed her eyes and was back in girlhood dreams—a slow boat to China—a sailboat in the moonlight.

Sounds of distant trucks wakened her from her reverie. Duck was standing beside her. He watched her rise from the floor—slowly, torturously, using her hands as props on the floor, the hall table, finally reaching onto one of the posts of the balustrade. They started to descend. She clutched the burnished wood of the banister for balance; her resistant body fought gravity to right itself. Duck walked ahead, her cane in his mouth. Not having the satchel made it easier. From time to time he would stop, a strange look on his face, as though he knew something she did not know.

Finally they descended the last flight of stairs. When they reached the bottom of the staircase, Edith sat down on the first step. She could have stayed there forever. Every part of her hurt and her heart seemed to be jumping about. But looking at Duck, she had a feeling of shame. The dog lay there, splayed out, ears fallen, mouth half-open, panting. How selfish I have become, she thought, and, forcing herself up, in a soft voice, "Come, Duck," she said and led him into the kitchen. Water, he must have water. She filled his bowl to the brim and watched him eagerly lap it up, not stopping until the bowl was empty. She filled it again, but he seemed to have had his fill. She took the bean soup she had made the day before from the refrigerator. Watching her heat the food, he whined and whimpered. She apologized as it cooled. "Only a few minutes and you'll eat, Duck. I don't want you to burn your mouth."

As she watched the dog eat ravenously, wiping the bowl clean with his tongue, her shame increased. This is a living creature, she admonished herself, and needs food and water as I do. "We're best friends, Duck, you and I." Duck gave a responsive wag of his tail, then, hunger appeased, thirst quenched, his eyes again seeming to see something she could not.

She emptied the remainder of the soup into a bowl, sliced some bread, brewed tea. The dog watched her as she ate and drank. If it had been feasible, she would have liked to have him seated with her at the table–her friend, sharer of the hidden treasure that would help them both when they were unable to help themselves. She recalled high tea with James. On weekends. He was away or too busy at the office during the week. And not every weekend. Cucumber sandwiches and deviled eggs–"As only you, my dear, can make them." Then they would go up to bed and he would make love to her–the way he liked. But as time went by, their lovemaking became less frequent. She wanted to talk to him then but could not separate thought from feeling. He would tell her to be clear. She would become more confused. Always, lurking in back of her mind, was the fear of rejection and her dependency on him.

She finished eating. Duck was regarding her urgently, trying to withhold a low plaintiff whine and again she was reminded of his needs and along with that came a feeling of appreciation. He asked for no more than food, drink, a run in the yard, and gave her everything without the asking. Duck was a true friend. He would always be loyal.

How cool it was outside. "Duck, dear Duck, you will have your run in the yard. You'd like that, wouldn't you?" She would have thought the dog would eagerly make for the door, but strangely he did not. "You're tired too," she said, "but a nice run will do you good," and she led him to the door and opened it to the evening coolness, first looking to see if the vagrant tomcat was about. She considered putting him on his leash, but no, Duck should have his freedom, let him romp as he wished. He always came when called, not one of those dogs who ran off.

She went back inside. She would call Alfred tomorrow, tell him she wanted to change her will. Edith felt the need for music. She went into the spare room, looked through the 78s, chose one. She put the record on the old Victrola, applied the needle and began to, not dance–but awkwardly move her arms and legs to the rhythm–*"Whispering so no one can hear me–whispering when you cuddle near me..."*

The musical chime of the doorbell broke into the dreamy song. Slowly, apprehensively, she went to answer. Who could it be? At this hour? A burly workman in coveralls stood holding the body of Duck. She knew the dog was dead; it was not only the utter stillness—it was the way the small paws dangled uselessly, the sightless stare of the eyes. Through a haze of shock, Edith heard the workman's stammered words–"Right under my wheels–sorry, ma'am, sorry..."

10

"Shambhala Festival." Alfred Seaman grimaced. "Ten thousand unwashed flakies high on pot and LSD and everything else they can get their hands on and making out all over the place like animals. Why the devil get mixed up in all that when you can go to Paris?"

Polly, his latest lover, swung her brown pigtail to the other side and sighed. "As usual, Alfred, you're making gross generalizations. For one thing, you seem to forget about the music. Six musical stages and each one a different scene. Five days—all those good vibes—woodland trails and birdsong and... Anyway, it's just possible that not all those ten thousand are unwashed flakies and will be high on pot and stuff and making out. Come to think of it, you might want to go too. Shake you up. A new experience. It would do you good to see different people and hear different music."

Alfred was about to say that the internet info on the Shambhala Festival in Salmo was a slick marketing job—music and nature and dancing abounding—but of course, not a word about all the drugs. No point in telling Polly anything; she had to find out herself. He regarded her vibrant face and wondered how to navigate the treacherous waters between truth and pride. This child was making life difficult for him. She had turned things around. He should be giving her advice; there were, after all, thirty-five years between them, but she often admonished him—affectionately —as she would—he flinched at the thought—a sweet old grandfather.

"Funky music is not my thing," he finally said. Polly laughed, "*My thing*. Oh, Alfred, that went out with the sixties. Sorry." She put her hand over her mouth apologetically.

"I wish you would call me Al. After all, I don't call you Pollyanna." He stopped and hoped she would go on to a more palatable subject. Unlike the others, Polly was inclined to conversation full of "how's" and "what's". Her curiosity about everything made him uncomfortable. He smiled at her–she didn't look thirty-five, she looked more like twenty-five. He decided to make a joke of his age. "Oh, Polly, you must remember I'm just an old man," he parodied in a voice that creaked.

"You weren't all that old last night," she said, winking at him.

He remembered. Hoisted on my own petard, came to mind. Literally. His obsession (which seemed–he was forced to admit–the word) for this irrepressible young woman was demanding more sexual energy than he could muster. He should say goodbye. A small diamond. No, an emerald. "So you don't want to go to Paris," he said and was relieved when she again told him no. The stock market had clobbered him. "Hedges," he said, shaking his handsome grey head. He hadn't meant to voice his dilemma.

"I didn't know you were interested in gardens." Polly leaned forward, avid for new information.

"The stock market," he said reluctantly. "That kind of hedge."

"Oh, the stock market–a lot of paper."

"The world runs on paper."

"Not for me. Well, what about your hedges? You don't look too happy."

He considered: With Polly it was safer to answer truthfully before she wore you down. "Some options didn't..."

"...come through. So you gambled and lost. Serves you right. Gambling's not a good thing."

He couldn't feel irritated. Her moralizing was just as bizarre as his being here in Lakeside Park.

"Isn't this mellow?" she was asking. "Aren't you feeling nostalgic? All your old-time favorites." As though she were offering something good for him. He took in the band–brass off to the side, alto and tenor sax up front, drummer, clarinet and bass off to the left.

It would have been a perfect day for a fundraiser–this time, for cancer research–if the haze from the fires in Slocan Valley was not covering much of Lakeside Park–the great firs, cedars and horse chestnuts–allowing only glimpses of an azure sky. Dusty smoke covered Elephant Mountain. As though it's hiding something, he thought. Suddenly, he felt lonely. In glittering Las Vegas, night never came and fun and games went on forever.

The String of Pearls Band began to play *In The Mood*. They had set up in the shade of an enormous tree–he wasn't sure of the name; Polly would know, but he didn't ask her. They were in the shelter donated by the Rotary, seated on one of the benches attached to a large wooden picnic table. All around them, on similar benches and tables, seniors sat, humming the tunes, smiling. He was sharply aware that the couples–husband and wife–were in the same age bracket. Did they think he was there with a daughter? How old had he been when the big bands were playing? He began to calculate but stopped. It occurred to him with a start that Polly would not have been born. He wished she were a bimbo. Too many things were happening too fast.

Polly was enjoying the music. But then, Polly enjoyed whatever she was doing. The band kept playing–*Song of India, Chattanooga Choo Choo, Moon River* and more of the big band songs. Right now they were playing *Begin The Begine* and the two sax players were caught up in the song, giving it their all.

A girl who looked like a pencil was in front of the band. She started singing, *"I'll get by as long as I have you..."* "I wonder if she's anorexic," Polly said–in a worried way that captivated him; he could not think why. Alfred had a talent for finding the right moment to say something sincere in an offhand way. *"I'll get by as long as I have you,"* he found himself singing, but the words weren't as light as he had intended.

"Liar. I'm going to get a gelato. Shall I get one for you?" He shook his head, watched her get in the long line, hoped it would take some time. He was grateful to be alone. He had a lot to think about, had almost been about to confide in Polly just how much he had lost with those damn options. Enough to replace the money he had taken from the account Edith didn't know existed. He closed his eyes but couldn't close his thoughts. Not an account. You could identify an account. The money James had given him couldn't be identified. Only he knew about it. Advance for the venture they were about to invest in. A sure-fire thing. If only James hadn't died so suddenly– that heart attack–leaving him free to use what no one knew about, what was really Edith's.

He watched an enormous woman in white pants, buttock cheeks bouncing, small feet in flip-flopping thongs, weave her way through the crowds to the Little Miss Gelato stand. The gelato line was moving more rapidly. He needed time. Still another pressing problem–Edith, herself. If only he had not made that promise to James: "Make sure Edith is all right, Al. You will, won't you?"

Polly was coming up to the gelato stand. Now she was waiting for her cone. With the ice cream cone in hand, she waved to him and mouthed, Yum yum. His hand waved back. Only his hand. The more he thought about the mess he'd gotten himself into, the worse his situation appeared. To top it all, the woman from the agency was threatening to leave Edith. "Impossible old witch," were her words. He had never particularly cared for Edith, but he could not shake his promise to James to see to her welfare. A nursing home was out of the question—she would not go. But she could not be alone in that old house. And now, with that funny-looking dog dead...

Polly appeared, chocolate edging her lips. "You missed a good thing. What's the matter?"

"I've been thinking..."

"A dangerous thing to do."

"What do you get out of this..." he searched for the right word, "relationship?"

"All the things I can't afford, for one thing." He waited for the inevitable, I'm fond of you, but she said, "What do you get out of it?"

"Youth, beauty..." he hesitated, "respite from time, I guess."

She surveyed him, her blue-grey eyes serious. "It doesn't seem right–having sex with a man old enough to be my grandfather."

"Why do it then?"

"Do you always do what's right?"

"No."

"Well, I guess knowing what's right doesn't mean one can do what's right."

He would tell her. He would confess. He had to talk—and who else could he talk to? Not another attorney. Certainly not Edith, who didn't seem to be all there, anyway.

"Hello, Mr. Seaman."

He turned. "I'm Quigley Biggs," the man said in a voice as polite as his pressed slacks and polo shirt. "We met a couple of times–when I took Mrs. Martin to your office."

"The Express Delivery man." He remembered that Edith had

liked the man, liked him enough to have him to Easter dinner. Trusted him enough to have him drive her to the bank. He thought, here's an answer to the Edith Martin problem; I've got to get this right. "I've been trying to contact you, but Express Delivery doesn't seem to be in business. Sit down, join us." He turned to Polly. "Polly, this is Quigley, and this..." turning to the smiling woman beside him, "is Sidonia," she said, supplying her name, as though this were a game she was delighted to play. "I'm going to get a gelato. Does anyone want one?"

Seaman restrained himself. He wanted to get on with this lucky encounter. He was wondering how to broach the subject of Edith and then Polly said, "So Express Delivery is out of business. What will you do now?"

"Go to Calgary."

"Why Calgary?" Seaman asked, as if he didn't know.

"That's where the jobs are."

"For the time being. It's boom and bust when oil's concerned."

"Oh, it won't matter to Sid and me—we're going to set ourselves up as a housecleaning team. A friend of ours said there's lots of work like that in Calgary. Anyway, there's nothing here in Nelson." Sidonia returned from the gelato stand, empty-handed. The band was winding up along with the day.

"Look, you like it here, don't you," Seaman informed them. "Well, you don't have to move to Calgary. Awful weather. Like having the sky right over your head–sun burning you in summer, wind whipping you in winter. I've got a job for the two of you–and you won't even have to think about renting a place to live."

The band was packing up and people were leaving. Without the chatter, the music, the sounds of life, the park was taking on the look of a place deserted–the old trees spreading their foliage over too quiet lawns.

"You mean old Mrs. Martin," Polly cut in. He nodded. With his eyes, he warned her to keep out of this. Just like her to detail Edith's abysmal experience with live-in help. Quigley and Sidonia were regarding him with interest. He said, "Edith Martin is a client of mine–but you know that, Quigley–you've taken her up to my office. She likes you, and I'm sure she would like Sidonia. She's fiercely independent–you know that too. Problem is she can't be alone now,

69

she's too feeble..." he caught himself in time. He had been about to say she was—what? Confused? Not all there? Given to illusions? Better not to say anything like that. "So," he continued, "you and Sidonia want to work as a team; well, you can. You can do the handyman jobs and chauffeuring," he addressed Quigley, "and you," he turned to Sidonia, "can help with her personal care and do the housekeeping. You'd have your own room and run of the house, of course." He stopped, realizing that 'run of the house' was not exactly the way Edith would see it, but it was too late to retract. "It would mean a lot to me. Her husband and I were close friends. He entrusted his wife's welfare to me."

"But we've been all through that!" Sidonia said. "Quigley asked her—and nicely too—and she turned us down flat. Twice. So why would she change her mind? Anyway, we've got our lives to live, we can't wait around."

Quigley was silent.

Seaman realized that it was to Sidonia he must further his case. "Because she needs you both very much now." He played his trump: "She knows she'll have to go into a nursing home, if..." he looked away.

"A nursing home." Sidonia's voice was grim. "What do you say, Quigley? Shall we try again?"

11

At first, Edith couldn't think who it was coming up the path to the house. She stood at the door, still feeling acutely the absence of Duck who would have been beside her, would have been –no, not ready to attack anyone bent on harm–more prone to licking them– but at least a living presence. She had lost more height. Her shoulders had rounded more. The arthritis in her legs had become more painful, and now the hamstrings of both her legs had become tight and contracted. Sometimes, when she lay sleepless at night, she traced her increasing physical infirmities to the day she had moved the money to the tower room–the day Duck had been run over.

The figure was coming closer. She could see it was not a woman. Edith could see that the figure was Skye. He was carrying a guitar case and when he was right beside her she saw the drawing of a bird on the cover. It must be his old case, she thought. Would the old Gibson be inside? He had pawned and retrieved it so many times she had wondered if his music had faded away like so much else of the boy she had loved.

He wore dark glasses and seemed thinner. He had a haircut—a real haircut. His smile was wide and open so that Edith opened the door wide and said "Come in," and was as though it was Matthew, not Skye entering—her dear grandson with his music and his special self.

"Better keep these glasses on," he said, when they were at the kitchen table, she with her tea, he with strong coffee—a plate of biscuits before them. "I had an infection in one eye," he said. Edith started and Matthew reached out to reassure her; "oh, its okay now, just better to be careful, the doctor said," then he added, "I've got some good news, gram."

The way he said it sent a jolt of pure joy through Edith's tired blood. His voice had a certain lilt in it. Matthew had had that excitement—a bird, tree, song; anything could evoke it.

"You're probably wondering why I'm here now," he went on. "Well, there's this band I used to play with—The Sunbursts—they're in a jazz combo now. They have a gig in Balfour and I'm playing with them." He leaned forward eagerly. "I know I've been—well, kind of wandering and stuff but getting back to my music—it's what I love." As he spoke, Edith had an image of Matthew playing his guitar, his young hands, face and body blending with the instrument, as though it were a part of him.

She made a special dinner—the chicken he liked and asparagus. He would have helped her but she said she was fine, to get some rest since he'd be up till all hours. She did not feel fine—not physically—every part of her hurt in one way or another. Another thing; she had a terrible time finding the roasting pan, condiments and even some of the things she used quite a bit. But Matthew (in her heart she was calling him by his given name) had told her he had plans all laid out—school besides the music, for one. So, she hobbled, her cane at hand. She moved slowly, laboriously; that's why she had told him to rest—so he wouldn't see her efforts to do what had, at one time, been, not a task but a pleasure.

She was rewarded by his, "no one cooks like you do." Yet he did not have second helpings and she thought his right hand shook a bit when he put down his fork. He still wore the dark glasses and she hoped the eye infection was gone and hadn't spread into some other place. She resisted an impulse to ask him to take the glasses off. Playing in the band would be no problem, he had said.

She gave him $150 for expenses he might incur.

"But gram, we'll be paid," he told her. She pointed out that Biff, the clarinet player, was picking him up and taking him and gas was expensive. "And then," she added, "there are contingencies." She wasn't sure why, but she wanted him to take the money. She guessed he had little cash, was waiting to be paid with the band. He seemed tired—and he was definitely thinner—too thin. For a moment she wondered if he was still smoking marijuana—pot they called it—or those other drugs. But he had told he was finished with all that.

She went to bed at midnight; far later than her usual hour. But Matthew said the jamming would really start then and somehow—she knew it was foolish—she wanted to try, at least in spirit, to be there with him. She had left the key under the large potted plant at the entrance to the house.

The next morning she could not wait to see him. He would tell her about the gig. She felt pleased with herself. Getting out of bed was hard—the need to turn carefully, to monitor each movement, to be constantly at attention lest her clumsy movements caused her to fall. She must not fall.

Perhaps he would play something—Simon and Garfunkel or even a jazz tune the way he did, making it different every time. But of course, she must let him sleep. She had said he could sleep in the sewing room which had a comfortable bed in it but, when she passed the room, the door was open and the bed untouched. She stopped, felt a prick at her heart. Had there been an accident? The grandfather clock in the hall chimed eight times. Usually she went to the kitchen had her breakfast but she wasn't hungry.

She hobbled into the living room. Rather she was led into the room by a mixture of smells—sickly sweet, alcohol, and something else, pungent, medical.

She wanted to cry but couldn't. She wanted to scream but couldn't. All she could do was look at Skye's body sprawled half on the sofa, half off, one arm dangling down, the dark glasses sunk in a pool of vomit. She waited until her heart came back. His strange breathing, the flop of his body. This wasn't sleep, healthy restorative sleep. This was stupor and worse.

Silence stretched itself all morning, as though to taunt her. As she painfully went about the endless tasks—washing the few dishes, sweeping the kitchen floor, tidying her bed—she resisted the terrible need to go into the living room. He would wake up. She would see his eyes and she would know what she feared to know.

It was nearly noon when he came into the kitchen. She was halfheartedly sipping a cup of tea.

"I took a shower," he said, "I didn't think you'd mind. I'll make lunch. An omelet. You have eggs, don't you?"

She hardly saw his neatened hair, the clean but unpressed shirt and pants. He was wearing the dark glasses.

"Take off those glasses," her voice sounded strange to her. It seemed to come from a part of her she didn't know.

He was saying he had cleaned up the mess. A band night, he

73

was sorry. He had thrown a tea towel over his arm clowning in a show of Maitre De but his arm began to shake. In horrified fascination, Edith watched the towel fall to the floor, exposing the arm, now shaking violently—an arm which seemed a backdrop for haphazard colors of blue and grey, lumps and welts.

"I could help you," he was saying. "I've been sick but I can get well. You and I, we're all alone. I could sleep in the turret."

Edith's heart yearned for him—her Matthew. He's my grandson she told herself. The feeling of aloneness now came to her—like being enclosed in a block of ice. And it was true, she needed help, she could no longer deny that. There was Leo and he was certainly helpful but he had many jobs to do. He was, after all, the best handyman in Nelson and the outskirts. She saw, as though before her, Leo's kind grey eyes. He was always ready to help her and others. Not just with the yard and garden but with the house which needed repairs. "A special house," Leo called it.

Skye had not moved.

"Take off your Glasses!"

He made no motion.

Edith was standing now. She was coming closer to him and he was drawing back with a speed that was impossible—surely she could not move like this—Edith's arm reached and in one swooping motion pulled off his glasses. Huge black pupils looked out on nothingness from swampy white orbits.

"Gram, listen to me," he was saying. "Let me explain." His voice was soft and wheedling. What was he thinking or feeling? She could not know. For this was not Matthew, the eager boy open to life, standing before her but Skye, a prisoner, devoid of will, enslaved by his jailors —marijuana that had progressed to something else and something newer. And still, the alcohol.

He was telling her that she was jumping to conclusions, and in a way, she was, but this conclusion was like the bottomless gap in the road that had been preceded by a long series of warning signs. He was saying that they had always been friends, good friends, but she knew another friend— not in human form—had replaced her and was holding him captive.

She stood there forcing herself not to fall. Outside, the day moved on. Cars started up, children chattered, the day didn't know what was happening here inside this house on Victoria Street.

She handed him his dark glasses. He didn't put them on.

"Say it," she demanded and she thought, if he would just say the word, the way the AA people did; "I am an alcoholic"—then maybe he could escape from his jailor.

"Say what?" His voice had an edge to it.

"That you are an addict," the word a red hot iron seared her heart. She went on, unable to stop herself. "It was all the same old play-acting—your wonderful plans."

He still had not put the glasses on. He tried to focus but the pupils of his eyes had become black, opaque ping pong balls. She looked away.

"Okay, I goofed," he said irritably contrite.

"Say it." If he could say the word, she thought still again, he could expose his jailors. It would free Skye to change back into Matthew.

"I don't know what you're talking about," he said. "Okay, I have some problems. Who doesn't? So last night didn't go the way I thought it would. I can get back on track. I can. I just need a little rest. I wouldn't be any trouble. And then…"

Edith felt afraid, a monstrous visceral fear. "Just go," she said. "Just go!"

For a long time she stood at the door watching him go down the drive and down the road. He did not look back. Then she sank heavily into an easy chair. Her leg throbbed; her hip threatened to come apart; her head was splitting. She could bear pain but how could she bear this loss which flooded her heart?

Minutes passed. He was clearly gone. Edith closed the door, put on the latch, drew the curtains. She got the hot water bag, started to fill it, but the bag slipped from her hand and the water spilled onto the floor. When the floor was mopped, she got the dry mop to make sure the floor was safe. Finally, she filled the bag again, but very slowly, carefully. Then, taking it, wrapped in a towel, to her easy chair, she sat down and placed it on her knee. But, as though playing with her, the pain kept moving around–her hamstrings–thigh–toes. Surely, it wasn't all arthritis. She thought of her last physical exam. Years ago. Dr. Helperin had advised this medication and that–for cholesterol–arthritis… She couldn't remember what else. And what was the end of all those tests? Medications that only made you sicker.

Closing her eyes, she let the hot water bag rest on her knee.

When she opened them, she saw the newspapers lying about, crackers dropped, stains on the carpet, on the tablecloth. The windows were grimy. She got up and went into the bedroom, thinking she would lie down a while, but the bed was unmade, sheets and pillows helter-skelter. The sheets hadn't been changed since that awful woman from the agency had left, but she felt too tired. It would mean putting them into the machine, taking them out, putting them into the dryer. The worst was getting the washed sheets on the bed. All that bending–when had it become so difficult?

She went into the kitchen, as though searching for more evidence for what she needed to do. And the evidence was there. The kitchen was a mess. The burners on the stove needed cleaning. A pot, half-heartedly scoured, stood on the stove. Traces of peeling from vegetables and fruits were scattered about the counters. She opened the refrigerator, then closed it. There was no way to tackle a job like that. Matthew had been right when he said she needed help. But whom could you trust these days? Certainly no one like that woman from the agency, nosing into everything.

On the fridge, the Express Delivery card was still posted, held by a magnet depicting a Canada goose. Quigley Biggs, Edith thought, and his name evoked not only his service but the tea and Easter dinner they had shared. Yes, Quigley had been good to her. Caring. Why hadn't she accepted his offer to come live here, care for her? A woman, of course. Always a woman. It had been like that with Tim. She started to dial the number of Express Delivery, then replaced the receiver, annoyed with herself: Express Delivery was no longer in service. How forgetful I'm getting to be, she told herself.

Her thoughts kept wobbling. How to get help? Do I really need help?

When the phone rang and it was Quigley, it seemed to her that it was providential.

"Mrs. Martin, I'm calling to ask if perhaps, you might now be interested in live-in help. If you are, we would be grateful for a chance to come and talk with you."

She hesitated, but only for a moment. "In a week–can you both come in one week–at three o'clock?"

"In a week–the seventh of September. Yes, we'll be there."
"To talk about–conditions of employment." She hastened to add, "It's best to be clear."

12

Edith looked at the bedside clock. Ten past six. During the summer the sun would be streaming into the room, but now, with fall on its way, the room was dim. She burrowed more deeply under the warm quilt and closed her eyes. The light drizzle outside the covered window sounded like music and enhanced her feeling of peace. If she lay there, not moving, the pain in her leg would go. Why not stay in bed? No more pain, no more striving, no more loneliness, no more having to do... If there were Duck to nudge her into the day...

She opened her eyes, saw the calendar on the wall and remembered–tomorrow was the 7th. Quigley Biggs and his girlfriend would be coming. She had to get up. She had to rehearse. Fortunately, she had the whole day to go over the way she must present herself. She began mumbling, as, laboriously, she managed her way out of bed, turning to one side carefully, placing her feet on the floor, first tentatively, then firmly. She stood up, holding onto the bedpost.

To an outsider her words might seem random jargon; in fact, they were full of purpose and determination. "I'll take them through the house–all the rooms, except of course, the tower." She would explain–oh yes, quite explicitly, what was required. To do this, she must appear in–she hardly knew how to express it–good shape, she finally decided. It would not do for them to see her weak and unsteady. No, it would not do at all for them to see her hobbling about. Fortunately, the leg spasms happened during the night. She shook her head. Last night had been difficult; an hour–walking slowly–before she could release the stubborn leg from bondage.

She turned on the light, dressed slowly, reached for her cane, hobbled into the kitchen, all the while reminding herself: "Tomorrow you must be erect. No stumbling. Take one of those Ibuprofen– maybe two–before they come." Quigley, he could understand weakness, but that sweetheart of his...who knew what she would be like? It was important to be strong. It was vital. In the nature programs on TV, lions pounced upon peacefully grazing gazelles, leopards crept up on unsuspecting fawns. Edith could hear the voice of the narrator: "That's another fawn that didn't get away."

She prepared her breakfast—a small glass of orange juice, a boiled egg—easier than scrambled, which she preferred but meant scrubbing the frying pan. She toasted the last slice of bread. Then tea. Breakfast and washing the dishes took a long time. She had to be terribly careful not to put anything near the edge of the counter or table. If a dish fell, there would be the scattered shards to deal with. Worse if a glass fell; there would be all those splinters hiding in corners least suspected. And then a cut that must not get infected, the arduous task of cleaning the cut, the dressing. Even if a spoon fell, it meant figuring out how to pick it up. The long metal retriever could pick up just so many things. So she would have to bend down and, of course, that would trigger the sharp incapacitating pain in her left leg. It seemed to Edith that much of her life was being lived in the future as she plotted and planned how to do the simplest things.

After her second cup of tea, she realized she was out of milk, also tea, really a good many groceries. She had become careless about the food deliveries. Anyway, food seemed less tasty; more and more, she was losing interest in her meals. But tomorrow Quigley and Sidonia would be coming. She needed to have food in the house. Then, an idea struck her. It would be nice to have a lemon meringue pie too. The lemon meringue was somehow a link to her pleasant relationship with Quigley Biggs and his excellent delivery service.

Edith went to the front door, opened it. Her old Packard was there in the driveway in front of the house. Moving about, she began to feel somewhat better. But then she had to go to the bathroom. She sighed deeply. Another struggle. Brought up to be modest about bodily functions, she did not like the time and effort this could take. But this morning all went quickly. She felt her easy bowel movement was a sign she was quite well. What was more, the pain in her leg was practically gone. The exciting idea began to circle round and round in her head, giving her pace momentum.

She looked inside her purse for her driver's license and found it tucked inside the little card case, along with her Care Card and Visa. Then she took Teddy down from his shelf. Not the top shelf.

All kinds of terrible accidents happened to old women who reached too high... If that were the end, it would be all right, but if your heart kept beating while the rest of you disintegrated... Sitting in a wheelchair, needing toileting, feeding... She didn't want to finish the thought.

She brought Teddy over to her easy chair, sat him on her knee. She knew he was a stuffed animal, but she had to tell someone:

"An Expedition, that's what it will be! It's time, time for another. I'll drive downtown to the mall, get groceries–a lemon meringue too. And I'll have lunch at that little coffee shop." Teddy was sitting there blandly. She went on–talking to him–talking to herself: "After all, Quigley and Sidonia aren't coming until tomorrow. I have all afternoon to rehearse." Rehearse what? she thought, then answered: "Rehearse the way I'll show them round the house–*my* house."

Teddy made no comment. Somewhere, in the background of her mind, she could hear James' voice: "Stubborn, you're just plain stubborn." She paid no attention. "Ted," she said, "I have to get out. I haven't driven for a while, but I was a good driver, and after all it's an automatic. The brake and the gas, that's all I need to remember. I still have my license." She would take Teddy along; you couldn't go on an Expedition alone. Still, it wouldn't do for anyone to see a stuffed animal beside her. She would put him in the back seat–a toy for a grandchild.

Edith started to prepare for her Expedition, her thoughts and movements taking on the rhythm of her will which was climbing within her. What to wear? What to carry? She would not take a purse. Too easy to lose. She would travel light. She searched her hall closet, chose a jacket with four large pockets, studied it. Into the bottom right-hand pocket she put her house key held on a bright millennium key ring; in the bottom left, she put her car key, held on a square leather fob. Her driver's license went into the top right-hand pocket; several bills—including, after some deliberation, one hundred-dollar bill—went into the top left. These she took from the canister holding her household money, stored in a kitchen cabinet. She patted each pocket, took Teddy and went out to the car.

Edith turned the key in the ignition. The car started at once. Then the windshield wiper. It swept back and forth, but the windshield was still misty. For a moment she hesitated. She had never liked driving in the rain. It's only a drizzle, she told herself, more like a mist. Tentatively, she placed her right foot on the gas, then the brake. She did this three times, feeling the space between, reminding herself that it was the left leg that was—as she put it—the bad one. A voice in back of her head told her that this was a crazy impulse, but she was already in drive, releasing the hand brake, her foot on the gas pedal. The Expedition had started.

"We're off!" she called to Teddy in the back seat and drove slowly down the long driveway. There were no other cars, but when she came to the turn for the road going into town and saw the cars speeding along both sides her hands began to shake. She turned off the ignition and sat there trembling. Her mind wandered back to long ago. Into her ear came the voice of James. "I'll drive," he would say, when they went to the theater—to visit—to dinner—anywhere. Pride and Fear waged an all-out war within her as she considered turning back.

In the end, Pride, buoyed up by a vagabond girl, won. The girl, knapsack on her back, had been standing on the side of the main road trying to hitch a ride—but apparently the right kind of ride, for she had refused a couple. Suddenly aware of Edith Martin sitting in her Packard, she came over. "Are you all right?"

"I'm fine." When the words were out, Edith made an effort to straighten, to steady her hands—to breathe more evenly.

"I need to get to the Greyhound Depot. In the mall. But you can let me off anywhere in town," the girl said. Edith told her that she was going to the mall. The girl, about eighteen or so, made her think of herself at that age. Which was odd, because the girl didn't look like her at that age. It wasn't just that she had an oval face whereas Edith's had always been squarish; it was the girl's attire. She had on a quilted vest, open, showing her plaid flannel shirt beneath. Her jeans were worn and turned up at the ankle. Tangled auburn curls ran down her back. Edith remembered wearing Scotch plaid skirts, frilly blouses and saddle oxfords at that age—or maybe before. She couldn't remember ever thinking of hitching a ride.

When the girl got into the car, she began talking. "I really appreciate your giving me a lift. I could have gotten a ride, but I didn't like the look of the fellows in the car. My name is Rainbow. What's yours?"

"Edith, Edith Martin. You have an unusual name."

80

"Actually, it's not my given name. My given name is Geraldine Feinstermayer, but I've given myself a new name. That is, changing the Geraldine to Rainbow; I'm leaving the Feinstermayer–I never seem to use it, anyway. Do you want to know why I have to get to the Greyhound Depot?"

Edith said she did. The drizzle had turned into a light rain, but the wipers were working well. She relaxed her hands on the wheel but kept them steady. Driving, after months away from the car, did not seem the problem she had anticipated. Whenever she glanced at her passenger, the girl seemed completely at ease, as though she were sitting beside an accomplished driver.

"These trucks think they own the road," she said, companionably, as they drove into the mall; "you're smart to just let them pass." Then, as though no time had gone by since she asked her question–in a voice trilling with excitement–she said, "I'm taking the bus to Vancouver–to meet someone–at the Depot..."

"Someone in your family?"

The girl shook her head, smiling happily.

"Your sweetheart?" Edith tried again, aware that the word was old-fashioned.

"Sweetheart–sweet–heart," the girl murmured, savoring each syllable. "What a lovely word. Well, not exactly, but–like–it could be...I met him on this chatroom: *Talk Free*. Do you believe in synchronicity?"

Synchronicity? Edith wasn't sure what the word meant. But she did not have to answer. The girl was talking again, rapidly. "He's got a job–at the Park Plaza–shuttling to the airport, and nights he drives a cab. He says there're lots of jobs around. It's the 2010 Olympics. Vancouver's in a frenzy–building–taking down– contractors making money..."

They were at the Bus Depot. Before Edith could ask important questions, the girl was saying, "Thanks very much for the lift." Edith looked for a space where she would not have to back out, found one and very carefully parked. But she could not take her hands from the wheel. Her knuckles were white. As the girl got out the car, Edith could not refrain from asking, "But where will you stay?" The girl turned around, all smiles. "He's sharing a flat with two other guys. He said there's no problem, always room for one more. Take care." She did a little skipping step, heading for the Depot.

It took a few minutes before Edith felt confident enough to move the car to another space. She kept seeing the girl (Rainbow, she told herself) skipping along, a book sticking out of her backpack–*The Power of Now*–whatever that meant. She had not wished the girl good luck. She would need it.

Edith had to get moving. Her Expedition had gone off-course. She relaxed her hands on the wheel. The light rain was somewhat heavier now. She set the wipers, looked all around many times, then drove the short distance down to Wal-Mart.

As she tried anxiously to maneuver the car into a space near one of the cart enclosures, a long box pulled into the next space. At once, a panoply of emotions–anger, fear, anxiety–forced her foot from the gas pedal to the brake. Only when the other driver slid into his space did she continue into hers.

"Got enough room?" the hefty young fellow asked, when she got out of the car. She looked up in surprise. The man had a smile that matched his courteous words. She nodded. Indeed, looking at the space between their vehicles, she had to admit there was space enough. "Have a good day," he said, whistling as he headed off.

The words, along with his smile and amiable manner, threw her completely off-guard. "And you too," she said. Patting the four pockets of her jacket, she closed the door of her car. As she took a cart, the anxiety and fear with which she had begun her Expedition gave way. She had come through the first of her trials. She had driven to the mall, dropped off a sweet and innocent talkative girl, and was now wheeling a cart, smiling at others doing the same; they smiled back as though she were one of them. After her long isolation, it all seemed extraordinary.

Holding onto the handle of the cart, she entered the mall, but not before noting that the drizzle had changed to rain. An obstacle starting out, rain did not seem like one now. Her Expedition, initially so hesitant, so fraught with danger, had taken a turn. After all, I might have gone back, she reasoned to herself, if Rainbow had not come along. And wasn't that what happened in all those adventures she had read about–a stranger coming along and changing the course of the adventure?

She regarded her watch. Barely twelve. She would have lunch before she bought her groceries. She wheeled the cart into the coffee shop, sat down at a table and picked up the menu. The waitress came over, looked at the cart. If she tells me the cart can't stay, it will be a bad sign, Edith thought, but the waitress only said, "What will you have?" Edith waited for some other remark that might set her apart from the others. "The special is a cup of corn chowder and a spicy chicken wrap," was all the waitress said.

"Sounds good to me," Edith said in a breezy voice, the voice she had used in her teens. She watched the waitress depart and smiled at the woman at the next table. Her smile was returned. Edith wanted to linger here, in this anonymous mall, amidst strangers who took for granted she was the confident woman they saw. She would make an afternoon of this adventure. She moved each arm then leg. No pain, not even a trace. The corn chowder tasted like ambrosia. She could not find words fine enough to describe the chicken wrap. She had a second cup of Earl Grey. When she finally reached into the pocket where her money was, she took out a five-dollar bill and two loonies, considered, then replaced the five with a ten. She would leave a more-than-usual tip.

She wheeled her cart down the mall, increasingly pleased with herself. She had dressed carefully; her slacks fitted well, not too loose and worn, like the ones she wore around the house. Her hair too was carefully brushed. She did not look like those bag ladies wheeling carts of empty pop cans up and down streets.

At Coles Books, she paused before a display of new *Dummy* books. A stand held a large number of the latest *Harry Potter*. She went inside the bookstore, suddenly recalling Quigley once mentioning a book called *The Secret*. "You want something badly enough, you get it," he had said. Well, there was of course more to it than that. They were all sold out.

She looked at her watch. Plenty of time. She had left the house in a terrible mess, but she'd have all afternoon to at least tidy it. And rehearse. As she walked past Victoria's Secrets, resolve walked with her: she, Edith Martin, could hold her own. She would tell—what was her name?—Sidonia—exactly what her duties were. The resolve grew stronger as she lingered before the discount rack outside Work World, peaked as she scanned the special items outside Shopper's Drugmart. It's my house, after all, she reminded herself.

After a while, her step changed. She began to meander aimlessly up and down the mall. "Buy me! Buy me!" the shirts, boots, pants, jackets, cheap jewelry and jogging outfits all seemed to be saying. She remembered the first mall she had seen. Long ago. In Vancouver. James was starting his career. She had wanted to be–of all things–a biologist.

"Excuse me."

The voice brought her back to the present. She moved away, murmured an apology. She had bumped into an elderly man in front of Stewart's News. The man was reading the headlines and shaking his head. She had a glance–TWO MORE CANADIANS KILLED BY ROADSIDE BOMB IN AFGHANISTAN–ICE CAPS MELTING–GENOCIDE IN DARFUR–TAINTED BLOOD SCANDAL... Her thoughts began to mingle, meeting each other, joining...Darfur is in Africa...Tim is in Africa; improper screening...tainted blood...AIDS...Tim is with an AIDS support group in Africa; where is he...will I ever hear from him again?

She moved resolutely away from the newsstand and the news disappeared. Her thoughts vanished too, as she continued to ramble on in the direction of Save On Foods. The safe feeling of the mall was with her again. She could have stayed inside this insulated world forever.

It was nearly one o'clock when she went into Save On Foods. She lost herself getting groceries. It was pleasant to go up and down the aisles, gathering this and that, even some expensive sauces she didn't really need. Winter was coming, after all. If she got back to the house in an hour or so, there would be plenty of time to rehearse for tomorrow.

The rain was coming down in sheets when she finally wheeled her cart outside. She wished she had worn her raincoat instead of her jacket. And her rain hat. Get to the car as quickly as you can, she advised herself. But where was her car? In the downpour, she wheeled the cart back and forth between the lines of cars. Inside the cart, her bags of groceries were quickly soaking. It took fifteen minutes to find the Packard–not next to the cart enclosure where she was certain she had parked it, but near another, farther away.

Her jacket was drenched. She reached into the pocket holding her car key. The pocket was empty. She felt inside the pocket again– then again. It was not there; only an old leather watch band. Frantically, she searched in her other pockets. Her house keys were in place; her license and her money too. No car key. Why were her parking lights on? Apprehensively, she brought her dripping eyes inside the car. The key was in the ignition.

As the rain beat down on her and her groceries, Edith tried to play the Pollyanna game her mother had long ago taught her: be thankful the motor is not running; that you are not on some back road... But her heart refused to play, kept racing wildly, as though, by itself, it must get her home immediately.

Pain, hard and punishing, streaked down her left side and leg. Her head felt about to burst. She stood there, her eyes blurry with the rain become a torrent, clutching the handle of the cart against the fierce wind. Her hands began to throb uncontrollably.

"Are you all right?"

In a daze, she turned. An old and wrinkled man was about to get into his old and wrinkled car.

She shook her head. "My key—is inside—my car."

"Do you have BCAA?"

Again, she shook her head. It had seemed like so much good money gone each year.

"I'll go inside and call Jake's Auto Service; he'll come and open your door," the old man said.

"Thank you." Guiltily, she watched him limp his way toward the mall, the rain beating down on him.

With a long strangely-constructed wand of wire, the man from Jake's Auto Service pried open the driver's door; shivering violently from head to foot, she watched him. "There!" he said, cheerfully. "Should start right up. Lucky the motor wasn't on. I'll put your groceries in back."

There seemed nothing to do but get into the car and turn on the ignition. The car started at once. "That'll be fifty dollars." She handed the money to him and he wrote a receipt. "You're on your way," he said with an expansive smile, as though, she thought resentfully, the incident had been a piece of cake.

Edith had not intended to drive home. Surely not. Yet she found herself driving, her foot on the gas refusing to hold steady, braking erratically, her movements jerky. "Lady, where the hell did you get your license!" a thickset man in a Cadillac bellowed. She tried to keep her head down. They must not see her. Her soaking hair dripped onto the wheel. To get home, close the door, not go out again—that was her one thought.

When she finally rounded her driveway–the fifteen-minute drive had taken twenty-five–she said, to her surprise, "Thank you, Lord." She had not spoken to God for several years.

She did not put the car in the garage. It was all she could do to park it. The storm had passed. The sun shone. The air was fresh. A glorious rainbow was right before her. She felt out of place with all this loveliness. She fidgeted, trying to fit the house key into the lock. For one terrified minute, she thought she had the wrong key. She gave thanks to God again when the key turned and she was inside.

She did not want to look at the messy rooms. She would tidy up tomorrow morning before Quigley and that woman came. Most of all, she did not want to look at herself, drenched, hair matted, face smudged–like one of those women who run with the wolves. I'm old, she told herself, putting into the word all that had happened during the torturous day: the way her body was shaking, her breath coming in gasps, and the aches and pains besieging her soggy self.

She was about to turn on the taps for her bath, when the door chimes sounded. She thought of not answering. Then she remembered that the paperboy was due to collect. The chimes sounded again. She patted her hair down and opened the door.

Quigley Biggs and his girlfriend stood there.

"Tomorrow–you said, tomorrow," Edith stammered, when she could get her breath.

"September seventh, three o'clock, Mrs. Martin, that's today," Quigley said–not reprimanding her but softly, in that way he had. Then she remembered what had happened. She could even see the early morning darkness, the calendar on the wall. It hung on one of those photo hooks. The page had flipped over. She had been looking at the wrong month.

"If you..." Sidonia was saying gently.

"No, no, come in." Edith felt depleted, exhausted, beyond caring. Let them see the crackers on the sofa, the papers on the floor, the stains on the upholstery... And let them see me in the state I'm in, she told herself. The Expedition had been too much.

"You're ill," Sidonia said.

"I'll put your car in the garage," Quigley said.

Edith gave him the key. She let Sidonia take her hand and lead her to a chair, take off her wet shoes and stockings. "The house..." she began, remembering there were things she had to say to

86

them–explain the mess, which they did not seem to notice or if they did, they did not indicate. Certain conditions–arrangements–had to be made. But all this seemed far away. Sidonia was running a bath, taking off her clothes, helping her to bathe, finding a nightgown, warm and dry. Then, there was tea and toast and soup, and they were saying she must rest.

Even as she welcomed their attendance upon her, she hated needing it. She wanted to explain: she was not always so needful. But she could not find the words to describe her Expedition, could not convey the difficulty of accomplishing what people did every day as a matter of course. As to the key left in the car, the pouring rain, her foot trembling with endeavor between brake and gas–how could she tell them of her terrible feeling of responsibility for the lives of those who might fall victim to her pride?

Then, she was getting ready for bed, and Sidonia was saying, "You can't take the stairs; it's good you have your bedroom downstairs." Edith wanted to protest, to say she could manage the stairs, although she could not imagine how she could after the frightful day, but Quigley agreed.

So she went to bed in her bedroom downstairs and they, after seeing to every possible need of hers, went to bed in the second-floor bedroom. The master bedroom. And Edith, while upset they would be sleeping on the second floor, for there had not been time to lay out sleeping arrangements, nevertheless found some comfort in the fact that the satchel was no longer in the closet.

"We never use the third floor," she managed to say, "so there's no need to go there." They nodded. "Your salaries..." she went on, but they said that could wait till tomorrow.

"The important thing is for you to get some sleep," Sidonia said and laid her hand gently on Edith's shoulder.

"Your health, that's what matters," Quigley said in his softly deferential way

They care about me, she thought. Though Quigley was in his fifties and Sidonia in her forties, they seemed young to her. Young and possessing the power of youth.

Although she was exhausted, Edith did not fall asleep. Enclosed by the dark night, she lay uneasily in bed, beset by doubt and fear, gazing at the shadowy branches of the trees on the opposite wall–whispering to each other.

PART TWO

13

All of Canada was in a deep freeze; December through January 2007, storms came along with outages and floods. Edith had only to look out the window, see icy branches, a leaden sky, hear the wind screaming, or listen to the radio and know there were homeless sleeping in alleyways, to feel how lucky she was—in her own home, safe and secure. She had taken Quigley and Sidonia more or less for granted, but was beginning to see them in a different light. It was they, after all, who made her comfortable and saw to her needs. Her grudging acknowledgment of their services over the last months started changing to a feeling of gratitude. "They care about me," she told herself, and this was comforting, as increasingly she noticed changes within herself that were unsettling but hard to define.

"Come now, Edith," Sidonia said one day, "everyone forgets, everyone mislays something. I couldn't find the key yesterday and it was right under my nose—the newspaper was covering it. And the other day I met one of our neighbors and for the life of me couldn't think of his name."

Edith didn't say anything more, but, age or not, she couldn't get rid of the feeling that she was not quite herself. Of course I am old, she thought, and I can't expect to be the same as I used to be.

"This winter is enough to make anyone go off the deep end," Quigley said, "nothing but cold, snow and ice." His face was flushed, his red hair matted. He had taken off his boots at the door but still had on his parka. "I'll have to get Leo to help me clear the ice-snow from the garage roof," he said, annoyed. "That is, if he's available. Looks like everyone in Nelson needs a handyman and it's got to be Leo."

At the mention of his name, Edith realized she had avoided seeing Leo. He, so quick to detect any changes in her, would ask if she was all right. And she wasn't quite sure what she could tell him.

Certainly not about this latest obsession. She didn't want to talk about the labeling. She put labels on the jars and containers in the refrigerator. She labeled a piece of cheese wrapped in plastic, some buns in a bag. She painstakingly put tags on the drawers of her dresser–blouses, underwear, scarves. Often, after some remark made by Sidonia or Quigley, she would go to her bedroom and note them in the little notebook on her bedside table.

One day, as she was putting some additional labels on the cabinets which held pots and pans and dish towels, she began singing: *"Tea for two and..."* she left off sing-songing abruptly. *"...Two for tea,"* Sidonia supplied, coming into the kitchen. "Why are you putting labels on everything?"

"You're always saying everything is so messy. If we know where everything is, it will be neater." Edith followed Sidonia's eyes to the cabinets. "And we're always mixing up dishes and glasses and..."

There was a certain amount of logic in what Edith said, Sidonia told herself silently, and there was usually a reason for her other strange behavior these days.

When Quigley came back, it was four o'clock, but dark outside. A wet sloppy snow kept falling. Elephant Mountain and the lake were the color of slate. He removed his boots, hung up his parka, put the groceries away, then came into the living room.

"Thank goodness you're back," Sidonia said, glancing at Edith.

"I stopped at Leo's shack to see if he can help clean out the garage," Quigley said. He turned to Edith. "I got those muffins you like."

"Thanks, Quigley. Thank you very much." Edith wanted to say more but she didn't know what. Most times he brought something back for her. She looked at her cane propped against an armchair. It had a nice broad base. That had been Quigley's idea– replacing the flimsy pointy base.

"I'd better start supper," Sidonia said.

"So early?" he asked.

Sidonia shrugged, annoyed. He knew very well why early supper was necessary. Edith would fall asleep afterwards. The early darkness conjured up the night and bed. They would have time to themselves. She said quietly, "We've been through this, Quiggy."

"Is something wrong?" Edith asked. It bothered her if she sensed any conflict between them—these two people she cared about and who cared about her. But they were shaking their heads.

"The kitchen is very neat, very neat indeed," Quigley said, looking around at all the labels. Sidonia said nothing.

When supper was over and Edith in bed, and she and Quigley were sitting in the living room in front of the fire, she asked, "Do you want to listen to the National?"

He picked up one of the mugs of tea on the side table in a desultory way. He's grown older, Sidonia thought. His red unruly hair seemed faded. There were lines around his eyes that hadn't been there months before. He shook his head. "It's all bad—the news; Darfur, the crazy housing market in the States, kids frying their brains on crystal meth..." he stopped for a breath. "Not to leave out Conrad Black, Mulroney and those other..." He shrugged. "Oh, what the hell."

They sat in the darkness, not bothering to light a lamp. Inside the house the silence deepened, broken only by the drip drip drip from the roof. Finally, Quigley got up, switched on the lamp on a side table. "Does it happen like that—I mean, her putting notes in the fridge and on the tables and marking up the calendars?"

Sidonia gazed into the fire. "Happen like what?"

"Come on, Sid, you know damn well what I mean. Is this what aging is about?"

"All those notes—it's her way, she's methodical, likes things to be in order. You know, Quiggy, her forgetting, misplacing something—people do that all the time. I do it. You do too. You went out the other day to get a pair of ice-grips for my boots and I must have told you at least ten times that I needed them and you came back with a snow brush, a flashlight for the car, anti-freeze—and no ice-grips."

Quigley pondered this for a moment but in the end, all he could say was: "I just plain forgot."

Sidonia grinned. Her dimple came back out of hiding.

* * *

Edith was about to go into the living room—she had left her book there—when she heard Quigley's voice: "Beau called. He says

93

Calgary is the place to be. Easy to get jobs, not like Nelson. He says there's a guy selling his delivery business—has to go south for his wife's health. Sid, it's a terrific opportunity for us."

There was a silence. Edith balanced herself on her cane and wondered if she should leave. Perhaps she should go into the room. But going into the room would not necessarily lead to taking part in their conversation, she felt. There was something secretive about standing there, unseen, listening, something not quite right. Still, she stood where she was, leaning on her cane, unable to go into the room or go away.

"We'd have to put up some money. But it's a good business, been going for years and what with the economy booming like it is in Calgary, it's going better than ever."

Quigley was speaking rather loudly—for him; he was inclined to speak softly. But now, he was accentuating certain words. Edith could imagine him gesturing with his hands, which he did when he was excited. A feeling she could not define was making her heart quicken and her pulse race. She realized her painful shoulders were up to her neck. She was hardly breathing. Would they come out? But no, they were too deep into what they had to say to each other.

She took a breath and backed further away from the room taking care not to make a noise. She held her cane so tightly that her hand hurt. Her whole body ached and wanted to lie down. Still, she stayed there, pressed against the wall. She had to hear. It was crucial for her to hear what Quigley and Sidonia were really like. The stuff they were made of. Now that she felt herself more vulnerable than ever, all her old fears about her money magnified. It was safe in the trunk in the turret room. But she could no longer make the trip to get a large bill when needed. She was in fact finding it more and more difficult to handle the small amounts kept in her room. She wanted— needed—desperately to turn the handling of her money over to an other. But not the bank. Quigley and Sidonia. They cared for her. They had always been honest. But temptation had come their way. It seemed providential to Edith that circumstance had placed her outside this room at this time. Her feet could barely hold her up, but she could not move.

For a few minutes, there was silence. Then Quigley said, "We shouldn't be thinking about Calgary, Sid, much less talking about it."

"Yes." Her voice was so low that Edith had to strain to hear her. Then Sidonia said, "If we went to Calgary, we would have to put Edith in a nursing home. We just have to do what we can, Quiggy."

Edith stopped listening at that point. With every ounce of attention she could muster, she took firm hold of her cane and moved torturously back to her room. There she slowly undressed, put on her nightgown with awkward twistings and turnings, and got into bed.

Edith felt terribly tired but she could not fall asleep. Her thoughts came and went. She moved to one side, then another. Her legs hurt, her head ached, a knife cut into her hip. In a miasma of long ago she saw herself doing all the things she could no longer do—taking charge of all the household needs, driving, dealing with insurance–and more–for the family who had once been hers, but whose names were receding to the background. She had wanted to make them happy. To be there for them whenever she was needed. But it had been hard, all those times–keeping silent when you wanted to shout, not answering back. "And where has it gotten me? A husband with a mistress, a son in the far corners of the earth, a ne'er-do-well grandson. I have trusted and I have been betrayed. Now, when I am old and need help…" She was talking out loud, and, hearing herself, was shocked by the peevish childish sound of her voice.

Then she smiled. She need not be afraid. She could trust Sidonia and Quigley. They were her family now.

The following afternoon, the three were sitting in the kitchen having tea. Quigley had been to Kal Tire to get two new winter tires. The tires had been a good buy. One hundred sixty for the two. Bud, the owner of the gas station, had told him the tires would be fifty dollars more. "Gas has gone up again," Quigley said, "and the word is it's going to keep going up." Edith scanned his face. He looked drawn, tired. "I think I'll walk to town after I tackle that snowdrift–unless I have to get a lot of heavy stuff. Anyway, it's good for the environment–not driving."

Sidonia poured more tea, then fixed the pillow behind Edith's back. Edith picked up her teacup carefully. She took another sip. Earl Grey–her favorite. Sidonia knows what I like, she thought. Then she scrutinized Sidonia's face and saw–what did they call them?–worry lines. Edith felt a pang. Worrying about me. Having to do all the things I can't—and more.

"Everything's going up," Sidonia said fretfully. "Harper and Campbell and all the rest of the politicos say we don't have to worry about inflation, not in Canada, but all you have to do is buy groceries. It's our being in Afghanistan and Bush being in Iraq and the whole crazy world. Of course, they're not buying the groceries, probably not even their wives. No, not them."

She turned to Edith. "Eighty-five dollars for groceries this week, and I was real careful with what I got—vegetables, milk, bread, some chicken breasts and..." she hesitated, "I did get some no-fat yogurt for me—no one else likes yogurt—and some other no fat things. The health food department, that's the most expensive—no fat, no sugar, no this or that. But I'm trying to lose weight, I really am." She looked accusingly at Quigley.

"You're too sensitive, Sid. All I did was call you Chub. It's a pet name."

"Well I don't like it." Sidonia folded her arms against her waist.

Edith put her cookie down. It missed her plate and landed on the clean tablecloth and crumbled. She tried to wipe up the crumbs but only succeeded in smearing them.

"Oh, don't!" Sidonia reached over and stayed Edith's hand. Then, seeing Edith back away, "It's all right," she said gently, "I'll take care of it."

Edith sat quietly. Although she could not have given details of what had been said at the tea table, she understood the underlying messages: Quigley and Sidonia were ever so careful about what they bought. And the past came to her—Quigley and his Express Delivery, his sensible choices of what was on sale. And then, Sidonia's almost frugal way of looking at what to buy. She bought what was needed, a way of seeing material things because she had grown up poor.

"Well, I guess I'd better get on with that snowdrift next to the garage." Quigley got up, took his cup, saucer and plate to the sink. He was about to leave but didn't. Sidonia was bustling about nervously, putting dishes in the dishpan. He went over to her, put his hand on her shoulder. "I'm sorry," he said. "For what?" she asked. "You know—for calling you Chub."

Sidonia's whole demeanor changed. Her face relaxed. She turned to him and smiled. "I'm okay. Anyway, it's true, I'm fat." He shook his head. "Not fat, you're not fat." She said with certainty, "Well, I'll go from chubby to fat if I don't do something about my weight." He said he loved her the way she was.

They were all right; they could talk to each other. That's how Edith felt when Quigley left. She had been afraid they might quarrel. Or, what in a way was even worse, grow apart. "Not much fun." The words came back, faintly. *On little cat feet.* That was from a poem but she couldn't remember the poet. That was the way words came so often now–in bits and pieces, in tidbits. James had said that to her. Hurt, she had kept bitterly silent, hiding in the pages of her books, while James had worked and played in the world outside. Long ago. When Tim was a baby.

"You're so quiet, Edith. Are you all right?" Sidonia asked. Edith nodded. Sidonia went over to the stove, and began stirring the simmering stew. "Maybe a drop more salt," she said, tasting it. Holding a spoonful, she came over to Edith. "What do you think?"

Edith felt pleased. "Yes, just a little."

The sound of snow blowing against the roof heightened Edith's feeling of warmth and well-being. Since this strangeness–that was the word she gave to the unpredictable erratic behavior of her mind and body–she found herself more careful in how she spoke. But now, in the warm kitchen, she had no need for caution; a tune was playing to her from long ago–*You're nobody till somebody loves you*–and she felt their love–Quigley's and Sidonia's–and their love affirmed her presence, which had always seemed tenuous, lacking, insubstantial.

Edith had a new sense of her mortality—new, because Death seemed more real. When young she had not thought of Death in relation to herself; Death was something that happened to heroes and old people, in wars and catastrophes. But with the passage of years, Death changed from its heroic or poignant metaphors in books and poetry to a fact. I'm seventy-nine, she told herself, and time is running out.

With that acknowledgement came another. I haven't been a good mother. Even before going to Africa on the AIDS mission, they had grown apart. She felt shaken by regret. If only she could see Tim now; face to face, she would be able to tell him what she couldn't before. She would ask his pardon. They could start anew, mother and son, with something that, while not perfect, could at least approach connection.

But even as she wished for closeness with her son, she knew in her heart it was too late. Tim was a middle-aged man, no longer a needful child. Their relationship had begun to falter long ago. Calls and letters became fewer and fewer then stopped. But then, Leo had become her friend, the kind of friend James could not be. So she had allowed the distance between Tim and herself to linger on and on, like a chronic disease.

Edith lifted her head from the table, where it rested on her arms. She should stir herself, help Sidonia prepare supper, but she was lost in regret. Tim is fifty-two now, she told herself. He found his way in the world long ago. He doesn't need me. She realized she had been lying to herself, telling herself he couldn't reach her because he was off somewhere, in an inaccessible village in Africa. That others had heard from him was too painful to bear. He wasn't going to get in touch with her.

She shifted her arthritic body but it was getting more and more difficult to find a comfortable position. She would call Alfred and tell him she wanted to change her will again. She would name Quigley and Sidonia as her beneficiaries.

"My money," she said to them that night, "is now under your management."

Quigley and Sidonia looked at each other with astonish-ment.

"I don't get out much, so I can't compare prices. Anyway, it's getting too hard for me to manage money now. I forget one thing or another. So, tomorrow, I want you to take the money I've been keeping and put it in a suitcase, whatever can hold it–the trunk's not good, too much trouble to take it down all these stairs. I want you to take the money to your room and take charge of it–for our expenses. You know the things the house needs and the bills that have to be paid and the insurance for this and that. And I want to raise your salaries." And to herself, she said, No need to tell them about the money I've hidden in the sewing machine.

Quigley and Sidonia looked at each other in disbelief. Edith Martin, who would not entrust her money to any bank, was putting them in charge of it. What was more, she had spoken clearly, without the stops and starts and breaking off of sentences that happened all too often.

"Edith, it's not good to have so much money in the house," Sidonia said. "It would be better to put it in the bank."

"No banks." Edith placed one hand over the other and plunked them down on her lap. In the shadowy dim light of the wall sconces, her face was gaunt, her chin thrust forward. "I took the money out of the bank and I won't put it back in. They lost it, you know—my safe deposit box. You think I don't remember, but I remember that all right. Having to go through hell—there, that's the word for it—until it was finally found. No banks."

"I'm not sure I want that responsibility," Sidonia said. She shifted uneasily in her chair. Then, turning to Quigley, "You haven't said a word. Say something."

"It's Edith's money and she can do what she wants with it." Sidonia was still frowning. "It's not all that complicated," he went on. "We keep the bills and receipts so Edith always knows what's being spent." He shifted his attention to Edith. "How much is there—in the trunk?"

"I've taken a portion off to keep in my room for expenses and such." She stopped, considered. "Two hundred ninety thousand."

Sidonia and Quigley sat on their bed, unable to sleep. It had been a long day. A strange day. Counting all those hundred-dollar bills, for one thing. And when they had brought it down the long winding staircase, Edith, waiting at the bottom, had spoken of an Expedition she had made that somehow or other had to do with the money. Sidonia, all her romantic notions prodded by a vision of a young and daring Edith, asked, "Was it to some foreign land? Some exotic place far from Canada?" But Edith had just smiled.

Now, they kept looking at the great big suitcase in the bottom of their closet. Every now and then, they looked at each other. After a long while, Sidonia sighed. She stroked Quigley's cheek, as though trying to discover what both of them were thinking but would not say. "Life is getting too complicated," she said finally.

But Quigley was hardly listening. Express Delivery, he was thinking.

14

"I kept thinking everything was going along too smoothly all these months," Sidonia said. "We were doing fine with Edith. I had a feeling it just couldn't last, things being so nice. Oh, maybe it's spring fever. After all, it is April."

"Spring's supposed to make you happy," Quigley said.

"Come on, Quiggy. Happy? It would take a lot to make Edith happy."

Quigley threw up his hands. "So what are we going to do about the change in Edith? Suppose she needs more looking after?"

Sidonia thought, she takes looking after right now, only she won't let on she does. "Maybe we should send to Japan for one of those mechanical helpers they're perfecting–a neat obedient robot who'll do anything you ask. They're even working on a way to have it smile."

Quigley tried for patience. When Sid got silly, it meant something was bothering her. "Some on, Sid, seriously." He grimaced. "Damn! She's got a son, she's got a grandson."

"Quiggy, I tried to get in touch with them. Seaman's tried too. Tim's still somewhere in Africa. And Matthew, her grandson–no one knows where he is. You and I, we're all she has.

We've got to get Edith to Dr. Helperin."

"You know how she is about doctors. Same as she is about money. Nuts." He shook his head. "She's weird, she's like some character in a gothic novel."

"She's old and scared, Quiggy, and some day we'll be old and—"

"Not scared. Don't say we're going to wind up just the way we are–nothing happening and scared to make things happen."

She got up. "We have to get her to the doctor, that's the first thing we have to do. We have to find out what's going on with her. I know, I know, she won't want to go, but she will, I promise you she will." Her voice softened. "Let's turn in early, Quiggy. It's been a while..."

He got up. "I know. What with one thing or another..." He waited. He knew what she was going to say, and she did. "I'll just check on Edith first."

"I wish you wouldn't close your door," said Sidonia still another time, when Edith finally answered her knock.

"I have a right to my privacy." Edith drew herself up as much as she could, but could not attain the kind of no-nonsense straight-back posture she wanted.

"Yes, of course you have a right to your privacy. Edith, remember how you were saying you keep waking up and can't get a decent night's sleep." And neither can Quigley and I, she thought. "Well, I phoned Dr. Helperin and he can see you end of the week after we go to do some blood work and stuff. I can take you tomorrow. Quigley will be working on the darned garage door again."

Edith's first reaction was to say she wouldn't go. After all, Saul Helperin had been their family doctor since she and James had married. Would he see something different in her–about her? Would he ask questions? She had a moment of panic. She would be found out and then... She didn't want to think about what would happen.

She was about to protest but then Sidonia said, "Look, Edith, you've been having trouble sleeping and that's not good. Dr. Helperin can give you something to help you sleep."

"Some pill, you mean?"

"Some medication. It's not good for you to lose so much sleep."

Edith was silent for a long minute, after which she agreed. It had occurred to her there was a vial of sleeping pills prescribed for James that he had never used, having died so quickly. It seemed like a good idea to get some more.

Sidonia hesitated, then, "Let me fix your nightgown, you've got it on backwards."

Remarkably, in an instant, Edith mustered her forces, as though she were going into battle. Amazed at the clarity of her mind and even more amazed at her easy words, she countered, "I want it that way. I prefer the back neckline to the front." Having said the words, she believed them. "Why must I always do what someone else thinks I should do?"

Sidonia looked amazed. "Of course, you can wear your nightgown any way you want."

* * *

Dr. Saul Helperin was often saddened by the weariness he saw in certain older women. This fatigue—for want of a better name—was many times accompanied by expressions such as 'well, what can one do,' 'that's the way things are,' as though the impersonal words put the issue at hand beyond contemplation and certainly beyond solution.

He had started as a family practitioner, but with the years had become interested in dementia, and now that he himself was old, his interest and research had developed into the field of senile dementia. A contemplative man, he wished at times he had chosen to interest himself in a field where conjecture did not play so large a part. Orthopedics, for example, gave you, at the very least, certain givens: bones broken to be put back together; worn joints to be replaced; vertebrae to be realigned.

Saul Helperin was an essentially kind man whose initial reasons for studying the many forms of dementia were still intact: he wanted to play a role—however small—in alleviating the pain and suffering of those whose cognitive abilities could no longer navigate the often difficult journey through life. A shy and lonely boy, given to books and introspection, his own excellent brain had provided a safe harbor in times of social awkwardness.

There were so many forms of dementia, and the term 'senile' added still another factor—age—which, in this society where youth was at a premium, often carried an implication of failure, just as death did for so many of his colleagues.

"It's good to see you, Edith," he said, as she hobbled into his office, leaning heavily on her cane. She nodded, attempted a smile, which did not quite succeed.

"And good to see you, Mrs. Biggs," he said to Sidonia. He motioned to chairs. Sidonia took off Edith's coat, then her own. They sat down. The office had scenes of the Kootenays on the walls, softening the paraphernalia of swabs and blood pressure apparatus.

He was about to direct his remarks to Sidonia; instead, he turned to Edith. "I'm pleased to tell you, Edith, the tests have come back from the lab and you're fit as a fiddle–no diabetes, cholesterol okay. Of course, your bone density has decreased but not alarmingly."

He stopped. Sidonia was looking at him expectantly. Edith's face, on the other hand, had a neutral expression. He continued, "There doesn't seem to be any problem as far as your vascular system goes. That is, the tests show your arteries aren't clogged, blood vessels seem to be doing their work." He kept on: "The report from the ophthalmologist showed decided macular degeneration in the left eye; the right eye, however, is fine."

What about Alzheimer's? Sidonia wanted to ask, but how could she when Edith was right there. As though in answer to her dilemma, Edith asked if she could be excused, she needed to go to the ladies' room. Her cane, propped against her chair, fell as she rose. Quickly, Sidonia righted it, handed it to her. Edith murmured a thanks, took it, hobbled in the direction of the washroom.

Sidonia leaned forward. "What about Alzheimer's?"

Dr. Helperin shook his head. "I can't say Edith has Alzheimer's at this point. Her medical exam showed no indications. Of course, there are other diseases, such as Lewy Bodies, that manifest in a similar manner to Alzheimer's—that is, sleep disorders, a wide fluctuation in cognition, and other factors. So we can't know for certain what is causing these changes in Edith. Changes occur with age, too. Forgetting things, misplacing this and that, having a hard time managing one's money or house—there can be any number of reasons for these symptoms." He was about to add that in many cases only examination of the brain after death could determine the existence of Alzheimer's, but, looking at Sidonia's intent face, he decided not to.

"So we don't know what will happen to her?" Sidonia finally asked.

"It's not possible to say." He clasped his hands in his lap and again wished he had a more satisfying answer. "I have one patient who has some of the symptoms of Alzheimer's but is still functioning fairly well after ten years." After a moment, he added, "In her own way."

"So Edith can go on more or less like this for years." The doctor did not answer. He merely shrugged his shoulders in a gesture of not knowing. Sidonia wondered how Quigley would receive this news. She could visualize him doing what he did when he was in distress– tracing circles on the arm of his chair. Round and round his index finger going, until she would reach over and stop it.

"Yes, it's possible for Alzheimer's to go on for years," Dr. Helperin felt compelled to say. "You've told me there are many times Edith is perfectly lucid, even reciting poetry from her childhood and making changes in her room–you might even say, redecorating. As for her insomnia, there's no reason why she should lose sleep–and you," he smiled. "I'll just write a prescription." He drew his pad before him, took up a pen.

Edith hobbled back into the room. "I'm sorry I was so long." She sat down, managed a smile. It had been a close call. She had barely made it to the toilet. In fact, she had dribbled several drops in the bathroom. That had not happened before. Incontinent. The word leaped into her head. One more indignity.

"I'm giving you a prescription that will help you sleep, Edith," Dr. Helperin said.

"That will be a big help." Edith gathered herself together as well as she could. It was strange how terribly clear she could be at times. "Losing sleep," she went on in a calm and rational manner, "makes me do all kinds of crazy things." She watched Sidonia take the prescription and silently ordered herself to be sure, to be absolutely certain that Sidonia did not keep the pills, that she, Edith, had possession of them—and she saw this new little vial beside the one that James had never used.

Dr. Helperin kept thinking he needed to be tactful. Even in the old days, Edith had not been the most outgoing of women. Hard to know–talk to–which, he supposed, compelled James to... There he was, going off in his head on all kinds of conjectures. He came back to the moment.

"May I ask you a few questions, Edith?"

"Are you trying to trap me, Saul?" She tightened her resolve. She could do that now–exercise her will, plan, that kind of thing. But for how long? So she must be crafty, take advantage of the time allotted her, pretend—and all the while be planning.

"What's today's date?"

"April 10, 2007."

"And my name?"

"Oh, come now, Saul, I've been saying your name since I came in."

She named them all–James and Tim and Matthew. She had rehearsed all morning. Yes, she could do that now. She could know it was winter or spring or summer, but one day she would not be able to rehearse. One day there would be an end to knowing.

"There's nothing wrong with my head," she said, careful to keep her voice calm, her hands still. "I forget things. So does everyone. I bump into a wall. So does everyone at some time. I can't find my pen. Neither can you, I'll wager, now and then. Are there any more questions?"

He shook his head. It would serve no purpose, he knew, not at this point. Edith had no recognizable cognitive decline. She seemed, in fact, to display a kind of spunk she had not possessed years before when she had been rather subdued, even withdrawn in social situations. A memory surfaced then. "I recall giving James some tablets for his insomnia before he passed away…"

"I threw them away," she said.

* * *

Fern Helperin put down her knitting–a sweater for another grandchild. She looked at her husband who was in one of his reflective moods. "What I can't understand is how a person can be perfectly lucid one moment or even a day and totally out of it the next moment or day." She took up her knitting and waited. Saul had an uncanny way of knowing what was being said, even as he was deep in reflection.

Indeed, he did look up from his pondering. His arm reached carefully to the side table; his fingers just as carefully lifted the fine liquor glass, and he sipped the nectar with appreciation. *There are more things under the sun...* he began, then stopped. Fern was raising her eyebrow. Then she sighed in resignation. "At the very least, dear," she said, "you might get another quote–and one not even from Shakespeare."

Fern, of course, was right. The line from Hamlet, he supposed, was like the teddy bears or Morgan dogs their children had carried about as toddlers—always there for comfort. "There's no certainty at this point that Edith has Alzheimer's," he said. He went on heavily, "And even if it were, there's a lot we don't understand about the disease. One thing though, it can progress slowly or not so slowly." He thought, how little of the brain was mapped out when I started my career, and how little we know now, in spite of all the new information.

"Is Edith Martin doomed?"

"I wish you wouldn't use that word." He willed himself to stifle his annoyance. And yet, what did her unquestioning use of a word matter? She got things done: raising the children, working for the community, and yes, making his life comfortable. He had only to look at her, white hair cut short and in bangs, brow smooth, as she dropped a stitch, picked it up, and continued knitting, to know how much he loved her.

"What word would you have me use, Saul?"

"It's not a question of words. We'll have to wait and see." He did not speak of his clients' problems to his wife, but Edith Martin was an old acquaintance. They had known each other since starting their married lives.

Fern decided to let the matter pass. Saul would go into his philosophical mode, and—there was irony in this—besiege her with long and impenetrable words. "Poor Edith," she said, "she never did seem able to express her point of view—if she had one." She paused then. "Maybe she expressed it to her house? She sure loved that house. More than Tim, I used to think." She put down her knitting. "Would you like an espresso? It's only nine." She winked at him. "And the night's still young."

15

The soft white abundant flakes of the last snow covered the ground, cars, fields, roofs, trees and bushes, hid the ugly ochre-colored remnants of the previous light falls mixed with sand, salt and gravel. It was going to be a real old-fashioned Kootenay Christmas. The fog had burnt off by mid-morning. The winter sun shone down. Elephant Mountain and the calm lake were a painting in black and white.

Edith left the window. There had been days like this. Long ago. She saw them, bright and sparkling; then they disappeared. James had been there, and Tim. James was my husband, she reminded herself firmly. Tim was my son. Is? The thought detached, drifted away. Her brow knit, her eyes grew anxious, her whole body reached out, trying to catch the thought. But it was gone. What is happening to me? she asked the air. My notebook! I must get it!

She hobbled slowly back into her bedroom. It had, in a way, become *the* room for her. Teddy was there. She was careful not to let him out. She got the notebook where it lay–atop the small dressing table. Always there. Nowhere else. "Not now, Teddy," she told the bear sitting in the closet. "Later, we'll talk later."

She picked up her cane and made her way painfully toward the kitchen. There was something she must do, something that the Christmas carols on the radio–Sidonia had them on all the time–told her she must do. Sidonia was out. Grocery shopping. And Quigley was–where? In the garage, she told herself, triumphant. To make sure, she called, "Sidonia? Quigley?" No answer.

She looked at the oven: Why am I looking at the oven? She opened the oven door: Why? Why? Fright came into her eyes. She picked up her notebook and thumbed through, but there was no mention of the word 'oven'—and it was hard to read her own writing; the macular degeneration was going into the good eye. She sat down heavily in a chair. Why was she in the kitchen?

A car was pulling up. She could hear the scrunch of wheels on snow. Sidonia! Sidonia was back, and now it struck her that Sidonia must not see her in the kitchen. But it was hard to get up. A terrible tiredness was holding her down. Edith was still sitting in the chair, when Sidonia, parka and tuque snow-topped, arms filled with packages, came in.

She put the packages on the table. "Why is the oven door open?" She tried to keep her voice even, tried but failed. Sidonia was furious. Her voice was crisply sharp, accusing. Edith looked away, needing an answer–the right one–but, "Cookies," she said, suddenly, the word springing from her mouth like a wild beast.

Sidonia closed the oven door and wondered for the hundredth–or five hundredth–time how to get it into this poor woman's head that she must not cook or bake anything. But, of course, it was no use, no use at all. She saw the fright on Edith's face. "I'll make some Christmas cookies later," she said, gently, and waited for Edith's desperate attempt at all-rightness–the smoothing of her dress, the attempt at a smile.

"You'd better have your rest before lunch," she told her. "I'll just take off my parka and help you."

"I know how to lie down in a bed," Edith glared. She started to get up from the chair, rose a bit, came down, tried again. Sidonia stood there, waiting. After a few minutes Edith said, "I try, you know, I try." Sidonia nodded, touched her gently: "I know you do. Edith, I know." She must be absolutely firm with Quigley about leaving Edith alone.

But back in her room, Edith said to Sidonia (who wasn't there), "You don't know, you don't know." She wasn't tired anymore. Unbearable loneliness engulfed her. She made sure her door was closed, took Teddy from his shelf and sat down in the little lady's chair. On the table beside, she propped him. The lady's chair–that's what James had called it–who was James? Sometimes a child came to visit and called it grandma's chair. Who? What child? Someone had gone far away. Someone. And long ago there had been a man who loved her. "Do you really love James?" he asked. "I married him," she said. (James–who was James?) And the man said, "People marry without love." The sentences in her head began, staggered, splintered, broke apart, floated...

Teddy was regarding her seriously. "I know what they're thinking, Ted." Encouraged, surprised by the fullness of her sentence, she dared more. "A nursing home. And you sit there and sit there and they say, 'How are you dear? Looking well today.'" Her eyes searched Teddy's. Sit? Who was sitting? A profound stillness. Only the soft pit-a-pat of gentle snow on the roof. If you could climb up the snowflakes—all the way to where the snow began. Slow and peaceful...

There was a soft knock on her door. "Lunch," Sidonia said. The voice propelled Edith to effort. She took the brush from the dressing table, clumsily stroked her hair. She looked at the sign above it: SMILE. She smiled. She smoothed her dress, cajoled her voice into response. "Coming."

"What do you suppose Mr. Seaman will do?" Sidonia asked.

"Put her in a nursing home," Quigley said.

"She'll die there."

"She'll die anyway."

They had lingered in the living room long after Edith had gone to bed. The weather had changed. A freezing rain clattered on the windows and roof. But the logs in the fireplace burned brightly and lit the dark room; they had not bothered to turn on the lights.

"When is he coming?"

"Who?"

"Seaman."

"Should be here tomorrow. He's been in Vancouver—some business deal. Anyway, his office is there." Quigley stared into the fireplace. "We'll have to tell him about the money. I mean, it's Edith's money after all."

Sidonia was bent over, head in hands, elbows on lap. She lifted her head. "I feel awful, Quiggy. It's wrong."

"Damn it! Stop doing that! Stop talking as though we're committing a crime."

"Lower your voice. You see what's happening. You're cursing. You've never cursed."

"I used to wish my father would burn up in flames," he said. "After one of his rampages. When I was little."

"What a thing to wish!" But then she reached and put her hand softly on his shoulder. "You were just a kid; you felt helpless."

But Sidonia didn't feel as easy as she sounded. Quigley seemed to be undergoing some kind of change.

He sighed and said he was sorry. "She's asleep, isn't she?"

Sidonia brushed her hair from her eyes, lifted a shoulder in a questioning way. "I put some valerian drops in her tea. It's only an herb, but still... It's hard to know what she's doing. I worry she'll put an empty pot on the stove, turn it on–start walking in her sleep right out the house. She almost drank the metal polish the other day."

"Sid, she can't see, that's the trouble. She couldn't see the letters on the box. She thought—"

She shook her head. "No, it's more than her eyes; she didn't know what day it was yesterday. Said it was Wednesday instead of Tuesday." She hesitated. She had meant to scold him but she couldn't. "Listen Quiggy, we mustn't leave her all alone. Sometimes I think you don't take that seriously. Tell me you do."

He put his hand on hers. "Okay, okay."

She frowned, sighed, shook her head. "Who would have thought Edith would get like this —I mean, we don't even know exactly what's wrong with her. Maybe we should have stayed with your Express Delivery, maybe things would have picked up, maybe..." She stopped, suddenly hearing herself. Then, as though posing the question more to herself, she asked, "We're good people, Quiggy, aren't we?"

"What's good?"

"Doing the right thing."

"What's the right thing, Sid?"

The light from the winter moon cast an eerie green shadow on the snow. Edith stood at the window in her room at attention to herself, seizing the moment, for her mind was perfectly clear. It was this clarity that seemed to be clouding—like the small chandelier over the dining table that you could dim if you wished. But this dimming was not obedient to her wishes.

She knew what she had to do, and she knew she could not wait too long. She must go on a last Expedition. Remembering that first Expedition–the arduous trek up the flights of stairs to hide her money—and then her second Expedition–driving to town in the rain, car key left inside the car–she could feel again her exhaustion and more than that, the fear and trembling of doing more than she really could.

But the fear and trembling on those Expeditions had been largely concerned with her weak physical state–legs that were clumsy and weak, reflexes no longer sharp, senses slow to seize the turn of a traffic light from red to green. That kind of thing. And then, she knew her final destination: it was home–this house, these rooms that had sheltered her for most of her life.

The fear and trembling when she thought of this last Expedition was different than anything she had ever felt. Before there had been a known place to go and a known place to return. "I do not know, I do not know," she said aloud. She had never accepted heaven as a certainty, nor hell. Did one simply return to dust? Become compost? Was there a soul? She had never pursued these larger questions, and now she was afraid, she started to tremble, knowing there would be no coming home on this last Expedition.

"*Joy to the world–Oh, little town–Silent night...*" The bright voices of children were a welcome antidote to her fear of the unknown. From the window Edith saw them in the driveway, so real, some five or six animated little ones, bundled up with scarves and mitts and woolly hats that came over their ears. So alive. Singing their hearts out.

She heard the door open downstairs. Sidonia was giving them Christmas cookies. Sidonia liked to give. She gives to me too, Edith thought, but it didn't help the feeling of sadness. An ache, dull and thudding, in the region of her heart. Christmas should be merry, but this wasn't merry, this feeling of loss.

She left the window, sat down on the bed and looked around the room. There were no photographs. Her family seemed like a dream that had floated away. Her feet were cold. She got up painfully, dragged a blanket from the bed. Why am I taking this blanket? she asked the air silently. A sliver of moonlight came through the window and lit on her feet and she suddenly felt their cold which she had forgotten, and put the blanket over them.

She knew something bad was happening to her. Only months ago her mind could command her body. Tell her legs to walk, albeit clumsily, instruct her bony arms to wash and cook and carry. Tell her eyes to open and close. Only months ago her mind could–one way or another–order her body to do what she needed.

Not now. They spoke in whispers–but she knew what was

happening to her. She didn't need a doctor to tell her. She knew. Even as she stood there her heart was beating faster, and, from the pit of her stomach, a sense of dread arose like a serpent uncoiling, ready to strike.

She sat down on the edge of the bed. Suddenly–she had not thought of Dylan Thomas for years and years–that first line stole into her ears: *Do not go gently into that dark night,* and she froze with terror, because the words had come alive, were engulfing her, threatening to swallow her, and now, more than any other time, she longed for someone to talk to. There was only one person, and in the dark night, in a hushed voice, she began to talk to Leo:

"Leo, my dear friend, doctors will try this and that. But I know where this thing that has taken me over will end, and what toll it will take on those around me. So I will have to make a final Expedition and this time I won't come back. I don't know how I'll do it. I have no idea how to go about it. It's just an idea, Leo, but it's there. It comes and goes. And Sidonia and Quigley mustn't even suspect that I'm thinking about this."

Edith felt exhausted. The voicing of what had been simply an idea had taken all her energy.

"Seaman said he would make arrangements for Edith to go to a nursing home," Quigley sighed. "I don't trust him, Sid. He looked different when he came back from Vancouver, almost haggard. He's hiding something."

There was a silence. Edith waited impatiently.

"I told him it was out of the question."

"Quiggy, what will we do if—when Edith starts going downhill?"

"I thought Dr. Helperin said it's not possible to predict with certainty what will happen."

"But he did say there are symptoms of Alzheimer's. It won't be little things–forgetting and labels and that kind of thing. Oh, what's the point of talking about it now. It's not going to be much of a life for her."

"It's a life, Sid, it's Edith's life."

By their deeds shall you know them. And surely, they had proven themselves faithful and loyal. Not like You, God, Edith found herself saying. For God had not always been faithful, had not always been loyal, had time and again deserted her. And now this disease—whatever it was—that came and went like a trickster, leaving her well one day and the next in pain and confusion, so that at times, looking out, trying to find Elephant Mountain, hidden by fog and mist, Edith had the frightening feeling of not being there at all.

16

2008 settled in, and with it, a massive cold front that blew through the country from Toronto to the Kootenays. Along with the below-zero weather, a steady snowfall blanketed trees, bushes, earth, houses and cars.

As January went into its third week, Quigley's work began early and ended late. The snow and ice demanded constant attention. Muttering under his breath, he shoveled, sprinkled salt, de-iced.

Worst of all was the problem of Edith. "Don't call her a problem," Sidonia told him. "The cold gets to all of us, and it gets to Edith most of all. She's old and the cold makes her arthritis worse, and anyway, she's having more trouble with her eyes and..."

But she didn't voice what they both knew. Edith's sudden bouts of clarity and reasoning were just as suddenly disappearing. It was getting more and more difficult to deal with her. It wasn't only her frustration when she couldn't finish a sentence or forgot where she had put something or needed you to repeat something a hundred times and even then didn't get it; Edith, so full of good manners and proper behavior, was changing—getting angry, nasty or moody.

"But she must get outside, even for fifteen minutes," Sidonia insisted. And that meant the driveway had to be kept walkable and Edith's boots had to be laboriously put on and the two of them walking with her, one on each side and Edith wanting to shove them off.

Home Hardware was out of snow shovels and Wal-Mart was out of snow shovels. Quigley had to go to Canadian Tire in Castlegar to get one when theirs broke.

"Listen to this, please," he said one day. He tried to keep his voice even, which was the opposite of how he felt. We're both just slaves, he told himself, as he watched Sidonia taking towels and sheets from the laundry basket, folding them, placing them on the table in the laundry room.

"I just want to finish the laundry," she said, without turning around.

"Leave those damn towels alone and come into the living room! I have to talk to you!"

A chill ran down her back. She put down the towel she was folding and followed him into the living room. He pulled up two chairs in front of the fireplace. They sat down. "What's so important?" she asked, trying to keep her voice neutral.

"Beau called again—this morning—when you were giving Edith a sponge bath. Are you listening?" She nodded, thinking that Edith should be getting up from her nap soon. "He's making big money, Sidonia. He wants me to come in with him, says the money's flowing. They bought a house. We could—"

"There's no point talking like this, Quiggy." But he seemed not to have heard her. "We could start a new life," he said, leaning forward eagerly, "a real life, not have to cater to anyone."

"Edith isn't just anyone. She depends on us, she trusts us. We're her family; she told us that."

"She's nuts, Sid."

Sidonia kept looking at the dying fire as Quigley got more and more excited. "We're not old—not yet. We could be having fun, enjoying all the things we've never been able to buy." He stopped. "There are really good nursing homes. Seaman says."

But you don't trust him, she thought. *You* told him no. Quigley was regarding her expectantly. She turned her eyes to his. "You're forgetting one thing," she said. "We're the guardians of Edith's money. It's in our room. And she told us it would be ours when she dies."

He turned away and looked at a spider spinning a web on the wall. The spider went round and round. It seemed it must inevitably weave itself into the web. "Whenever that is," he said.

"What do you mean by that?" she asked.

"She's got a good heart. The doctor said so. Everything's going, but her heart keeps right on tickin' away—tic toc, tic toc." He started to rhythmically stamp his feet on the carpet—one, two, one, two... "It's not going to be Express Delivery right up to heaven for Edith. No such luck."

"Quigley!"

He stopped stamping. "Don't look at me that way! Don't say you've never thought about it: wanting Edith dead–all that money ours."

Sidonia got up suddenly, swiftly. "I don't know what's gotten into you, Quigley." She wanted to cry but couldn't. "Nothing but work," he was saying. "You used to be fun but you're too tired for anything these days. And that means everything."

The room became very still. Then the clang of a cane against a wall in the downstairs bedroom broke into the stillness. "She's awake, I've got to see to her."

"Yes, go see to her!" he mimicked. "All the same, you'd like her to be dead; yes, secretly wishing she would just disappear–die in her sleep, maybe fall down the stairs, slip on a banana peel..."

Sidonia clapped both hands over her ears. "I'm not going to listen to this," she said, getting up. But before she got out the room, Quigley was up and holding her and turning her round to him. "I'm beat, Sid, just dead tired. That's what made me talk that way. You're tired, too. You know you are."

She was listening. "So what's the answer, Quiggy?"

"We've got to get some help. It's too hard for just the two of us–looking after her along with the house and all. We could get Leo. He's kind of a friend of Edith's...or used to be. And he can do just about anything."

"Are you mad, have you gone completely off your rocker? Leo's old—he must be pushing seventy. We'll end up with two old people. Anyway, what makes you think he'd be willing to leave that cabin of his and come live here?"

"Because his cabin is freezing this winter, and he's only got that old wood stove and the windows need replacing. He was saying to me he was going to look for some other place. By next winter for sure. He's healthy, Sid, he's as healthy as we are. Maybe healthier."

"What about the money?"

"It's in our room. He could sleep in the turret room."

"Still..."

"Leo's different—Leo really doesn't care about money."

"Everyone cares about money."

"Come on, it's an answer looking us in the eye."

17

Leo Mann, wool jacket loose around his tall skinny frame, bent over with the weight of his backpack, plodded his way through snow slickened by intermittent rain. He could have done without this weather. Mountain weather–snow, hints of sun, mists like vaporous veils covering the town. And then, the freezing nights, laying a sheet of ice over the snow. He had liked winter in the Kootenays all the years he'd been here–nearly half a century–looked forward to its challenges. This was the first winter that was hard for him, though anyone seeing him at any of his many and varied handyman jobs would not know this.

He took his steps carefully now, telling himself he was fine. An ache here, a pain there. Well, what could one expect at sixty-eight? Still, it would have been nice to be in the car. He smiled to himself: if you could call that ancient pickup a car. "Give it up, Leo," Buzz, his mechanic friend kept telling him, "let that poor heap go to the happy metal heaven."

Leo figured that was fine, too–not having a vehicle. Foot power. Eliminate some carbon emission. Good for the environment. "No sweat," kids today said. Said it about anything, as though everything had equal value. Like pressing a button on a computer, getting an answer, not thinking the problem all the way through.

He shook his head, told himself he wasn't being fair–putting the young in one big heap, as though each was not different from the other. A crotchety old man? he questioned. Is that what I'm getting to be? He knew the type. Living alone in a rented room, they tended to delay laundering their clothes, which took on a musty smell. Leo scrupulously took his laundry to the laundromat in the mini plaza on Front Street. Sometimes he would stop by the table where the old codgers gathered mornings. It would be at the A&W or Quiznos. They would be discussing the cost of gas, the super bug at the hospital: "You go in with a hernia. Supposed to be out next day. End up staying two months." The talker would shake his head prophetically: "Those damn bugs are gonna kill us in the end." Another would ask Leo to join them: "C'mon, sit down, have a cup of coffee." But Leo would smile and say he had to get to a job, he'd only stopped to pick up some paint. He wondered what would happen if he didn't have those jobs. Would he be sitting at a table, chewing the fat with other lonely old men who had plenty of time and nothing to do with it? The question made him uneasy but he didn't think about it much; he was too busy with all the work he kept getting.

Leo had walked from his cabin near the orange bridge through Lakeside Park, rather than go the downtown route. He had enjoyed being in the midst of the old firs, cedars, oaks, maples, seeing the snow-glistening foliage—like a painting—but now he was tired. A sit-down would be good. Still, he had told Quigley he'd be there by ten, and his watch said two minutes to.

As Leo neared Edith's driveway, he surveyed the snow-topped house, the icicles hanging from the roof. It made him feel good to know Edith had Quigley and Sidonia right there, caring for her. Edith, Edith, Leo thought. They had been friends so many years. Nowadays he hardly saw her. Well, she had that troubling arthritis and, he knew, other physical problems that could come with age. Still, as he'd gone about his various jobs, he would sigh profoundly, remembering their long talks, their confidences—their friendship. Leo had wondered why Edith had been keeping to herself the past months—even longer. True, their friendship had never been tied to schedules but it was long and deep. Something was not quite right, he thought. He was happy to finally be here.

When Leo got to the garage, Quigley was trying unsuccessfully to remove a huge snow mound leaning against it. Suddenly, the sun came out, glistening the mound. Watching Quigley strike, pick and hit with all his might, Leo had the impression of David trying to vanquish a huge icy Goliath.

Quigley looked up and Leo could see his face was almost as red as his hair, which was flopping off in all directions around his bald spot. He was breathing hard and irregularly, clearly exhausted. When he saw Leo, he leaned on the ice pick and the shovel and grinned with relief. "Hi, Leo, thanks for coming."

Leo had the feeling of rescuing him. From what? he asked himself. Well, from a heart attack maybe; that could happen. You could land in a hospital. Every job–fixing a fence, seeding a lawn, whatever it was–gave him that feeling. He knew he wasn't Superman (how he had loved that comic as a kid); still he was there when needed, doing what he could.

"Snow mound? No way!" Quigley said. "Ice mound would be more like it. Right up against this old garage!"

Leo nodded. "No problem." Which was what he was inclined to say no matter what the job. He took the shovel and pick from Quigley and got to work. For a few minutes Quigley watched him, admiring the way he pick-axed and shoveled and chopped the mound, his bent-over body never stopping, with a kind of flow that seemed effortless. All the while, however, Leo, ignoring aches and pains in his arms and legs, fingers colder than cold, was concentrating on doing what he had to do to not only get on with the job but finish it.

"How's your cabin?" Quigley asked, when he came back an hour later. The snow mound was dismantled, the pieces in two wheelbarrows ready to be taken off to the lake. Leo was brushing snow and ice particles from his wool jacket, and blowing on his hands every once in a while.

Not too bad, he thought of saying, but finding it too troublesome to lie, he amended this to, "Freezing. And my water line froze." He took the money Quigley gave him; without looking at the bills, he put them in the pocket of his wool jacket. Then he picked up his backpack, and was about to go off when Quigley said, "Your age–you should be nice and warm."

Leo stopped short. *Your* age. As though he was an old man. He was almost about to ask him, what do you mean, *my* age?

"Aren't you going to look at the money?" Quigley was saying. Leo shook his head. Quigley looked at him as though trying to solve an extremely baffling puzzle. He shook his head along with Leo then said, "If you have a few minutes, Sid and I would like to talk with you. In the house."

"Okay." He started to follow Quigley, down from the garage and up the lawn to the house, the snow crunching or slippery underfoot, depending where the sun shone. It would be warm in the house. There was only the job at the Fraser's and that wasn't until later in the afternoon and not too tough–just weather-sealing their garage.

They sat at the kitchen table having tea. Leo would have preferred coffee, but tea was good too. He ate three cookies in a row–a peanut butter, an oatmeal raisin and a chocolate chip, savoring each at length, then thought he'd better stop.

"You make them?" he asked Sidonia.

"Edith helped me," she said, pleased. Catching Quigley's little smile, "Well, she mixed the batter," she added.

"Is Edith all right?" Leo asked, leaning forward, his face concerned.

"She's having a nap now," Sidonia said. She hesitated. "She's having some problems–after all, she is eighty."

"What problems?" Leo's voice rose.

"We don't know exactly what's going on," Quigley said. He looked at Sidonia.

"She's got arthritis, for one. Her eyes are worse. And sometimes she gets confused." To herself, she wondered if sometimes was the right word. She went on, "We'd like you to move in with us, Leo—for the winter, anyway."

Quigley jumped in. "Your water line's frozen."

"About Edith," Sidonia said. "Could you spend some time with her, when we have to be out?"

This explained the distance Leo had felt between him and Edith. Obviously, she was not well. How alone she must feel. True, Sidonia and Quigley were there but her own family—her son and grandson—were not in her life. How hard that must be for her. "Of course," he said. Then, "But have you discussed this with Edith?"

"Sure we did—as much as you can discuss something with her," Quigley said.

"Anyway," Sidonia continued, "it's clear she considers you her friend and likes the idea."

PART THREE

18

When Leo Mann was a youth, friends and relatives would say to him, "One of these days your big heart will get you into trouble." It was commendable to be of service to those less fortunate, they would go on, but Leo simply didn't know where to draw the line. They were talking about the young girls he was forever rescuing from parents who did not understand them, dreams that could not be fulfilled, or even vague states which seemed like some lingering low-grade illness. Leo felt in his heart their yearnings, their impossible dreams, their fears, their loneliness and wanted to comfort, to do whatever he could to make their lives happier.

Even as a small child, Leo showed a heightened sensibility. When his mother became ill with flu, he insisted on staying at her bedside, applying compresses to her fevered forehead, and had to be persuaded by his father to go to bed. Even when she was well, Leo would be attentive to a glance, a hesitant step, anything that might indicate distress, and ask what he might do to help her. "I'm fine," his mother would say. Looking at her little boy, so fair, his grey eyes unchildishly grave, she felt apprehensive.

"The boy's too sensitive, too serious. He's only a child, yet he feels for others like one of The Just," she said to her husband one day. He smiled. "Come now, we're in Canada, not in a nineteenth-century shtetl in Russia." He went on, chiding her gently, "Our little Leo—one of the Thirty-Six Just Men taking on the suffering of the world?"

His wife was silent. "You're making too much of the child," he continued. "He's only acting with the kind of feeling one should have." And he pointed out the state of the world with its endless conflicts and lack of compassion, how fortunate they were to be in Canada where all people could go to school and were free to live a good life.

Leo went to one of the best elementary schools in Toronto, then to a fine junior high and afterwards to an academically excellent high school. Busy with his studies, making friends, joining the swimming club and basketball team, Leo became less intense in his relationships. He would go to medical school, he told his parents.

"You see," said Leo's father to his wife. "He will be healing the sick and sustaining their lives and this is certainly a good and useful life without taking on the suffering of the whole world." Leo's mother agreed, but at times, seeing her son sitting quietly in a long meditative silence, she felt afraid for him.

At a certain point in his studies, Leo decided he could not dissect anything. Not a frog, not a worm, certainly not a human cadaver. His parents were distressed when he left medical school.

He worked three jobs for two years to repay loans which fortunately, were not staggering as he had won a scholarship.

One day he told his bewildered parents he was going to Vancouver.

"Vancouver? What's in Vancouver?" asked his mother.

"And how will you live?" asked his father.

"By fixing things."

In the end his parents gave him their blessings. Looking at their son, so confident, they were drawn into his benign and open face. They told each other that, after all, he was a man and had to find his own way. But to himself, his father thought his son a fool to give up a chance at a good life and a good living. And beneath her farewell smile, his mother was somber.

Leo, a knapsack on his back, set out one spring day in the sixties to hitchhike from Toronto to Vancouver.

It took him a week to go from east to west. In Vancouver Leo got his final ride. Her name was Pegasus. She was driving a Volkswagon, one of whose windows had a large winged horse with a wreath of red flowers round its head. Pegasus had long red-gold hair, sea-green eyes, a lithe figure and ended her sentences with a question.

"I'm going to Nelson," she said when they happened to meet at Granville Island. "It's one of the magical centers of the world. A real neat mountain town. Why don't you come?"

Why not? he thought—she really is a pretty girl.

"What's your name?" she was asking.

"Leo. Leo Mann. What's yours?"

"Pegasus. I don't believe in last names. What do you think?"

"Think about what?" Leo watched her assume the pose of a tree, which was difficult since the scarves she was wearing over her shirt and jeans kept falling off.

"About going to Nelson together. What do you think?"

Leo hesitated. He sensed danger. She seemed overly friendly and they had hardly met. And why was so young a girl wearing a bracelet of skulls? Small skulls, but still... And why a sandal on one foot and jogging shoe on the other? It was as though she were intent on getting attention. But just then the setting sun leaned down and crimsoned her red-gold hair, and Leo wondered what it would be like to have his head next to hers.

This thought caused him to reflect. What if she is a little flaky, he told himself. We are, all of us, just human beings doing the best we can.

"Well?" Pegasus was saying, tapping the sandaled foot on the ground.

"Thanks, I'd like a ride."

"Can you fix cars?"

"Your Volks?"

She nodded. "You might say it's mine," she said enigmatically. The feeling of danger grew stronger. He was about to ask whose it was, but the next moment she said, "It's borrowed. Can you fix it? I don't think it'll make it to Nelson."

"What's wrong with it?" he asked.

"That's for you to find out," she said.

But, when he had the hood up and checked the battery and the water and gone through all the other steps, there was nothing seriously wrong with the car. "How come you know how to fix cars?" Pegasus asked. He said, "I took a course in auto mechanics," and let it go at that. She shrugged. "Jack of all trades, master of none," she scoffed. Then, "If only there was a course in..." and her eyes clouded. A course in what? he wanted to ask, but once again, her mood changed. "You'd better get some sandwiches and pop, if we're going to drive all night," she told him brusquely.

Leo had the eerie feeling of being a character in some movie. Reason told him to get out of the movie and back to himself, but he couldn't listen. His body told him he was dead tired, but he couldn't hear it. Now that he was on the very last leg of his journey, the momentum that had kept him eager and enthusiastic had worn off. He wanted to get to Nelson. He wanted to settle in, to start his new life.

"Do you mind driving a while?" he asked Pegasus, when they got to Hope. It was night. In the sixties, the highways from Vancouver to Nelson had not yet been fully constructed. The road was narrow and the lights were interspersed and dim. Pegasus, however, seemed alert and even cheery.

"No problem." She settled herself at the wheel. Leo leaned back in the seat adjoining the driver's. He made an attempt to keep his eyes open but didn't succeed. Finally, to the humming of the motor, he fell fast asleep. In the black night he felt himself being carried along a road that went on and on.

He awoke to a jolting, then another, and another. With fascinated horror, he saw that Pegasus was zigzagging back and forth across the narrow deserted hardly-lit road. He reached over and grabbed the wheel. He had thought she might have fallen asleep, but he saw that she was wide-awake—her eyes were fervid, her lips drawn back, her jaw set. Crazily, a phrase from medical school flashed through his head: cranial nerve. It was as though all her senses had gone haywire.

But when his hands covered hers on the wheel, she suddenly slumped and he was able to steer the Volks back from the wrong side of the road without resistance. At first his anger made him fear he would lose control and strike her. If she wanted to kill herself, that was her affair, but he wanted to live. They sat on the side of the road in the black night.

"Where are we?" he finally asked.

"Near Osoyoos."

"That's halfway to Nelson."

"About."

"Are you mad!"

In the silence he could hear her labored breathing. Slowly, she lifted her face. Some moonbeams played about her eyes. Lost. Yearning for something irretrievable.

"Leo, save me." A crow cawed overhead. After a few minutes, she went on: "I try, but I can't stop thinking about it. My father used to play secret night games with me. It began when I was eleven. He'd come into my room and whisper nice things and undress me." Her voice broke. "And then he'd play these games—dancing his fingers, first one then the other, on my nipples, my belly button, going down, down, slowly. And then...I don't want to talk about it."

"But your mother..." Leo said.

"When I told my mother, she threw me out."

"I'm sorry." The expression sounded inadequate, as though he were apologizing for something he had done, but he couldn't think of what to say. Her story sounded too dark, too hideous, too removed from the bonds of parent and child. "Why not get in the back and get some sleep," he told her gently. She obeyed without a word. When he looked behind minutes later, her eyes were closed and her breathing even.

Driving along the deserted road in the night, Leo gave himself over to sad reflection. This unfortunate girl, asleep in the back, was without question, the most tragic he had ever met. He recalled how she had seemed to relax when his hand touched hers over the wheel.

Toward daybreak he saw the lights of Nelson. He drove to Lakeside Park. Birds were singing, flowers were blooming; the sun shone on emerald grass, a sparkling lake and soft furry mountains. The firs and maples and pines were not as tall as they would become years later, but the horse chestnut at the entrance spread its branches wide even then. As though reaching out to the universe, Leo thought, and felt uneasy at what he was going to say.

"Goodbye now, and thanks for the ride," he told her.

"Is that all you're going to say?" She looked straight into his eyes.

"Take care of yourself." He started to walk away and kept on walking. If he looked back, he would be caught in her unbearable stare of disbelief and turn around.

"Pegasus!"

"Joe! Penny!"

He slowed his walk. From the periphery of his eyes, he glimpsed a couple and Pegasus hugging each other. He heard her laughter. Then they began talking low. She had friends, Leo told himself. She would not be alone. It occurred to him that perhaps she had been lying, that her outrageous story was just that–a story. He quickened his pace, going as fast as he could without running.

Leo rented a two-room cabin near South Slocan. It was bare, except for a wood stove, a rickety table and two chairs, a lumpy narrow bed, assorted cracked dishes and cutlery from the Salvation Army. There was also a goat, the owner said, if Leo would like to have it. The goat wandered into the cabin and was about to chew on his backpack, when the owner led it outside. Leo hesitated about keeping the animal but decided not to. He feared an attachment. Even now the little animal had wandered back into the cabin and was attempting to put his front hooves on Leo's lap. "He thinks he's a dog," the owner explained.

This was a new beginning, this handyman business. The Slocan Valley in the sixties was peopled by many enthusiastic counter-culture young eager to take up a rural communal pioneer lifestyle different from the ordered suburban and city lives of their parents. There were calls for help with lawns, plantings, building a shed, painting and staining, as well as a great need for help in digging up vast quantities of rock in order to work the soil for the eventual lawns and vegetables, herb and flower gardens. Occasionally, someone would want an outhouse built. Leo would research the city's requirements, improvise the wooden structure according to the space allowed, make certain the plumbing was in keeping with the sanitation code.

"Where did you learn to do so many things?" the happy residents of the Valley asked him. Leo would answer by a slow sunny smile. It seemed to be enough in the same way his ability to diagnose a case of chicken pox or measles, to suggest relief for a case of flu and various other ailments came to be accepted as, "That Leo knows everything."

It was early fall, when he drove from Slocan Valley to Balfour one morning in his ancient Ford truck which he had retrieved from a used car lot. Working on it whenever he could get the time, he had restored the old truck to function; at least, well enough for his needs.

On the long deserted stretches of Highway 3A, Leo could see knapweed on the shoulders, their rough tough branches reaching up and out like kingly scepters. Here and there, a workman or two would be digging, engaged in battle with the rapacious roots.

Leo left the truck at the bottom of Franz Muller's road and walked up. Mid-way he encountered Franz, a huge plastic bag beside him, digging out knapweed with some sort of small incising instrument.

"I'm Leo," he said, stooping down to offer his hand.

"Franz," said the other, in his forties, in dungarees and T-shirt. He lifted his free hand, took Leo's. "Thanks for coming." He shook his head. Two sun-bleached dreadlocks fell down his back. "We can start with the road. Used to be all kinds of wildflowers. Now–" He spread out his arms, "this damned weed has killed them all."

Suddenly, his eyebrows ran together, as he frowned. "Deutschland Ubber Allus. That's what knapweed makes me think of. Kill off everything that's not your own filthy tribe."

"How can I help?" Leo asked. He wanted to put his hand on the other's shoulder as a gesture of understanding, for the man was clearly upset by more than the knapweed. Instead, he said, "I can dig on the other side of the road, and you on this side."

"Good idea. Come to the cabin first and have a cup of tea." But Leo said he had had a large breakfast and, if it was all right, preferred to get to work. At which the older man smiled broadly. "So it's true what they say about you."

Leo did not want to think about the world. He loved his days full of work and his evenings all to himself. He would at times recall the words of Voltaire: *Il faut cultiver mon jardin*. Yes, that was enough. But sometimes when there was a steady drizzle outside his dark window and the only voice in the silence was the murmur of the mountain stream, he yearned for the voice of another.

* * *

Leo had been in the Kootenays for a couple of years when he got a call from a Mrs. Fern Helperin.

"So you're the best handyman in Nelson," Saul Helperin said, as he shook his hand. Leo smiled. "I'm Fern," the petite woman held out her hand.

They were in the garden of the large but hardly extravagant house on Mill Street. Leo looked around. The yard was large. One portion was planted as a vegetable garden. The rest was lawn interspersed with small islands of rock. They have minds of their own, he thought. And now they wanted a rock wall on one of their borders. "It's native to the Kootenays," the doctor was saying. "We don't want to put up a fence, but we want a natural kind of barrier to keep the dogs and cats out."

"How do you want to get the rocks?" Leo asked.

"It's not a huge area. Can we collect them from the North shore and—well, you know there are lots of places where there's plenty of rock for the digging."

"I'll need a helper."

"Yes, of course." A look of sorrow crossed the doctor's face. "Do you think you can find someone? We had an excellent young woman doing all kinds of odd jobs around the house, but unfortunately, she's no longer available."

"No longer available? What an odd thing for you to say, Saul." His wife turned to Leo. "She's dead. Pegasus is dead."

"Pegasus dead?" Leo heard himself saying, the words, like a bell, tolling him back to what he had forgotten—Pegasus, eyes fixed, zigzagging across that dark road. A bird chirped. He looked up. It was a small bird. "Save me," it chirped.

"Are you all right, Leo?" Fern Helperin was asking. Her husband was regarding him intently. "Did you know her?"

He composed himself. "I'm all right. She gave me a ride once," he finally said. "I'll get to measuring now, if that's convenient." And he went to his truck to get his surveying equipment.

Leo left the Helperins feeling sad, wondering if Pegasus would be alive if he hadn't left her in the park. His pace quickened. He must not allow himself to sink back into his old patterns; he could not save every woman.

Tomorrow he would go to the Martin's home on Victoria Street. His face brightened. It's a beautiful house, he thought. The grounds are lovely. It can be the beginning of a steady job. Little did he know in those early years just how steady the job would be.

19

"Perhaps there are miracles," Sidonia said to Quigley one day. "Edith seems so much more lively since Leo's moved in." She waited for some confirmation from him, but he only nodded–or seemed to nod. He was listening to his own silent voice: And where does that leave us? "Edith said to take advantage of the bulk sales at Save On. Here's a list." She handed the slip of paper to him. "She told me the stuff to get. I wrote it down. And what a fight that was; she wanted to write it herself and you know how awful her handwriting is. Strange, I was looking at some of her old notebooks and her writing was beautiful, every word precise, every letter perfect."

"I thought she was leaving all the shopping to us. I don't like it, Sid, her telling me to use the car less. I know damn well the price of gas. Where is she, anyway?"

"Watching Oprah. Hollywood stars and their babies."

They were in the living room. He had started to gather up the newspapers for recycling. Sidonia kept gazing at the back of his head, as he put together the sections of the Globe and Mail, then the Vancouver Sun. "You're getting bald, Quiggy."

He looked up sharply. "Does it matter?"

Instead of answering, "You're fifty-three and I'm forty-three," she said in a reflective way. "I don't even know if it will work."

"If what will work?"

"If we could make a baby."

For a minute, he could do nothing but stare at her. She had gained some weight. There were small lines around her eyes. "Are you mad?" he finally said.

"Is wanting a baby madness?"

He pointed to the headlines–MASSIVE EARTHQUAKE IN CHINA–CYCLONE DEVASTATES MYANMAR, FORMERLY BURMA—DARFUR GENOCIDE CONTINUES... "Not exactly the kind of world to bring kids into." Sidonia was folding the cover of a carton over the pile of children's clothing and blankets to be brought to the United Church for shipment to China. She had found them tucked away and Edith said she didn't want them anymore. Sidonia considered keeping them, but then she thought, but they need the clothes right now and they should have them right now.

"All those poor people," she said, "thousands and thousands, buried under their homes come apart–swept away by raging waters..." She stopped. Then, "Alive one minute, dead the next. Quiggy, we're getting older all the time, but we're still here. Don't you see that?"

He gave up collecting the newspapers. "But you never wanted a baby. You left Nova Scotia to get away from too much family."

"That was different." She shook her head. "I don't want to go into all that. It's different for me–for us."

"You forget one thing," he mocked. "We're stuck here."

"I know."

"I don't know what's worse–having Edith acting like she has been, with all those notes and labels or the way she is now–giving orders, acting as though she owns us." He looked at her and sighed. "Beau called again. I told him we couldn't leave, not now."

There was a demanding summon from Edith's room. "Don't forget to take those beat-up cartons to the dump," Sidonia called as she ran. Quigley's eyes narrowed. Garbage man and maid-in-waiting, he told himself.

* * *

"Going to church makes me feel so much better," Edith said that Sunday. Leo looked at the majestic stone ivy-covered building that seemed to shine under a benevolent sun. Then he looked at Edith. A large hat with a blue ribbon round the brim, a light blue suit, a soft white blouse showing through the well-tailored jacket. Special shoes that supported her weak feet but still looked fashionable.

How happy she is now, Leo thought, as he watched this one and that one greeting Edith–so nice to see you–lovely sermon... But then, their voices seemed too low, too even, their smiles too polite. Edith's careful, poised, "So nice..." Surely, her smile masked who knew what. But he found himself smiling too, his voice turning into the other's low polite, "So pleased to meet you." He thought, *A painted ship upon a painted sea*. But there had been an albatross, falling, a crossbow in its breast.

"Leo?" Edith was tapping her cane on the sidewalk. The street was nearly deserted. A few children ran to their parents about to get into their cars.

"Yes, let's go," he said, and looking around at the empty street, he murmured, *"Our revels now are ended. These our players have melted into air, into thin air..."* For wasn't he a player too, smiling, saying polite nothings?

But after he helped Edith into the car, he couldn't help being aware of her need for dignity. She straightened her jacket, put her hands to her hair, smoothing; in her lap the kid gloves she had insisted on wearing.

He began the drive home. From the outside Edith might appear an elderly lady out for a Sunday drive but inside the car, Leo could not help seeing her right hand in constant motion, tapping her knee then the dashboard, her knee, the dashboard... He tried not to sigh.

* * *

Edith woke up in good spirits all that week. Dawn was beginning to pearl the May sky; right outside her window, a lark was singing then another bird joined in, and another. She lay in bed listening to this bird symphony of trills and chirps and tweets and chirrs, until she reminded herself that she must get up. The repairman from Benny's Appliance Service was coming this afternoon.

As the first rays of the sun came into the room, she got out of bed. She moved, slowly it was true—but more smoothly than usual, from a lying to sitting position. The lovely feeling of purpose was stronger in her now. Still in her nightgown, she took her cane and hobbled to the window.

As the day danced in, sun pouring into the room and birdsong outside her window, Edith felt a surge of newness. Am I really in such a bad state? she wondered. True, the arthritis was there, in hip and leg, hindering movement, and her eyesight was worse, but the budding bushes, sunny skies and shimmering lake caused her to forget winter's ice and cold and furious rages, the many days she'd awakened to a desire to sleep on—not get up at all.

The change of season called for action. A garden to be dug,

then rows of peas, beans, radishes, lettuce... The house to be vigorously taken in hand, dusted, scrubbed, shaken out. The yard to be raked and seeded. It was time for spring-cleaning. She began to plan–the closets, the drawers in the bedroom, the kitchen. Winter clothes put away; summer garments taken out. Curtain to be taken down and laundered, carpets to be cleaned. Things to be done. Not all today, of course. But towels and sheets and that kind of thing must be ready for the washing machine, which had not been working for a whole week. She looked at the calendar on the wall. Yes, three o'clock. Saturday.

As she dressed–the new spring slacks, the pretty blouse Sidonia had gone with her to buy, shoes, not slippers that she usually wore in the house–her feeling of purpose soared within her, a wave rising high. She brushed her hair with vigor.

The clock on the wall said eight-thirty. Usually, Sidonia knocked on her door about this time, but then she remembered that Sidonia had mentioned going out early for laundry supplies and that Quigley and Leo would be working on the roof of the garage. So they trust me to be alone here and handle things, Edith thought.

As she moved from her bedroom along the hallway to the kitchen, she almost felt she could throw her cane away; she was walking more easily. She blinked and blinked, but the cloudiness that so often smudged her vision seemed to be gone. She felt as new as the day.

"I am all right," she told herself, as she shook corn flakes into a bowl and sliced a banana. The craziness in her head, or whatever it was that had taken hold of her, was not there. "I am not senile," she went on, just the usual things that happen to all of us in old age–forgetting this or that, misplacing one thing or another. And then, the winter had been grey and icy enough to have an effect on anyone–certainly an old person who had to be so careful on the streets. As for that terrible word–Alzheimer's–it could not apply to her, not the way she was carefully measuring the water as she filled the kettle, not the way she was watching the water come to a boil and turning off the burner.

It was nearing ten o'clock when she finished breakfast and even swept the floor. The appliance repairman would be coming at two, she reminded herself. She must get busy, surprise Sidonia with a tidied kitchen, maybe cook the stew that Quigley liked. And then, there were the towels and sheets to be gathered up for the washing machine.

But suddenly she felt tired. It came on like that–the great exhaustion, she called it. She had to sit down and rest. She went into the living room and sat, leaning back, on the recliner. Quigley came in. "There's a hailstorm coming up," he said. "I hope Sidonia doesn't get caught in it." Then seeing Edith relaxed in the recliner, "I came to see how you're doing," he said, "but I can see you're doing fine."

"I'm waiting for..." she began, but Quigley was on his way out and telling her that he and Leo needed to get the garage door fastened quickly.

Hail began to fall, big blustery white nuggets that clattered the roof and windows. Suddenly, it grew dark. Edith looked at the clock and it was only eleven; it was strange to have this darkness so early in the day. She felt so comfortable there in the lovely recliner, in the darkness. Her eyes closed, then opened, then closed, and finally gazed at the windows where the white nuggets rolled down and banged against the glass as though trying to get inside.

A warm contentment came over her. Long ago, on days like this–dark and stormy–there were chores she loved to do. Others called the neatening of spice jars, the tidying of drawers and closets bothersome work but she loved–yes, loved–the orderly clothes, the clearly labeled jars, the closets with their racks aligned. She would polish the handles of the kitchen cabinets. The metal would shine, as though smiling at her, thanking her.

She opened her eyes. She told herself she had dozed off and must be careful. She must not miss the repairman. But looking at the clock, she saw it was only past twelve, so she could rest a little more. Sidonia must be taking shelter in this storm. She settled back in the chair.

The hail had changed to a downpour. Listening to the rain slamming against the windows, Edith smiled. Her thin dry lips grew softer, her bony jaw relaxed and her faded eyes glinted just a little. The smile was for long ago, for herself in the large kitchen, for the roast ready for the oven, the vegetables to be cleaned and cut. The smile was for Tim, too–Timmy, they called him–three or four he was–rolling a toy car on the floor. And for James, who would be coming home.

The spirit of the house would be smiling too, keeping her

company, waiting with her. They would sing together—*"Just Molly and me, and baby makes three. We're happy in my blue heaven."*

There was a crash. Edith sat up. Lightening streaked across the angry sky. She did not open her eyes but rubbed them, as a child does, with her fists. But her hands hurt; the arthritis was bad, and, when she sat up straighter, her back hurt too. She was waiting for someone or something. She looked at the clock. It was nearly one. She would have some tea, some toast, and then she would gather up the towels and sheets for the washing machine. She liked that—the machine working, everything nice and clean. James had called her a good housekeeper. For a moment she wondered who James was. Then she remembered: he was big and strong, the man who took care of her long ago. Now Sidonia and Quigley took care of her. As usual, even their names brought on the feeling of love for them. Where is Sidonia? she wondered. She said she would be here when the repairman came.

But two o'clock came and the Benny's Appliance repairman did not show up. Saturday, she told herself, he said he would be here Saturday, and today is Saturday. She felt terribly tired but she did not want to lie down. The happy feeling with which she had awakened was gone; her head felt blurry. Flat, like a drink with no taste, although she would not have been able to describe it so.

She went into the kitchen, suddenly thirsty. She took a glass from the cupboard, turned on the tap, filled it with water. But, returning to her chair, she spilled the water onto the floor and she slipped—would have fallen if she had not caught hold of the kitchen counter. The glass fell to the floor and shattered. She stood there, uncertain what to do.

"My God!" Sidonia, still in her outdoor jacket, was looking at her. "Haven't I told you a thousand times not to mess about in the kitchen, Edith? And where is Quigley?" She took a dustpan and broom and began to sweep up the shattered glass. "Don't move," she said to Edith. When she had swept up all the glass, she led her to the living room.

Still breathing hard, Sidonia sat down. Trying to be gentle, she led Edith to a chair and helped her sit down. "The repairman didn't come," Edith tried to explain. "I waited and waited, but he..." Suddenly, she could say nothing.

"Of course, he didn't come. He came yesterday." Sidonia told herself she would have to have it out with Quigley. One day she had asked him to keep tabs on Edith, one day so she could go join the demonstration against the Olympics in China, so she could really do something to help those unfortunate Tibetan people who had had their freedom taken from them–and look what had happened!

"No, today," Edith said. "He said Saturday and today is Saturday."

"He said Friday, Edith dear." Sidonia sighed. The poor woman was not to blame.

"Friday? I was so sure."

"Never mind. I'll make some tea and sandwiches. You lie down now and rest." She led Edith to her room, helped her off with her clothes and into a nightgown.

"I wanted to..." Edith began.

"You wanted to help. Of course you did." Sidonia put the cover over her. "Just rest now."

Edith raised her head. It throbbed and hurt, but not like any pain she had ever known. It came to her that this was not a pain at all. She could not think what it was making her head feel so strange. She wanted to tell Sidonia she was sorry, but for what? Like those bits and splinters of shattered glass, words gleamed, flashed, disappeared. Then, everything seemed to be floating–the room, Sidonia, the curtains. She could not keep her head up. She lay down.

It was nine at night. The room was dark. Edith sat on her bed, shivering, until she thought–if that was the word–to put the extra blanket over her flannel nightgown. She could still know when she was cold or hot, hungry or not. But for how long? The images of a nursing home haunted her.

The moon came through the window, lighting the wall. Gazing at that screen, Edith saw scene after scene unroll: the college application unfilled–the job left after two weeks–one course after another abandoned. The moon left the room, and, like a child, she wanted to follow it. She reached for her cane and hobbled painfully to the window. But the moon was gone.

She could see the scudding clouds. My days were like those clouds. Like a sudden spark in a dying fire, the thought lit the muddle of her brain. Yes, the days had come and gone–the job not taken–the seminar not attended–the degree started and left after a year. There were always reasons–good, virtuous reasons, so it seemed at the time: a family member gravely ill, James away and she the mainstay for Tim at a vulnerable age (and every age seemed vulnerable).

The moon disappeared. The room turned black. And the blackness was what happened in her head more and more. She finally fell asleep. Was it a dream? It seemed too brief–only moments–herself, Edith Martin, shrinking–smaller and smaller, until only tiny bits and pieces were left, falling away. Then, nothing.

The next morning she felt for her cane, which lay propped on the bedpost. But the cane had fallen. She must have it. Somehow. Above all, she must not call Sidonia. She took as deep a breath as she could, positioned herself, bent tentatively, and then the pain came, sharp, a dagger cutting into her bad leg. Slowly, she straightened, then, taking another deep breath, changed the torque of her reluctant body so she could, in spite of the pain, bend and retrieve the cane.

"I can do that now," she told herself. "Even with the pain I can bend and reach and walk, but for how long?" She was quiet. Then went on: "And I can still figure things out–not everything, but some things. I can retrieve, a word, a sentence, a moment, a time, but the handwriting is on the wall: one day I will no longer be able to think, to move, to speak, and then it will be too late." And it seemed to her that Death would tease her, play with her. Hide-and-seek. And then, wouldn't her death be like her life–taking her as Life had taken her–as though Edith Martin had no say in dying as she had had no say in living.

She sat bolt upright. There was a way to redeem her lost life. This time, she, Edith Martin, would have her say. She, not Death, would choose her time of leaving earth. She, all of her. It would be an act of wholeness. She must go on one more Expedition. Her last. She must venture into an unknown territory, unafraid. A shiver ran through her. She must rekindle the daring to set out on this Expedition, find the courage to carry it through to its end. This time she would not be within the sheltering pages of a book, nor maneuvering the winding twisting staircase or the dangerously difficult automobile; this time her equipment would be the guarded pills, the bottle of whiskey. This time she would not be coming home—she would be going...

Edith made sure the door was closed. She put a chair against it too. Sidonia was courteous, did not intrude; still, she worried and might come to check if she was all right. Edith went over to the chest of drawers farthest from the door and bent tentatively. Every part of her resisted, but with successive attempts she was able to reach the last drawer and open it. Rummaging through panties, scarves and socks, she found the small vial of sleeping pills that Dr. Helperin had prescribed for James. But he had died suddenly, using only one pill. From her pocket, Edith took another vial and added it to the first. She was conjuring up another way to get more pills from Dr. Helperin, when there was a knock on her door.

"Are you ready?"

Sidonia's voice propelled Edith to a level of movement that surprised her. Quickly but softly she closed the drawer, straightened herself, stood, took up her cane, went to the door and opened it. It occurred to her that Sidonia would grieve. Yes, her dear Sidonia would grieve. And Quigley too. But grief, like everything else, would fade with time. And then, of course, they would have the money—the money to bring to life the dreams of the two people who had cared for her, rather than keep alive a body that could not function and a mind that could not think.

"I wish you wouldn't close yourself in like that, Edith, it worries me." Sidonia was dressed for outside—her new jacket and skirt and a pretty blouse.

"You look nice."

"And so do you," Sidonia smiled. "You'd better take a jacket and scarf; there's a wind out there, and it's cold." She shook her head. "What a crazy year this has been. Here it is end of April and brrr." They got into the car; thankfully, Leo had the heat on.

"How's the sleeping?" Sidonia asked from the back seat. Quigley sat beside her.

"Not too good," Edith said. "But, you know, it's all right when I take one of those pills Dr. Helperin gave me. I just take one and I sleep like a baby and feel fine."

"I'm not crazy about medications," Sidonia said. "Still, it's not good to go without sleep. We'll talk to the doctor. I'm glad you're sensible, Edith, I'm really pleased you're willing to go see him, instead of the fusses you used to make."

Edith was pleased too. She would get more pills. Actually, it was easier than she had thought it would be.

139

20

"At this point I believe we are dealing with Alzheimer's," Dr. Helperin told Edith, Sidonia, Quigley and Leo, who sat in their chairs like spectators at a show. Edith had started to fidget with the fringes of her long scarf, which she would not take off; her eyes were cast down. Leo took her hand. Sidonia and Quigley exchanged quick nervous glances. The doctor suppressed a sigh. If only one could tiptoe around some words, soften them with the usual platitudes—research, medications, that kind of thing. But they had said that they wanted the truth.

"What Sid and I want to know is why after all this time—it's going on two years now—Edith has changed so much in some ways, yet, in other ways, she hasn't changed that much." Suddenly aware he was speaking of Edith in the third person, Quigley felt ashamed. He looked at Edith. She didn't seem to mind. She seemed almost alert. It was strange how often Edith's mood or attention could momentarily change. She was not fidgeting anymore, her foot was not tapping; her body was still, her eyes focused on the diagram on the wall behind the doctor.

Dr. Helperin had been careful to choose a picture of the brain, not out of *Grey's Anatomy*, just a diagram to clarify their confusion at the wavering course of Edith's Alzheimer's. "This is the cerebral cortex." With his pointer, he indicated the ridged and creased greyish matter surrounding the skull. "It's the shell, you might say, enclosing the sections of the brain. Medical science has come a long way; we can now identify the functions of each area."

He paused, suddenly aware he had not answered Quigley's question. "What happens in this disease," he continued, "is an overlapping of symptoms." He turned to Edith. "It's what is happening to you now, or, at least, explains part of what is going on inside your brain. We always have to remember we can't explain everything." He paused, wanting to let this sink in. Most of the time he succeeded in sticking to the facts, but there was in him a chronic ache for those who fell through the ever-widening gap between knowledge and what his grandchildren would call 'unknowing.'

"So part of your increasing difficulties," he went on, addressing Edith, "is this overlapping of symptoms, due to the overlapping of various sections of the brain. Edith, does this make sense to you?" She nodded vigorously. Extraordinary, he thought, considering the extensive damage to her brain.

"You okay?" Leo said softly, still holding her hand.

Suddenly Edith straightened herself. "I want to hear more," she said in a voice verging on strident.

And there you have it, Dr. Helperin thought, there's no doubt she understands me, yet her area for understanding language has atrophied considerably. All eyes were on him. They want to know how long the disease will go on before death, he thought. They want a time frame. But he could not give them one. "The way the disease progresses and the time it takes to progress varies with the person," he continued. "The progression can be fast or slow or very slow— years, in fact. Edith, you can go on quite well for a long time with the good care Sidonia and Quigley give you." He smiled at them. They did not smile back.

He took up the pointer again. "This section is the frontal lobe. It's responsible for our ability to plan, organize, make strategies, sort things out. Also our self-control, so we can behave in a socially acceptable way." A sigh came from Sidonia, who was telling herself that the scan must have shown how damaged Edith's frontal lobe was. "The first scan showed about twenty percent of the neurons gone. This area is quite damaged."

"Will they come back?" Edith asked.

"There's work going on about the plasticity of the brain." She was looking at him, puzzled. "About the brain's ability to build new cells, but it is ongoing research—something for the future." He cleared his throat. "The second scan shows no further loss of cells. And stress is always a factor." He turned to Sidonia and Quigley. "Your handling Edith's finances and housekeeping allows her to do what she loves—read poetry, that kind of thing, which may be keeping her memory from going as rapidly as it often does."

"So that's it," Edith said. She turned to look at Quigley and Sidonia. "At least you have the reason I behave the way I do." They

hastened to reassure her, "Not all the time—look at you now…"
And it was true; from somewhere within, something had fired up in
Edith. It had happened; it could happen again; but this disease was
not one with a prognosis or cure, and it came to her now, in these
minutes of clarity, that she was eighty after all and time for making
decisions was fast running out. Quigley and Sidonia were trying to
hide their confused feelings of loyalty and their desire for a life of
their own; time was running out for them too. A feeling of fierce love
made her rise to her feet, go over and embrace them.

A look hard to decipher came over her and then Edith sat
down again. She placed her hand in Leo's.

Dr. Helperin continued. He indicated the area at the bottom
of the diagram. "The temporal lobe. Surprisingly, both the first and
second scan showed only about twelve percent damage to the cells,
so it may be all that reading and memorizing is helping this section
which assists in making sense of sounds and language, as well as
being able to name and recognize objects and faces. And with this
slow progression, with the proper mental exercise and physical too,
perhaps the damage will not increase—at least for the time being."

Dr. Helperin paused. The silence in the room was not simply
rapt attention; it held a tension that was surely due to more than the
April wind raging outside the windows as though it were January.
What were they all thinking? He wondered. And how much thinking
was going on within the unpredictable brain of Edith? There was an
odd stillness about her.

He pointed again. "This section beneath the temporal is the
hippocampus, where memory is organized, encoded, stored and
retrieved. The scan showed all these areas have been affected. The
nerve cells have died or are dying because they can't connect with
each other. Plaques and tangles in the brain become more frequent as
the disease progresses."

"How far along is she? Could you say?" Quigley asked.

He considered. Only death and examination of the brain
could be so specific. "I would say, Edith, you're in a mildly moderate
stage," he finally said. "With the good care you get and if you keep
exercising your mind and the apparent slow progress of the disease,
why you could have years ahead."

Edith turned to Leo. "Years ahead," she said in a leaden
voice.

Years ahead, Sidonia thought, and the thought spiraled into all the cooking and cleaning that would have to be done and dishes that would have to be washed. The thought kept spiraling, until it seemed a gigantic metal spring that would snap in her head. All the spilt tea that would have to be cleaned up and the blouses taken off and put back on, front to back, the shoes, right on right. And what about my wanting a baby? Sidonia's eyes drifted.

"The answer to those occasional night wanderings, Edith," Dr. Helperin said, "could be a more effective sleeping pill. The one you now have is rather mild." He thought, the occipital and parietal lobes do show more damage, and was about to mention this but Edith was getting restless. Sidonia and Quigley were looking at the darkening windows.

"We'd better get going," Leo said.

A light rain had become hail. They could hear the pounding on the windows.

"I'll start the car," Leo said.

Dr. Helperin pulled Quigley aside discreetly as they were leaving. "It might be a good idea to have a meeting with Alfred Seaman at this point. I seem to recall James telling me he'd placed additional funds in his keeping..."

When they were gone, Saul sat in his swivel chair looking at the diagram, immersed in introspection. *Grey's Anatomy* had been his Bible long ago, when medical school took up his days and nights. A different time that was, a simpler world or so it seemed. You probed until you found the site of the disease. You tried to take care of the problem: surgery, medication... How sure he had been in those days. How certain that cures could be found for just about every illness.

The hail had stopped. Blackening night outside the window. He took down the diagram, closed up the office. *Why? What?* How many times had he seen Alzheimer patients mouth these questions—or seem to—toward the end, before the blankness, the vacant stare, the drooped head, the leaden yet muscleless body. It seemed to him they were asking the very air around them, as though from out of the vast reaches of the universe an answer might come.

He got up. Fern would say he was being fanciful. He wanted to go home. To have a martini—the way Fern made them. Dry. An olive and a sliver of lemon. He wanted to sit across the table from his wife of fifty years, watch her eat, each mouthful savored. He wanted to see her smile, talk about her day. He thought he could look at her forever and not tire of her face.

* * *

Outside Edith felt the crisp air revive her. She thought of what she had to do. "I'd like to get some wine," she said.

"I thought wine made you ill," Sidonia said.

"For you and Quigley. An Easter present from me."

"That's sweet of you, Edith," Sidonia smiled, anticipating the night–she and Quigley slowly sipping their wine, looking at each other, then... Delicious.

"I'll gas up," Leo said.

"I'll stay in the car with Leo," Quigley said.

Inside the Government liquor store, Edith watched Sidonia looking through the shelves of wine. "White," she said, "and dry." Edith wondered how to get her out of the store. It turned out to be easy. "Safeway's having a special on strawberry shortcake." Her voice took on a holiday gaiety. "You know how Quigley loves strawberry shortcake. Why not go over–it's right next door –get some. I'll just take a look at the wines."

Sidonia hesitated. "I'm going to do the big shopping in a couple of days."

"The Special is over tonight. Anyway, it's for Easter."

When Sidonia was out the door, Edith purchased a bottle of 40 proof bourbon. "An Easter present for my daughter and her husband," she explained to the clerk. "A surprise. Please put it in a party bag," and placing her finger on her lip conspiratorially, she put the bag inside her backpack. She was getting the hang of it, as Tim used to say. Tim?

* * *

When Saul got home, Fern was looking at the TV. Peter Mansbridge and The National. Chaos in Gaza, genocide in the Sudan, another roadside bomb kills four in Afghanistan. "I wonder if Barack Obama really understood what he was taking on running for U.S. President." She shook her head in disbelief. "Imagine, Saul, eight hundred billion dollars to stimulate the economy, most of it to Wall Street, the crooks who caused the meltdown in the first place."

She turned off the TV, came up to him, kissed him. "You're tired. I'm sorry—venting my political ire when you walk in."

"I saw Edith today," he said.

"How did it go?"

"It went."

They both laughed. Then she was taking his hand and leading him to the recliner.

"I had to tell them Edith's Alzheimer is progressing very slowly."

"Had to? Is that bad—the disease going slowly?"

"It's good that Leo's come to stay with them. He'll be an enormous help. I could use a martini."

But even as he spoke, she was mixing the martinis. He thought how, after long relationships, one person could know the other's need without words. He leaned back in the recliner and closed his eyes. *"Falling, falling, falling, we are all falling…"* he murmured. That had been in a poem; he could not remember the name. Long long ago, he had read it—when he read poetry. He sat up, took the drink Fern handed him. "Come sit beside me," he said, moving to the sofa.

"I never could quite understand Leo's relationship to Edith," Fern said. "I always had the feeling he was as much a friend as a handyman."

It was dark in the room, only a lamp on a side table. After a few minutes, Fern said, "Jilly said she was going to run for Premier when she is older."

"Premier of B.C.; that's ambitious, considering she's eight years old."

"Premier of Canada."

He smiled. Jilly, his youngest grandchild. Then his mind switched tracks, went from pleasant thoughts of his grandchildren to Edith. "Years and years, and in the end, death."

He must have spoken out loud. "You can't take on everyone's problems," Fern pulled him up. "Let's eat. It's coq au vin and Fern's supercalafragelistic salad. Let's take our drinks."

"What about dessert?" he kidded.

She smiled broadly. "Strawberry shortcake. The real sweet stuff comes later."

21

Sidonia walked down Vernon Street, trying but unable to succumb to the allure of the gorgeous May day. The West Kootenays was a special place—one of earth's magical centers—that's what she had heard when she left Nova Scotia some twenty years before. The low sky, the soft mountains, the lakes—all changing with the weather—could do something to you. Make you change too. But it had not been like that. Head bent, she walked on moodily, thinking about the jobs she'd had to take to keep going. Always managing. Just.

"Fat ass!" A boy of fourteen or so, stopped on his skateboard, was rubbing his shoulder and looking angrily at her. Lost in discontent, she had bumped into him. "Sorry," she said automatically, but the kid was already whizzing past her, careening down the street. She stood there for a couple of minutes, resolved not to let the nasty word bother her. It was only a word after all. Still, she couldn't help feeling hurt.

Two teenaged girls were standing in front of the Bulletin Board on the Recreation Building. "So I, like, told him we had to talk, and he, like, said there was nothing to talk about, so then, I told him to piss off," the one in mini skirt and halter said. The other, in short shorts and a ribbon of bandana over breasts, nodded. "It's like they want what they want but like they clam up when you tell them what you want."

Sidonia watched their skinny bodies sprint—oh, so easily—across Vernon against the light. Being thin gave you a kind of power. No matter what anyone said to the contrary, being thin made life easier. She looked down at herself and sighed. Breasts bulged her T-shirt, pants near to bursting with thighs and buttocks.

She should be getting back. She had finished her errands—stops at the Government building, the Provincial building, City Hall—doing chores Edith could no longer do. In a way Edith was lucky, not having to deal with all that stuff–medical premiums, questions about utility bills. Immediately she felt guilty. Poor Edith, doing less and less, needing more and more help.

Yes, she really should be getting back. There were things she had to do. Endless things. But Sidonia couldn't get herself going. She leaned against the building. A drag–that's what life was. She closed her eyes and saw how it would be. She would come into the house, and the house would be full of Edith: Edith and her needs. Edith and her frustrations. Edith and her listening for them. Edith, the prim old lady. Not knowing which Edith was there, not knowing how she would end up. How they would end up.

She sighed deeply. Idly, she watched a young woman holding a leash to which a toddler's hand was attached by a ribbon bracelet. She closed her eyes, as she thought about how Quigley would be seeing her: too full T-shirt and pants, too full of the body he had–only months before–called plumply perfect?

She opened her eyes, gazed absent-mindedly at the notices stick-pinned to the Bulletin Board: MEET THE MANGOSTEEN–BIRTHING FROM WITHIN–RHYTHMIC GYMNASTICS–LAID BACK YOGA–MARKET FEST ON BAKER–THE DROP DEADS IN CONCERT...

One of the notices had fallen. Habit made her pick it up. A frieze of small hearts and rockets framed the sheet which read: LOSE WEIGHT WITH A WHOLE LOTTA LOVIN'–THE ULTIMATE DIET. SEXASIZE. REDUCE STRESS. BURN CALORIES. RELEASE EUPHORIC CHEMICALS AS YOU BOND MORE DEEPLY WITH YOUR PARTNER!

Firmly, Sidonia folded the sheet and put it into her pack. As she walked home, she straightened, quickened her pace. She wasn't frowning now. Her dimple was deep, the corners of her mouth turned up, her eyes bright. Talk about Providence. Talk about someone out there listening. Hadn't Quigley said they both needed to get to a gym? Hadn't he said there just wasn't the time? She had to stop a minute, take the sheet she'd picked up from her sack. There it was–a half-hour of sex equals seven minutes on a treadmill. She quickened her pace. She had things to do. Those chemicals. She'd heard about them–from that animal Leopold who kept talking about all the dopamine and endorphins he was releasing when they were climbing Pulpit Rock. Only, she wasn't releasing anything but misery.

Sidonia walked more quickly–almost a run. All those endorphins and dopamine and serotonin right there in her brain, just waiting to be released. The right way. Making love. Her smile broadened. "What the hell are you so happy about?" the shaggy-looking man encased in a sandwich board–REPENT WHILE THERE'S TIME–called out.

She hardly heard him. And losing pounds all the while, she was telling herself. She remembered the note on the bottom of the sheet: *For more: www.bedroomolympics.com.* She would have to get to the internet at the library.

* * *

As May passed into June, Sidonia spent every moment she could spare from her duties as housekeeper and caregiver trying to track down *bedroomolympics.com.* It was hard to get away for Edith had become possessive. "You're going to leave me," she would cry, and Leo would have to patiently deflect her attention away to a nice walk or some other distraction.

First Sidonia tried the internet stations at the various little cafes, but they were always busy with giggling young teenaged girls hiding the screen and whispering to each other manically: "That's Lotto–I told you–isn't he..." Or, "Can't use my computer, my mom's practically standing over me all the time."

* * *

As June deepened into July and the temperature soared, Edith began hiding her eyeglasses in the refrigerator and putting various articles–a brooch, an old compact, a small magnifying glass–in the freezer. Then, she would accuse Quigley or Sidonia—or even Leo—of stealing them. This behavior, so different from the rather benign Edith of a couple of months before, made it harder for Sidonia to get away.

But Sidonia felt she had a mission. She felt she could climb every mountain and every hill to find what she was looking for. As it was, she had only to get to the internet. She went to the Municipal Library.

The three new computers at the library were fronted by three pre-schoolers. Sidonia made out strange little creatures chasing one another round and round at the first screen, a hodgepodge of lines going in all directions at the second, and, at the third, what appeared to be an article on the killer African ant. The small girl at this computer was taking notes on a pink posy-covered pad.

The librarian had said her time was up, so Sidonia asked the girl, "Excuse me, are you through with this computer?" She shook her head without turning around. Sidonia realized that once again—and now to a small child—she was asking instead of telling. "Your time is up," she said as firmly as she could.

This time the little girl shook her head more briskly, her Shirley Temple curls tossing about, and brought up a page headed AARDVARK. "Not till my mother comes," she said, still focused on the screen.

"When will your mother come?"

"I don't know, she's walking Attila, and he has to find the right place to poop and that takes a long time." Sidonia watched in awe as the little girl brought up a page headed MAN EATING TIGER, then returned to writing furiously in her pink pad.

Sidonia left the library and headed off to the internet at the Tidy Boy's Café. But two twelve year old girls were sitting at the computer, looking at something on the screen which was hidden from view by their arms, and whispering conspiratorially to each other. "Are you..." Sidonia began.

At her voice, the girls jerked nervously around, still shielding the screen. Seeing Sidonia, they relaxed. "Whew! Thought you were my mother," said one. Smiling at Sidonia, "She'd kill me if she knew I was on *Trick or Treat*, but it's the greatest." The girl had rings on her nose, eyebrow, upper lip and lower.

They weren't going to leave so Sidonia did. What with the heavy metal music and young people dancing with each other, away from each other, into each other, all the while holding gigantic lattes in one hand, she had a sudden image of bodies drowning in a sea of foaming liquid while the drums beat out: Kill me, baby, kill me.

Walking past some demonstrators on Baker—Free Tibet—Boycott China's Olympics—Sidonia went to The Greenery, Bo's Bistro and The Candyman, but all three cafes had the Olympics on their large TV screens and OUT OF ORDER signs on their computers. It was late afternoon. She had to get back. Quigley would be furious. But wasn't she doing this for him as well as her?

She finally found a hole-in-the-wall cafe–Tiny's–and, in moments, was on the *Bedroom Olympics* site. Eagerly, she learned that a half-hour of sex could do away with fifty-three to one hundred calories. There seemed to be some figures milling about in the small café but they were merely shapes in the background configured into strange outlandish proportions by the shadows playing about, for the last rays of the dying sun were creeping into the café. What was relevant–what was important–was the screen before her. Overwhelmed with so much information with so little effort, Sidonia kept bringing up studies. Abundant health, neatly contoured bodies, joyful relationships were there for the asking. Or rather, the giving oneself over to the frequent coupling with your partner.

But it was the hands-on experience of a thirty-year-old fashion model that kept Sidonia's eyes on the screen; with so much concentrated looking, they were feeling tired. Hands-on, she giggled to herself–feeling giddy by now–turned on would be more like it. "Three weeks of endless fun and delight," exclaimed Lotus Greenhouse, about her honeymoon. On the edge of her seat, Sidonia scrolled down. With the Sexercise Program–lovemaking at least seven days a week, more if possible—there were hints of opportunities for sexual coupling between meals, in the swimming pool and on the roller coaster (although here one had to proceed with caution).

Dizzy with possibility, Sidonia exited the website. She was about to leave, when a soft voice said, "There's a club, you know." A man was standing there. "Tiny," he said. Everything about him was huge–his bulky body, the hand he held out to her, the smile on his round and fleshy face. She had been so engrossed she had not paid attention to what was going on around her. Now she saw a number of large men and women talking amiably and drinking what seemed to be a new kind of latte topped with quivering heaps of heavy cream and nuts. Dishes of pork rinds and greasy-looking dips sat on the small tables. "The idea," Tiny explained, "is to grow larger and larger so as to necessitate more and more sex in order to shed the pounds we put on." He winked at Sidonia. "We welcome new members." A total of two hundred and forty-two pounds had been lost among the members in the last two weeks.

Sidonia declined. She felt rather a woman of the world now that she had surfed the internet. And fearless too. This was obviously some kind of cult. All the Sexercise experts had been clear that sex must be with your one and only for the program to work. Well, Quiggy was her one and only.

She found herself whirling down the streets, carried by an irresistible momentum. Words kept dancing in her head: Search out every nook and cranny of your lover's body! Pinch! Bite! Nip! Dive right in! Hold nothing back! Repeat performances, Lotus had urged.

Sidonia arrived at Lakme's Lingerie on Baker Street. Many times she had stopped before the window, gazing at the shimmering nightclothes. Now she went right in. Lakme was there, a limber slip of a girl-woman who wore a bright beaded headband, reminiscent of the twenties.

"I'd like to see a negligee," Sidonia said. Then, her courage suddenly failing, "Something not too–revealing," she added.

Lakme went into the depths of the store and was back in minutes. "This," she said, "is what you want." She held up a long sheer gown, the color of mother-of-pearl.

"You can see right through it."

"Exactly."

"It's a little–daring."

"If you've got it, flaunt it." Then, Lakme sighed. "I sure would like to have all those curves." She nodded appreciatively at Sidonia's body. "It will drive him crazy," she exulted, rolling her big brown eyes round and round.

Sidonia bought the negligee. Somewhat guiltily, for it cost ninety-five dollars. As she watched Lakme nestle it into a bed of soft tissue in a mother-of-pearl box, it occurred to her that Quigley was rather set in his ways, followed certain steps in his lovemaking—and starting off with a see-through negligee wasn't one of them.

For more than a month, Sidonia waited for a chance to display her see-through negligee, as a prelude to putting it to use (very good use, she told herself) in the Sexercise Program. In all the novels she had read, a filmy negligee seemed the first requirement for tempestuous lovemaking. She, careful and cautious Sidonia Grout, making tempestuous love! And getting slim while doing it! As she went about her chores, she felt full of daring, of brisk resolve.

But there didn't seem to be an opportunity for sex. The Olympics were long over and Quigley no longer watched the games on TV every chance he could get, but now the worsening economic situation in the States had him listening to the news every night. He couldn't get enough of it. "How many times do you want to know about the sub-primes and Fannie Mae and Freddie Mac and the seven hundred fifty million bailout by the U.S. Government?" Sidonia said to him, when she turned off the TV and he turned it back on. "It's eleven o'clock," she repeated, always aware of the shimmering negligee waiting in a hidden corner of their closet.

But Quigley shook his head, worriedly. "Canada's not immune to bad economic times." She pointed out that the banking regulations were stricter in Canada, but he was in a mood to brood. "You know," he said, "it's a good thing we didn't talk Edith into putting her money in a bank, when she put us in charge of it. She wasn't as nutty as she seemed—she sure was right about keeping your money right with you." He was all wound up. "Those crooks in the financial world!" he ranted on. "Criminals, that's what they are—trading worthless paper! Getting their millions in bonuses, flying around in their jets..." he took a breath. "And here we are, the rest of us, trying to get by while factories close and gas goes up." He threw up his hands. "Oh, what the hell."

Sidonia saw what she had to do. "Listen, Quiggy, you put in a hard day's work what with putting the garden to sleep and trying to find the cheapest gas and all the other jobs you do around here, and then, you had to stay with Edith while I went traipsing around to get on the internet... Quiggy, you deserve some fun."

But he hardly heard. He was thinking Leo was really a big help, doing whatever needed doing and more, and then, Leo didn't mind staying with Edith and she liked him too. Not much of a talker though. Quigley was about to turn the TV back on, but Sidonia put her hand on his and stopped him.

"Quiggy, you're all stressed out. You need to relax. Let's go to bed."

"Why are you looking at me like that?"

She put down the nightgown she was hemming for Edith. "Like what?"

"Funny like."

"Funny ha ha or funny peculiar?"

He stared at her. "What's gotten into you, Sid?"

"Come on, I want to show you something."

"Don't you want to check on Edith?"

"Edith's fast asleep. She took a sleeping pill. Come on."

She took his hand and he followed her, surprised at the strength of her grip, up the stairs. There was a no-nonsense way in which she closed their bedroom door. He wondered why she didn't switch on the ceiling light instead of the small lamp with the rosy bulb.

"Sit there, Quiggy," she said, "on the bed and wait. I'll be right back."

She took something shiny from the depths of their closet and walked to the bathroom, all the while looking at him in a strange new way. "Are you all right?" he asked. She smiled mysteriously. Like that Mona Lisa painting, he thought.

"Do you like it?" she asked, reappearing, her long hair trailing in back, the pearly white gossamer negligee slipping from one shoulder. He didn't know what to say. Sidonia usually wore flannel pajamas when autumn came. He wanted to ask if she wasn't chilly, but somehow, that didn't seem appropriate. She wants me to make love to her, he thought, but then, Sid had always been—not exactly shy—but still not like this—almost brazen.

"Nice," he finally said, and wondered if he meant the negligee, which kept sliding down, or her creamy shoulders and melon breasts. She smiled as though she had some secret and started undulating her ample hips from side to side. This, too, was not part of their ritual. Quigley gazed at Sidonia, as though he hadn't seen her before. Or, at least, not like this.

"I better get undressed," he said, but, before he could take off his shirt, she was standing in front of him stark naked, the negligee glistening on the floor in a pool of moonlight.

"Let me," she said and began to undo the buttons of his shirts slowly—like those burlesque shows he had gone to now and then as a youth. Then she just dropped the shirt on the floor, not even hanging it up. He reached down to unzip his pants but she pushed his hands away.

"Let me," she said again, and remembered what came after this in the Sexersize Program ...if she could really be so bold. Then she thought of all the weight to be lost and slowly unzipped his pants and let them drop to the floor too. His jockey shorts. Drop. His undershirt. Drop.

153

There was Quigley standing before her, stark naked too, looking at her for guidance. Because he wasn't sure about the next step and they had always followed a procedure in their love-making. Polite conversation to begin with—talking about this and that—before... His thoughts slid away. Things were happening before he could make them happen. Sid's hand was snaking down to his penis, and, looking down, he saw he was aroused.

"Let's have some fun." When the words were out, Sidonia couldn't believe she had said them. It wasn't exactly the words that surprised her; it was the way she said them—drawing out the last word and winking. For a moment she wondered if that had been in the Sexercise Program, but then she was beckoning Quigley over to the bed and he was following her, mesmerized and giddy.

The hotter the sex, the more weight loss. That was on the Sexercise site. But Sidonia was no longer surfing the internet; she was surfing Quigley. Her fingers were scratching gently and not so gently, his shoulders, chest, all the way down to his groin. She pinched his nipples. With her index finger she dug into his navel and stirred. She licked his ears. Her mouth opened his. Her tongue probed deep within.

"Hey! Take it easy!" Quigley managed when he could get his breath. Still, even as he cried the words, stirred and shaken, he was trying to enter her, fumbling in his eagerness, so that she, as frantic as he, had to put him in. Then, she was astride him, plunging and bucking and it was he who was rising to her and the air in the bedroom was thick with the smell of their sweat.

She began to groan, then cry out words Quigley had never heard her say before. She was writhing, heaving, thrashing about. Their lovemaking had never been so—not like this. Her face was distorted, her hair matted. Was she sick? In pain? Quigley stopped. "Are you okay?" he said, barely getting the words out. She only clutched him more tightly to her, into her, holding him with her thighs. Then, as the heat within her forced him to climax, she gave a final convulsion and collapsed upon him.

Spent, their breathing labored, they lay that way for a few minutes, she sprawled upon him, her face on his. He tried to move to one side to breathe more freely, to see; her hair was all over his face and eyes.

She rolled off and lay beside him. He waited for her to speak

154

but for a long while she remained silent. Then she said, "I shocked you, didn't I?"

He wasn't sure what to say. "Not shocked; surprised," he finally told her. She moved closer to him. "Why are you smiling, Sid?"

"Quiggy, you're smiling too."

He turned to look into her eyes. "I feel real good."

"Do you know how many calories we've burnt between us?"

"What?"

"You know we've been wanting to lose weight but can't get to a gym. Well, we've used up eighty or even a hundred calories right in our bed." She told him about the Sexercise Program and the *Bedroom Olympics* site. "And all those great chemicals that make you feel so good—they're positively flooding our brains now." Her smile broadened. "Maybe it happened."

"What happened?"

"A baby. Maybe we made a baby." In the silent night, the walls echoed, "Baby, Baby..." Suddenly, Sidonia sat up.

"Did you hear something?" she whispered. He shook his head.

But Sidonia was out of bed and opening the door and peering into the hall. She came back. "I thought Edith might be roaming around, but she's not. Those sleeping pills Dr. Helperin gave her really work." She snuggled closer to him. "I love you, Quiggy."

"I love you, Sid."

"Quiggy, so you think we can do this five times a week?"

"How would we get the time?"

"Well, we could manage the chores better now that Leo's staying up in the turret room."

"What about Edith?"

Sidonia reflected. "There's her naps. Love in the afternoon." She grinned.

Quigley squeezed her hand. "I guess we can manage."

"We better get some sleep; Edith will be up in a few hours." Sidonia pulled the covers up, smiling. The weight was going to pour right off.

But Quigley couldn't fall asleep. He turned uneasily from side to side. How peacefully Sidonia slept, smiling as though everything was fine, as though they weren't saddled with Edith. Edith, Edith, he thought. Their whole lives were regulated by her demands and needs. Why shouldn't Sidonia have the baby she wanted? She deserved to have what she wanted. They both did. He was sick and tired of information that didn't go anywhere. Plaques and tangles in the brain. Parts that were still working; parts that were not. Not possible to know for sure exactly Edith's state. That's what Dr. Helperin had said. Alzheimer's, yes, but it could go on for months, for years. Only an autopsy could tell how much of the brain was not working.

Edith stood outside the closed door of Sidonia's and Quigley's bedroom, perplexed. "Wha–wha..." she asked the air, trying to place herself. There had been voices from beyond the closed door but she only heard them as sounds–wild and frightening, then low, murmuring. She was cold and her hands and feet were icy, but she was shivering more from fright than cold. Go–go where... Her forehead creased. She frowned.

Now there was silence from behind the door. Who? She closed her eyes and leaned against the wall. She opened them, looked fearfully around. Everything was quiet. Dark. She fidgeted with her nightgown, feeling the flannel with her fingers, pinching it over and over. She lost her balance, brushed against the wall. Go... Go where... There was a faint light at the end of the hallway. Go...go to light. She did not have her cane. She groped along the wall.

Forced by terror, she reached the end of the hallway, perspiring profusely, her nightgown soaked with cold sweat. She looked down the winding staircase. It did not occur to her she had come up by this staircase. Down... Down... Her legs, feeble with arthritis and poor circulation, started to buckle. Down... Down... Down... She could not have explained the terror that flooded her. Then, turning, she saw a door. She looked once more at the staircase, then hobbled to the door and opened it.

The linen closet was large: sheets and pillow cases on one shelf; blankets on another; towels... She reached to close the door, lost her balance, and tumbled then fell onto the chenille carpet on the floor. Soft... Her eyes closed. She slept.

She had a nightmare. She was in a room heaped with things. All kinds of things. Small and large, table and chairs, radios, flowerpots, pillows, stands, books and more. She had to find her beautiful silver evening bag; she needed it. At the far end of the room, something glistened. Painfully, she tried to get through the jumble. She hobbled, stumbled, holding onto whatever she could, a table, chair, lamp. Finally she reached the far end. There was the bag. She tried to pick it up but it moved. She went toward it; it moved again, this time a little farther. She must have it. She tried to grasp it but her hand had dissolved.

Edith awoke to a draft of cold air and a shout. The closet door was wide open and Sidonia was standing there, looking down at her: "So that's where you were! Oh my God!"

22

March 2009, wet and raw, lingered into April. Although the Canadian financial markets had not fallen into an abyss, the impact of the economic meltdown was evident. Food prices and gas were up and so was unemployment.

It was five in the afternoon and the sun was still shining, but inside the living room all was dark, except the television. "Get a job! Get a life!" Judge Judy was saying to the youth in jeans. "Turn around!" she commanded. "Yes," she said to the courtroom, "it's what I saw, his behind all patched up." She addressed herself to the youth again, "How about patching up your life instead of your behind!" Taking a long tortured breath, she turned to the young woman standing before her. "You never never never lend money to anyone, especially a loser who makes a career of borrowing! Judgment for the plaintiff."

Sidonia leaned back in the recliner as Quigley came into the room. "I don't know what you see in that Judge Judy," he said. "She's tough as nails, not the way a woman should be."

"And how should a woman be?" She leaned back further. "I'm tired, dead tired. Even when Edith's asleep, I keep hearing her."

"It's not Edith's fault." Quigley wondered whether to continue this conversation or leave. There certainly was a lot to do— all the lights to be replaced by the environmentally-friendly low wattage ones—the washing machine needed attention—the car needed a new battery. And he had to do it all himself; Leo was busy clearing the debris off the garage, driveway and yard, aftermaths of the spring thaw. He said, "She's okay a lot of the time. The problem is not knowing when and where she can get really hard to manage."

Sidonia rose slowly, almost painfully, holding her stomach: her six-month pregnancy extended before her like a football. "The point is, what are we going to do? You know how much the weekly shopping was? Two and a half times more than a month ago, and it's going to be more. First, we had to let that Express Delivery opportunity in Calgary go, and now we've had to let go the chance in the Yukon." Her brow furrowed. "Sometimes, I wish there was an Express Delivery for..." She stopped abruptly.

Quigley was at a loss. This wasn't like his Sidonia, certainly not the seductive, fiery Sidonia whose joyful abandon had resulted in the baby to come. "What about Goody, that young woman from Slocan who was helping you with the housework?" he finally managed.

Sidonia was about to wheel away the vacuum that stood in a corner. She stopped, turned and scowled. "I've told you a hundred times I had to fire her." Her voice rose. "What's the problem, you ask? I'll tell you the problem. The problem was Goody sitting on the toilet seat, smoking pot, and the pail of dirty water sloshed all over the bathroom floor and Goody exulting dreamily, 'What a beautiful sea this is.'"

Quigley wondered how to get Sidonia back to herself–the terrific Sexercise self. Then it struck him. "Sid, the answer's right here in the house. We'll ask Leo to pretty much take over the care of Edith. Then I can find some work outside, whatever it is, so her money won't run out, and you won't be run ragged."

Leo came into the living room and sat down, not on the sofa or in an easy chair, but in one of the straight-backed chairs. He sat down the way he did everything: mindfully, placing his lean flanks carefully on the seat of the chair. He sat up straight but not rigid, relaxed and easy.

"Leo, there's something we want to ask you," Quigley said. He exchanged a glance with Sidonia, seated next to him on the sofa. She nodded: "It's about Edith. Because you understand her and we can't. We try and we want to do the best for her, but..." Quigley took up her sentence: "The way Edith is now, needing more looking after, and what with Sidonia pregnant and having to do all the housework and me having to do the repairs a lot of the time, we just can't manage it all." He blurted out, "So we'd like you to take over more of the care with Edith. We know you've been doing a lot and it hasn't been easy. It would mean more money for you, of course."

"I'm not interested in money," Leo said. He watched the

dancing figures on the wall cast by the flames in the fireplace. He couldn't help thinking that the fireplace needed repair and the walls needed painting. This old Victorian, he went on to himself, it's falling apart like Edith; parts of her falling away. "I like being here and I like helping Edith. Sure, I'll take care of her."

"You say that as if taking care of her was so easy," Sidonia told him. "All her moods and the way she wants to do everything and can't and ends up burning herself or cutting herself…"

"And what would you do if there wasn't someone to take care of her? What would happen to her?" Leo fixed his gaze on the two of them and saw Quigley look at Sidonia in what seemed a questioning way. She'll be the one who decides, Leo told himself silently. Oh yes, he went on to himself, she's got him under her thumb. And he felt a kind of gratitude he had escaped all those young women with their demands and their pleadings and his need to give them whatever they wanted. Too tender-hearted, people had said. A fatal flaw, Leo thought, like being born with a vestigial tail. He came back to the moment.

"We don't want to think about it," Sidonia was saying, "but maybe we'll have to see about a nursing home, if the Alzheimer's gets worse and we just can't manage."

"She would die." Leo came down on the last word like a hammer. His face flushed. A dart of pure anger shot from his mild grey eyes. "That's what happens in those places—people rot away and then they disappear, like some fruit or vegetable or piece of meat."

"She's going to die anyway," Quigley said. "Listen, I'm sorry, I didn't mean that the way it sounds. The problem is we *do* care about Edith. She took us in, gave us a home. That's why we're asking you. We want her to live comfortably in her own home, but we need help. You're the only one we can ask, Leo."

They waited for Leo to speak, but he was gazing at the dancing shadows. The flames of Life, he was thinking, sacred, inviolate, to be honored and cherished until the Ineffable extinguished them. His face softened.

"I'm not interested in money. And don't worry, we're friends, Edith and I—I want to take care of her." He rose from his chair.

"Even though she's got this Alzheimer's?" Sidonia said.

"Because the Alzheimer's got *her*," Leo said.

When they could hear his footsteps going down the hallway

toward Edith's room, Sidonia said to Quigley, "Can you make him out?" He shook his head: "Maybe he's some kind of Jesus freak." She shook her head: "No, he doesn't go to any church at all and he gets angry if you call him a saint."

"The things he does, though–picking the lice off a field mouse–doctoring that stray mangy cat..."

Sidonia sighed. "He says every living creature has a right to its life, no matter how weak or sick it is."

* * *

Sidonia heard the shouts first. "Murderers! Baby killers!" Turning, she saw the large group of demonstrators in front of the Government Building. Men and women walked quietly, carrying placards depicting fetuses in various stages of development. Small children wore placards. Babies in strollers and childpacks. People in wheelchairs kept pace with the others. Several young people walked unsteadily with canes. The shouts had come from a couple of men whom others were trying to restrain.

In front of the ivy-covered courthouse farther up the street, an opposing group marched silently. Some carried placards: THE RIGHT TO CHOOSE; DEATH WITH DIGNITY. This group was much smaller.

Sidonia felt a tug on her arm. "Are you my mother?" an old woman asked, taking firmer hold of her arm. The woman was dressed in what could have been a lounge suit...or pajamas. Her grey hair was messy. She was wearing slippers, wet and soiled. The woman was clinging to her arm. "Take me home, mother."

Sidonia led her to Stanley Street and the police station. The constable in charge thanked her. There had been an urgent call from a family in Ymir. An old woman with Alzheimer's had walked out of the house.

Sidonia had to backtrack all the way to the post office. She couldn't stop thinking about the lost old woman. At the post office, she took a package out of her shopping bag. How pleased her mom would be with the pretty things for her. But while she was making easy conversation with the clerk, paying for the stamps then finishing the rest of her errands, she was thinking about Edith. Would they be getting a call about a lost old woman? Would it come to that?

* * *

Leo knocked on the door to Edith's bedroom, feeling uncertain. What he was going to suggest to her now (not tell her; that wouldn't do) was not that simple.

Her voice, "Come in," interrupted his thoughts. He entered and found her sitting on her bed, dressed in one of her long loose dresses, trying to put her feet into her slippers. He knelt down, gently slippered each arthritic foot. "I've come to suggest something to you, Edith," he said, and added, "if this is a good time."

Her mouth worked itself into a bitter smile. "If this is a good time," she mocked, as though to say she had no good times. She was getting up from the bed. The lines of her face tightened, her jaw set; she reached for the cane leaning against the bed. "What do you want to see me about?"

"Would it be all right if I sat down?"

She was immediately contrite. "I've forgotten my manners. Sit down, Leo. I'll take a chair too." Each time he saw her, he was struck by certain almost imperceptible changes. Now her eyes held a grim determination as they shifted to the walker next to the bed, within reach. She was making a careful appraisal of the distance between the walker and herself, then, in one sweeping motion, as though this were a game and she must reach the goal, she grasped the handle and swept the walker to her.

Seated next to him, she said, "Well?"

He took her in closely now—the squarish jaw, the dry lips, the faded eyes. Her white hair had not been combed into its neat bun. She held her hand to it in sudden recognition of its messy state. Not the Edith of long ago: bright-eyed, sturdy, in command of herself. But the Edith now. Time made changes in one way or another but friendship weathered all changes.

She was looking at him curiously.

"Everyone is kind to me," she said, after a silence. "Sidonia and Quigley are good to me and you are good to me."

"Edith, we're friends. I want to help you even more."

"They have asked you to take care of me," she said.

"To help take care of you," he replied quickly. "They're concerned about you."

"I don't want pity, Leo."

He moved his chair closer. He looked at her intently, searching her eyes for what might lie behind them. Once he had known how to comfort women, but this woman was old, and more, falling prey to a terrible disease. The room was quiet. None of the words that came to him seemed to fit the moment.

In the deep stillness they sat looking at each other. It was only minutes but it seemed to Leo hours had passed when she said, "But why, Leo? Why do you want to put so much time and energy into helping me…considering the way I am?"

"Because we're friends, Edith—the way you are now, the way you have been, the way you will be."

PART FOUR

23

Spring. Sometimes mistaken for fall. A melancholy season, haunted with drizzling mists, so that Elephant Mountain, shrouded and mysterious, seemed surreal. Edith's Alzheimer (strange to say it that way, as though she owned it, instead of the disease owning her) had progressed to that slippery slope of never knowing what she might do, regret doing, forget doing.

Nor could Edith herself predict her behavior, her frustrations and rages, her consequent melancholy, contrite remorse. And her body, too, refused to obey her, turning right instead of left, mistaking a mirror for a window, a wall for a door, so that the house was no longer familiar, known, trusted.

Decades before, she had walked briskly throughout her house, purpose in every step: beds to be made—and properly, curtains to be laundered, clutter to be excavated from the abounding nooks and crannies. Always picking up after James, she would think. And when the child, Timothy, came later (they had thought they would be childless), the little boy had to be coaxed to put toys back in the toy box. But she came to not mind picking up as she came to not mind the long absences of James, away on business. Tim was put in nursery school at two and a half. People said this was young but Edith explained that an only child needed other children.

The house had been her domain in that long-ago time. Her kingdom. It would be spotless. Beautiful. So the iron balustrades of the long winding staircase shone and the banisters gleamed. On each of the landings, mimosa, calla lilies, asters, roses and other lovely flowers rose gracefully from splendid oriental and alabaster vases. Although the house was Victorian in style, still Edith was fearless in its decoration. A reader of poetry as well as other literature, entranced with the Stately pleasure dome of Kubla Khan, she filled certain parts of the house with extravagance and splendor. In deference to James' business dinners, she kept the Victorian flavor in the dining and living rooms. There were long velvet drapes, antimacassars on armchairs, rotogravure photos and Currier and Ives prints on the walls.

As time went by, Edith began to see the house as a friend. You felt safe with a friend, and she felt safe inside her house. Although the streets of Nelson in the fifties had been quiet and peaceful—the Shangri-la flavor of a nestling mountain town, the sixties and seventies saw disenchanted young people flocking in—resistors against the Vietnam war, hippies in unwashed clothes, seekers of this and that. In her house, Edith was safe from strange frightening substances–LSD, marijuana, magic mushrooms, cocaine. Safe from the mad tumult of the world–the searing conflicts, the violent wars, the bloody revolutions.

As the world outside receded into the background of her life, her girlhood dreams of adventure became as vaporous and misty as the fogs that covered Elephant Mountain. And when Tim, her only child, decided, at nineteen, that he would go off to see the world, Edith would find herself conversing with her house as she went about her various chores.

"What you need," she would say to the large mahogany dining table, "is a good polishing," and she would instruct the cleaning woman, who came twice a week, as to the cloth and polish to be used. But then she decided she could do it better herself. In the subsequent shine of the table, Edith thought she detected appreciation. "Everyone has left me," she would intone to herself. (It did not occur to her that perhaps she had left them.) "But you, my friend, are always here for me," she'd told the house.

Now decades later, the house was her enemy. A battleground where walls thrust at her, knocked her down, chairs poked her and mocked her efforts to sit upon them, rise from them; hallways would not allow her to traverse them, at every turn making her stumble, catching a wheel of her walker. Everywhere she could expect to be attacked.

When the Alzheimer's had first been diagnosed, Edith pretended to be her former self. She steered herself from room to room with a kind of stubborn resolve. She touched tables, put a hand on a chair, in what she thought was her old familiar way. But now

168

that she could do less, the house *knew* she could not give it the love she'd given before. And the house was angry. "I have Alzheimer's," Edith sometimes pleaded, but instead of understanding, the house and everything in it provoked her more, as though they knew her defenses were down.

Cane in one hand, pushing the door with the other, she tried to open it wide enough to hobble out of her bedroom. The door refused to make way. Push here, push there, but it would not budge. Her face flushed with effort, she spoke: "Let me through!" The door refused to move. She poked it with her cane but the door knocked the cane down. Edith hesitated. Her hair fell in a white mass into her face. She could call out to Leo. He was in the kitchen waiting for her. Leo would help her. The next moment she pushed her hair back with one hand, set her lips in a grim line. If the door wanted to fight, she could fight too. The cane was a good weapon. Jerkily, she tried to bend down to retrieve her cane, but at that moment the door moved and imprisoned the cane underneath it.

Perspiration pouring down her cheeks, she hobbled painfully back into the room, holding onto the table near the door, then the bed until she came to her walker near the window. "The walker must be next to your bed," Leo had said. The walker knew that and started to roll away. Without cane or walker, she froze. Her heart pounded, her hammer toes curled up and would not uncurl so that she gasped in pain.

Leo was making tea. If she called Leo, he would not hear her; she was too far from her door. And she had forgotten to wear the whistle round her neck. She looked around the room. She had to get to the door. Slowly, she groped her way along the length of the bedroom wall until she came to the walker, which had rolled against the bed.

She grabbed the handles, then pushed down the levers beneath. The walker would not move. Up, not down. She pushed them up and they walked together to the door. But the walker could not go through. Jaw set, furious, she rammed the walker into the door. A split appeared in the wood but the door stood still. Holding the handles so tightly the veins in her hands stood up, she crashed the walker into the door.

Leo came running. He looked at the warped and beaten door but said nothing. The door squeaked and groaned as he opened it

169

wider, picked up the cane, took her trembling hands in his. "Why didn't you call me?" But, even as he said the words, the thought came, unbidden–what have I gotten into?

Edith's eyes were on the sagging door. "Did I do that?" she asked, her voice contrite, her eyes perplexed. Leo put her hands on the walker. He touched her shoulder gently. "Never mind," he said. "Let's go have tea." Meekly, she followed him out of the room.

They moved slowly along the hallway. In all his years as a student and then handyman, he had been, not hasty in his studies and in his jobs, but fluid, his brain and body moving to a rhythm of competence and good health. Now, trying to keep to Edith's unsteady and labored pace, he had to make an effort to withhold his own vigor and force. His job now was to walk in the slow steps of Edith. It's a job, he reminded himself, as he braked his step, paused, advanced a couple of inches, but annoyance sat on his shoulders, directing her, choosing his words: "I think, if you try, you can go just a little faster." Her face turned to him, a question mark. "Yes?" he asked, surprised at the sharp tone of his voice. But she only shook her head.

At the foot of the long winding staircase, she stopped suddenly. She looked in the direction of the living room. "I hear them talking," she said. Leo tried not to sigh; she was hearing voices again. He wasn't sure what her tightened features meant. Distress? Fear? Or was she frowning?

"They whisper, but I know," Edith was going on. The kettle whistled then and he seized upon this as a way out. "Let's have our tea," he said. "Yes, tea," she said, but turning to follow him, she lost her balance and struck her elbow on the banister. It began to bleed. She looked at it in consternation. Drip. Drip. She began to wipe at her elbow with a corner of her blouse.

"It's all right, I'll clean it in the kitchen," he said. Had he gotten more gauze for bandages? Maybe the large bandaids would do. And alcohol. Or iodine. He put his hand on the walker. She looked up at him but didn't take it away as she sometimes did. He steered her as straight and quickly as was possible without mishap.

The kettle was whistling loudly when they came into the kitchen. He took it off the burner, made sure a pillow was on her chair and helped her sit down. She kept looking at him in a way that made him uneasy. He had to search for some disinfectant, finally found alcohol swabs way back in a cupboard. Now why would Sidonia put them there when she knew darn well Edith was forever bruising or cutting herself? And why were they both out so long?

With a clean soapy cloth, he washed over the wound, trying to be gentle. Then he swabbed the wound. "Oh! Aaaa!" she cried out. "It hurts!" He looked up. Her face was contorted. What if she fainted? What would he do? "I'll just put the bandage on and it will be all over," he said, as calmly as he could. It's as though I'm talking to a child, he thought. But the next moment a sense of shame overcame him. She was not a child and this was not a job. All these changes didn't alter the fact that she was still Edith, his dear friend.

He made the tea, put the teapot on the table. She reached out with her good arm. He thought she was about to take it. The lady of the house pouring tea. Quickly, he picked up the teapot. There were scald marks on her hand. Her faded eyes were cloudy. Had the tea sparked a memory of the past? Leo wondered. It was impossible to know just how much she did remember. Or feel.

They drank from mugs. He had filled only a third of hers. She had wanted the china cups and saucers, but Sidonia had put the china in a high cupboard. "Shall I hold the mug?" he asked, feeling guilty. She shook her head, picked up a cookie, put it down. In the late afternoon the Victorian lamps cast grotesque shadows, like the distended little Leo he had laughed at when he saw himself in the mirrors of the Toronto amusement parks. A steady rain beat upon the windows. A wind had come up.

Edith had her arms in her lap. Scabs reared up on her wrists and forearms. On her gaunt angular face, forehead, chin, the bridge of her nose, blue and purple bruises made an eerie patchwork in the near dusk. Her eyes leaned toward him. "I hear them talking–'What will we do? What will we do?' Their whispers are everywhere." She fell back. She seemed exhausted in a way that eluded him. It wasn't ordinary tiredness, that straining of all her features, the stiffening of her body, as though there was something she wanted to say but couldn't.

Washing the mugs and plates, Leo felt he had been impatient. "Who whispers?" he asked, but Edith had forgotten or was no longer interested. "I'm tired," she said. "I want to go to my room." He settled her in her recliner. He was about to ask if she wanted to look at Oprah, but "I want to rest," she said in a way that dismissed him.

He wondered if he should read to her–he had the uneasy feeling of having offended her. But how was it possible to know? Even at this moment she was closing her eyes, as though to shut him out.

Leo went back into the kitchen and started to cut up vegetables for the stew. He worked swiftly, setting carrots, string beans, potatoes and onions on the cutting board, chopping to a steady rhythm, sweeping the lot into a large pot. He added water. When he was seated at the table reading Keats, he realized he had forgotten the tomatoes. He cut two large ones and threw them into the cooking pot.

That's what he liked about cooking. You began with a recipe or even one you somehow created yourself, added ingredients and a pot, and, after the required time, you came up with the finished product.

He set the pot to simmer, cleaned up the kitchen, all the while wondering if he should tell Sidonia and Quigley he couldn't do this. He hadn't known the challenges. He would explain. They would understand. But by the time the kitchen was all cleaned up he knew he wasn't going to tell Sidonia and Quigley anything at all.

"We're late because we went to the trial," Sidonia and Quigley told him, looking quite shaken.

"What trial?" asked Leo.

"Alfred Seaman," Quigley said. "It wasn't really a trial; he gave himself up, admitted to fraud and embezzlement. Apparently Edith was one of his unsuspecting victims. He'll be disbarred, of course," Sidonia said, an unusual edge to her voice. "I wonder if there was more money Edith's husband left her that Seaman was handling. Didn't Dr. Helperin mention something about that?"

Sitting around the dinner table, Leo listened as Sidonia and Quigley spoke of their day. They kept glancing at Edith as they talked of buying a baby's layette and looking for a crib at SHARE. "You'll like to hold the baby," Sidonia said. Edith kept silent. Leo had the feeling of the four of them trapped inside a holding pattern, some bizarre construct into which they couldn't all fit. As though she knew what he was thinking, Edith kept turning her filmy eyes upon Leo. From behind them he thought he could see a curious fleck of pink that came and went…talking to his thoughts?

That night, when they were sitting in the living room, softly lit by the wall sconces, Leo began to say, "There's something..." Quigley held up a forefinger like a child asking permission to go to the bathroom. "Before you say anything, Leo, we know you're worth a heck of a lot more than we give you. But we don't know how long Edith will live and what unforeseen costs will come up. And I haven't been able to find work yet. And with the baby coming..." He sank his forehead into his hand.

It seemed to Leo there were endless problems in this house, so much unknown, so many decisions left hanging. Suddenly he remembered asking his mother, "How did the Just Men know what to do all the time?" She had said, "I'm not a Just Man so I can't tell you. But when the time comes to make a decision, they know what to do."

"Leo?" Sidonia was looking at him, concerned.

"Not to worry," he found himself saying, Kootenay-style, then rolling on, "I'll help with Edith all I can, like I said."

But who is this new Edith? he thought with a hint of apprehension. This was succeeded by a great curiosity as he had formed a lasting friendship with Edith, the dignified controlled lady of the house, so he would continue with that friendship with the Edith at this time—unpredictable as to moods and behavior and who knew what other changes the disease would bring. How much more she would need him. Leo felt his heart lift. Whatever she needed he could help her. He knew he could.

When Leo finally fell asleep, he found himself in the middle of a Polish village during the Middle Ages–a hidden village far removed from the outside world, where God alone made the rules and exacted strict obedience and shame for infractions. He was a child, pale, skinny, with tiny black curls along his face. Along with other pale and skinny children, solemn well-bearded elders in long black caftans, women with moist eyes, he watched a cart driven by two large horses roll out of the village, dragging a man along a dry road dusty with dirt. Inside the cart, a lean rigid-faced cleric sat next to the driver.

Leo twisted and turned, trying to leave the terrifying scene, but he couldn't. Deep in sleep, he heard the petrified whispers of the adults around him: "The Inquisition–the Inquisition." The man—

more a tattered bundle of darkness—being dragged between horses and cart, would be unhitched sometime beyond the village to be transferred to Portugal, where he would be burnt at the stake. A Just Man....

Leo awoke with a start. His pajamas were soaked in cold sweat. His heart raced. He shook his head back and forth but the terror clung to him: the hoofs of the horses on his face; limbs broken on the rack; molten lead poured into ears, eyes, throat, anus, at the rate of one molten drop each day, running hot throughout his body; the fire consuming hair, shoulders... The Inquisition, the expulsions from Spain and Portugal, the pogroms, the Holocaust. Endless cruelty too dreadful to comprehend. Unbearable suffering. Long minutes passed before he could move from the bed.

He went to the window. To the east, the cloudless sky, blushing, announced dawn. Leo said to God, "Well, it's all the same to you, I suppose, whether one human tortures and kills another or a disease does, but I don't agree. A human knows what he is doing— bacteria and viruses don't." In his shower he scrubbed himself vigorously. He was scouring it away, the vestiges of the terrible nightmare.

Dressed, he stood before the mirror. A lean man looked back at him. Thinning sandy hair, firm legs and arms, flat stomach. A healthy man. A man who had not suffered. For whom the small and petty annoyances were like the bites of fleas. He could hear the voice of his father: "To live a good life, it is enough to be an honorable man." And an honorable man never walked away from a friend in need. Surely Edith's need now was greater than it had ever been. He felt lighter now; he could not save the world but he could help Edith.

24

Leo got out his tools and figured out where to put the shelves in the garage. Sidonia's baby was due in June and it was the beginning of May. There was clearing out to do. Since her pregnancy, Sidonia had become almost obsessive in her need to organize. Only yesterday she had called him into the sewing room, which she'd decided to use as a computer room.

"I wish you'd take that darn old sewing machine of Edith's to the Sally Ann. It doesn't work, and it's just taking up space."

Leo regarded the machine with experienced eyes. A classic Singer model. Although the metal parts were slightly tarnished, he had the feeling a good cleaning and threading up would do the trick.

"I'll fix it when I have the time. I'll take it up to my room right now."

He had intended to see about the jammed accessory compartment in the base but no sooner did he get the sewing machine to his room and Edith was calling, up from her nap.

The sewing machine could wait, he told himself, as he continued work on the shelving. He worked methodically and steadily, measuring, hammering, intent on the job. The rain started to come down in sheets. He heard a noise outside and looked out the window. A hawk was wheeling round and round in the pouring rain. The earth that had been so dry in the morning was sodden, the leaves of the maples and oaks dripping, the sky that had been so blandly blue was the color of smoke. The vicissitudes of the weather–of the world, Leo thought.

Finished with the shelving, he went back to the house and prepared a few sandwiches–cheese, tomato, lettuce and the imitation bacon bits that Edith liked. He put mayonnaise on hers, mustard on his. On the Kootenay Bakery's sourdough, he decided. He made a pot of chamomile tea. He would have liked to put pickles on the table but didn't. Edith would eat them all, and they upset her stomach. It pleased him to keep her well, to see her as content as circumstance allowed.

The phone rang. "I'll be back later than I thought." Quigley's voice seemed harried. "I've been to every place I can think of but there just aren't any jobs. I'm going to that factory on 3A. It's assembly line, but... Sidonia said to tell you she's getting a ride back to the house with one of the women from her Pilates group."

Leo was about to say, no worries, but Quigley had hung up. He looked at the clock on the wall. Yes, Edith would be getting up from her nap, or if she was still asleep, the radio going full blast from the delivery truck a few houses away would certainly waken her.

He walked quickly, with anticipation and some misgiving. "It's not unusual for an Alzheimer's patient to mistake one person for another," Dr. Helperin had said. Leo had persisted: "But who is this Pol?" "Pol Pitt–he belongs to a kind of legend, a secret ill-fated romance when Edith was young." Neither Sidonia nor Quigley could offer any help: "Nobody seems to have really known Edith even though she's lived here most of her life. And now, with her Alzheimer's speeding up, she can't tell us even if she wanted to."

At the door to her bedroom, Leo had to stop and remind himself not to correct her when she greeted him so delightedly. "You've come, Pol." At first, he had felt himself an actor, playing a part, but it was not like that, not like reading someone else's lines. There were no lines to learn, no plot to follow; he was playing a role in a script whose pages were blank—with only the need trembling in the depths of her eyes to dictate the plot.

There was a lock on Edith's door because she was apt to wander out and away. He knocked. "Pol!" The name danced through the door. He opened the lock and went in. He needed to right himself, maintain a sense of Edith as she was now. The Edith Martin before him belied the sprightly voice of youth that had welcomed him. Gnarled hands fumbled with a red bow, which she tried in vain to put on her disheveled stark white hair. Her blouse was roundabout, the puff of lace spreading airily in back like fairy wings. Her pull-on pants were back to front, compressing her belly and hips and ballooning buttocks and thighs, resulting in a bizarre silhouette. She was sitting on the bed regarding her feet, one of which wore a boot, the other an unlaced walking shoe. Dashes of crimson splashed color in the midst of her wrinkled face.

"Pol." Her voice, thin and weak, carried an echo of jubilant youth. "Is it time?" she asked. The disparate effect of youth and age made Leo pause. "The hiding place—" she continued, fearfully now, guarded, "we can go there," the words more plea than statement.

The look of her eyes, Leo thought, dots of light in the rheumy blue. He knew what to say; these trips—if one could call these strange communions by that name—had become a ritual. "It's all right," he told her, "no one knows." Would her secret love have said those words? He wondered. She sat quietly as he put on socks, walking shoes, laced them. He did not adjust her blouse and pants: it would mean taking them off and putting them on again. He wished he knew how to go about things, to have the assurance of the implements and tools before him, the job specifications. He found himself in the unexplored land of Alzheimer's—with no guideposts and no maps.

Slowly, they made their way along the hallway. Edith guided her walker but didn't seem aware of her hands on the handles. At the foot of the winding staircase, she looked at Leo. "Pol," she murmured. Then she looked up. Leo had the strange feeling of being back in his youth with a girl, heading toward some secluded spot, brimming over with excited anticipation.

But the trip to this hiding place was different—solemn and hesitant; from time to time, Edith paused, looked fearfully back as though someone might be following them. "There's no one but us," Leo pressed her hand, rough and veined. Ensconced in her own world, Edith, her walker left at the base of the staircase, held on to the banister, while Leo stayed close behind. Making sure she didn't fall, he assisted her nervous faltering steps trying to keep time to—a memory?—one of the romantic stories in her girlhood reading?

At the second landing he had placed a chair. She sat down. The sun came through the skylight exposing the lines crisscrossing her face. "Pol," she murmured again. "We're almost there," Leo said. He could see how tired she was and yet, how much it meant to her to go to the turret and sit with him there.

Going up the next flight, he was close behind her, keeping pace with her every move, every step, ready to steady her, letting her know he was right there with her.

On the third landing, her tiredness gave way to a kind of

177

gaiety and she turned in the direction of the turret room so quickly that she would have fallen had Leo not caught her. They walked along the landing. She passed the table with the tall vase of forsythia with unseeing eyes. Leo thought, those things don't seem to matter to her anymore. He would tell Sidonia not to worry about flower arrangements; she had enough to do.

He opened the door to his room, then took her hand to steady her. Her hand was, as usual, cold, but within his, became warm. It gave him a good feeling, giving her warmth, as though he were sharing his own vigor with her. "Pol," she murmured still another time. A mantra, Leo thought. She lifted her ravaged face to his. Points of light shone through the dimness of her eyes. "I'm here," he said, squeezing her hand gently. He made her happy, this Pol—whoever he had been. But we were friends and she never told me about this secret affair, Leo thought, miffed in spite of himself.

Inside the turret room, there were several bookshelves housing the plays and sonnets of Shakespeare, Plato's *Republic*, a number of other philosophical works, and, off in the recesses, tattered with much handling, *The Last of the Just* by Andre Schwarz-Bart, set apart from other novels. On a narrow bed, some volumes of poetry lay scattered. In another corner, table and chairs. On one wall, a Chinese rubbing of a tree leaning from a mountain.

Her eyes misted. What had they shared, these lovers, Leo asked silently, uselessly; she could not tell him—and would she if she could? He placed a pillow on one of the chairs, helped her sit down. She looked up at him; her thin lips and cheeks moved in a smile. He took the long embroidered scarf from the small trunk in the room, remnants of a time gone by.

Silence filled the room, enclosing Edith and Leo. Had Pol been a meditator? He found it hard to imagine: the proper lady and a man of silence, and, as the legend went in Nelson, somewhat of an iconoclast. Edith's hands lay loosely in her lap. She looked at Leo sitting slightly away, across from her. "Pol," she mouthed, and her eyes circled the room and everything in it. Then, she let them close.

For some time, Leo scanned her face, hoping to find some clue as to where she was. "The hiding place," she had called this room, but hiding from whom—or what? She seemed to be within a dream now or some other state; her eyelids moved, her head rose at times as though striving for something beyond reach.

He sighed. It was always like this. He could not enter Edith's world. He could not know what she was thinking. The very word, thinking, was faded and dry now, like fallen leaves. It was a Devil, this disease, a Dybbuk, stealing the person from within. Even her outbursts of anger, frustration or despair were as limp and weak as the dying cells in her brain. Wanting to help still more, to take upon himself her real needs, he felt powerless. What were her real needs?

Edith was still sleeping or in some state beyond wakeful-ness. Her head had drooped to one side. He rose and placed a pillow under it, careful not to disturb her. Then he sat down again. The room seemed isolated from the world. Intoxicated by the deep stillness, he let his eyelids drop, curtaining the room and all in it.

* * *

He was back in the kitchen in Toronto, a young boy, watching his mother light the Sabbath candles. Three times her short arms swept the air into wide circles, then, cupping her eyes with her hands, she welcomed Queen Shabbat: "Baruch atah Adonai Eloheinu meluch ha'olam asher kiddushanu b'mitzvosav v'tzivanu l'hadlik ner shel Shabbos." Talis round his broad shoulders, head slightly bowed, his father watched his mother light the candles. Golden buds of flame, gleaming brass candlesticks glowed in the dusky room.

Under the fond but stern eye of his father, the boy stands motionless, his eye on the small table where a large white napkin covers the challah. A pot of steaming chicken soup stands waiting on the small stove. Through the open window come the near-evening sounds of Yonge Street—children playing, a bus, cars, the ice-cream wagon. The family is about to sit down to eat.

Suddenly, with a desperate whirring of wings, a crow flies through the open window and drops on top of the challah. The challah turns red, as the bird quivers a few times, is still.

The boy starts to cry. He can't stop. Tears fall down his cheeks, his Sabbath shirt. The frantic activity of his parents—the phone—a basin of water—rags—is blurred. He feels only anguish, has only questions. "How was the crow wounded? Why?" he asks his parents. "How can we know," they say, and add, in the midst of their mopping up, a question of their own, "And why into our kitchen, as if we don't have enough to deal with?"

"Would a Just Man know?" insists the boy, in the midst of his tears.

"It was an accident. Stop crying and help clean up," they tell him.

* * *

Splattering sounds woke Leo. Shaken, the dream slowly eclipsed by the moment, he turned his attention toward Edith and saw he had been mistaken: it was not rain splashing the window he had heard—it was the drip drip of Edith's urine through her pants onto the wooden floor. Strangling sobs, bent over the chair, she was gazing at the puddle at her feet, clutching at her belly, tearing at it, as if to dam the flow. Red patches suffused her white face. Her hair flopped about as hairpins fell into the spreading puddle on the darkening floor.

The only word that came to Leo's mind was: Depends. A brand name. If Edith had been easy-going, able to joke about incontinence, to laugh about diapers for elders, he would not have been at a loss for what to say. But even now, straining for dignity, her hands still clutched at her stomach, trying to stem the flow.

It wasn't the cleaning up; that was nothing, simply a job. He didn't know the word for Edith right now. Not despair. Despair could be a gateway to hope, but, leaning over, ready to engulf her, stood Hopelessness. "I'll take your hurt away," his mother would say, when, a small boy, he cut or bruised himself. "How it hurts," she would say, "oh, how it hurts." Soon, his cries would turn to laughter.

"It's all right," he finally said, stupidly.

And then, looking at the puddle with interest–taking him by surprise, she said, "No, Leo, it's not all right."

The use of his name and the certainty with which she spoke shocked him. How was it, he wondered, that she, so brain-damaged, could travel from a time where a lover named Pol existed to here and now? And why, when moments before she had been petrified with shame, did she sound so, well, calm?

Edith was quiet and patient, cooperating, as he attended to the puddle. "I'll wait for Sidonia," she insisted, when he mentioned her soaked pants. There was nothing he could do; her modesty was fixed within her, like another organ.

* * *

"What a lark that will be," Sidonia said to Quigley, having just changed Edith's underclothes and pants. "Two sets of diapers." She put her hand to her head. "I just don't see how..."

"But Leo—" Quigley flopped down on the sofa.

"She only wants a woman. What's the matter?"

"The factory is closing in a month. They're moving to China. So no chance there."

"Jesus!"

"Tell me about it. And Beau's been calling again with an offer."

Outside the living room, Edith stood against the wall, listening. Words, sighs, exclamations all ran together, soft at first, then, magnified within her, the whispers turned to screams: "What will we do? What will we do?"

* * *

"You'll go. I'll be alone," Edith said.

"I won't go. You won't be alone," Leo said.

"When the disease gets worse, you'll go."

"No."

"Everyone leaves. Sidonia and Quigley are leaving."

"Why do you say that?"

"Because I know."

"I'm staying."

Edith examined Leo's face as though she were trying to put together a puzzle. Her eyes hurt with the strain of trying to see him clearly, but the macular degeneration had progressed too far; she could only make out his blurred head.

Leo was getting her jacket from the closet, his wiry body moving quickly. He helped her into the jacket, then took her hands and lightly pulled her to her feet. "We can go to Lakeside Park and sit under a tree. I'll read the *Rubaiyat of Omar Khayyam*. Would you like that?"

"No." She was walking slowly with her walker, eyes downcast. She saw her feet move awkwardly—her hammer toes were

181

painful; she saw her bony veined hands clutching the handles of the walker. "No," she said again.

"You don't want to go to the park."

"I'm afraid." Her voice trembled.

"Of the park?"

She shook her head, then looked down like a child who has broken some rule. "Not like the others," she muttered.

"Neither am I," Leo said.

It would be good for Edith to get out, he felt. Increasingly she wanted to isolate herself. He would have to entice her. "Edith," he said, "the greenhouses will be open. And you can sit on your walker seat and I can wheel you so your feet don't hurt. I'd love to see the greenhouses."

"So you'd like to go to the park, dear Leo."

"Yes," he said. "Very much."

"Then we'll go."

After they had been to the greenhouses, they sat down in the Rotary shelter and had sandwiches and tea. Leo was glad they had come. Edith seemed almost happy, looking around at the children playing, the people eating, the burgeoning bushes. Nature could do that, he thought.

Then suddenly Edith turned full around to face him. Her almost serene expression had become troubled. "Leo, why do you want to stay and take care of me, when you know how hard it will be, when the disease gets worse?"

He saw the ravages of the Alzheimer's—one foot circling the other and back again, eyes focused on him with an intensity so fierce he wanted to turn away and, all over her arms and face, blue, purple, black and red welts, bruises, abrasions, scars, as though an army of multi-formed and colored insects had invaded her.

They sat in silence. It was her dignity, Leo told himself. It was hard for a woman like Edith, so used to caring for herself, to be in this position. He felt at a loss.

"You can be free, Leo. You are not to feel you must take on this burden." And the way she said this—sternly with a surprising measure of authority reminiscent of years ago—made Leo say, "A burden. Edith, I don't think of you that way."

"You think you are one of them—those sixty—sixty—sixty-three," she finally said.

"I don't understand," he said.

"You don't understand," she mimicked in a voice so different from her own that Leo winced. But even with this show of bravado, she looked utterly vulnerable, like a child, frightened but trying not to show her fear.

"You want to help me because I'm part of suffering humanity. There, that's it!"

Then he understood. Somewhere in her crumbling brain the Legend of the Lamed-Vov had taken root. "You think I'm one of the Thirty-Six," he said.

She said angrily, "Sixty-three—thirty-six—what does it matter—you're one of the saviors and I'm just a part of the suffering world."

"Oh Edith, it's a legend. You know I don't believe in legends. It makes me happy to take care of you," he said, "and it will make me even happier to be able to take care of you more of the time."

"Why?"

"Because we're friends." Then, because she was regarding him as though she wanted to hear more, he said, "I'm just a man, an ordinary man. It's not suffering humanity I'm thinking of, Edith, it's you."

"When the disease gets worse, then what will you do?"

"I will help you any way I can."

"Any way?"

"Yes."

"I believe you mean that, Leo."

"Yes," he said again. He thought, this gives meaning to my life, which has been so predictable and comfortable. "So it's settled," he smiled.

She was smiling too.

"I'll help in any way I can," he had told her, but when the incident occurred he was not prepared.

The day was bright and sunny. They were at the Prestige Inn. Edith, at first, had not wanted to go but Leo had persuaded her. "You love the lake and the Prestige is convenient. And it will be quiet." She was wearing the Depends—not with acceptance but rather with concession to defeat. Being soaked in urine was too disagreeable. She could, however, sit for quite a while on the toilet for bowel functions.

They looked out at the sailboats, the pirate ship tied at the wharf, the shimmering lake. A large dog held on a leash came by. Edith quivered. But the dog passed peacefully, even wagging its tail, and still Edith's quivering persisted. She began to shake. She cried out. There was something primal in that cry.

She was wearing a long summer dress and the Depends underneath. On her feet were the only summer shoes that fit, a kind of white canvas slip-on. At first, the odd brown and mushy configuration on the sandals seemed like mud or sludge but they hadn't been through any mud. The next moment, as though a dam had given way, a torrent of fecal matter gushed forth.

Impossible though it seemed, they had to go back to the house. There, Edith lay on the bed. Under her was a rubber-backed pad. She lay utterly silent, as Leo, towel in hand, finished cleaning her. As the towel passed over her pubic area, her face blanched; her eyes went to the ceiling and closed. Her jaw, usually set when she was required to do something she didn't want to do, went slack with helplessness. He took another towel and dried her.

"Almost done," Leo said as he pulled up her Depends. He tried to speak easily, as though nothing extraordinary had happened but his words were lost in the shame and mortification that filled the room.

* * *

Leo called on all his resources to make her subsequent days as comfortable—happy was too much to ask—as he could. He tried to counter her devastated but helpless resignation to still another indignity by renewed and patient attention to her needs. He devised certain games to get her to eat, massaged her curling toes and in many ways tried to create some measure of comfort in the midst of her vanishing world. But he had been living in his own reality.

Some days later, as they sat in the flourishing garden, Edith said, in a surprisingly clear voice, "Leo, I must ask you something."

Delighted at this sudden clarity—which, of course, could eclipse in moments or minutes —he said, smiling, "Ask away."

"Be serious." Her tone and the stern look she gave him—like a mother to a teasing child —frightened him. Her words came down on him, crushing the vision of care and hope he wanted so badly to sustain for her.

She leaned forward in the lawn chair. Her eyes were filled with tears. "What's the matter?" he asked, but she only shook her head. "Oh, Edith, I know how hard it is for you–having to wear the Depends—but—"

"Just one more thing." Then she surprised him by ticking off on her fingers, misshapen with arthritis: "Names go, things get lost, times get mixed up, eyes can't see, ears can't hear... And now this." Even as she spoke, she was squirming, and he knew that by *this*, she meant her loss of bowel control. She suddenly erupted and said, "Leo, I can't bear this."

"I know this is hard for you, but it's just your body. You're still Edith."

"One day I won't be Edith anymore. And then—I won't be able to make anything at all happen in my head. I will only be hollow space, like the inside of a dead tree."

"You're not a tree, Edith. You're human." He moved his chair closer to her, took her hand in his. "I'm going to be here with you, Edith–no matter how long–taking care of you right up to the time Death takes you."

Without taking her hand from his, she rose a little in the chair. Her squarish body seemed to lengthen, her shoulders expand. Her words, when she finally spoke, echoed in the early evening air.

"No, not Death, picking at me, bits and pieces, dragging me along. Who knows how long. I've never made a decision in my life. This time I'll decide—I'll decide when it's time to go, not Death. I have it all arranged. Sidonia and Quigley have no idea..."

"Don't–don't say anything!"

"Leo, my dear friend, promise me you'll hold my hand!"

He could not speak. Already her face had changed. The clarity faded. He tried but could not shake off the ominous feeling rising within him. How could he have foreseen so long ago the devouring demands of friendship.

25

"The tests all came back, Leo. I'm pleased to tell you you're a healthy man. No diabetes, no cholesterol, and what's a bonus for a man of sixty-nine, no sign of any prostate problems." Dr. Helperin smiled. "Sit down, sit down. You look so solemn. Aren't you happy?"

Leo sat down and steeled himself for still another lie. For wasn't withholding information a deception? And cunning too, wasn't that a lie?

"What's the matter, Leo?"

"What? Oh yes, I'm fine, just a little tired."

"Edith wearing you down. It's to be expected. I don't like increasing the Memantine, although using it with the Aricept at this stage seems to have slowed the disease. Still, Alzheimer's is like a beast trying to survive: it eats up its prey when it's hungry and goes off to sleep when it has had its full. Well, was there anything else you wanted to see me about?"

Leo gazed around the office: the charts posted on the walls—skeletons in various positions –two small paintings–a totem pole and an Inuit bending over a fishing hole in the ice. On his desk, some files, photographs of a smiling woman in her sixties surrounded by her children, another of several grandchildren.

"If there's nothing else..." The doctor was getting up from his chair. Here was a chance to say the truth: Edith intends to put an end to her life and has asked me to be with her. But that was another omission–that he would be there only to hold her hand. There was an unmistakable quickening of the progress of the disease. He would have to mix the pills, see that she kept them down, and that terrible plastic bag...he would have to do it all. Even as he thought the unspeakable, God hammered into his ear: "Thou shalt not kill." And like a sad persistent counterpoint, "Promise me, Leo, promise me."

Leo kept silent. "Only that I'm not sleeping that well," he

finally managed. "Could I have something to help me sleep?"

"I shouldn't think that necessary. You get plenty of exercise with all you do. You want to take advantage of the Alzheimer's group in town, get some help with Edith. There is help, you know. You take too much on, Leo. There's a number of herbal teas that are very relaxing."

Leo nodded. "Thanks, Dr. Helperin."

After Leo left, Saul had a distinct feeling of things left unsaid. There had been something in Leo's demeanor that was different from his usual easy manner. There I go pondering; it's always one thing or another, he told himself.

Leo passed the High Street Condos, continued on to the mall. He found the Cadbury chocolate Easter eggs that Edith had requested. At the checkout, the man behind him said, "So you're living in Nelson now, Leo." It was Jake, a handyman he'd known years back, when he first came to Nelson. Leo thought of asking Jake if he'd been to Mexico recently. He got drugs there; Pentobarbital was one of them. But the thought slipped away and the next moment they were exchanging pleasantries, a bit of social amenities—crazy weather, crazy world...

Leo moved quickly out of the store. Another close call. What if he'd said, I am going to help an old friend kill herself? Another lie by concealment. *And let concealment like a worm...* There were so many silences, one forgot to call them lies.

He was almost back at the house when he saw a young woman trying to maneuver what seemed to be a barrel out of a wheelchair. "Can I help?" he asked, and realized he had been mistaken: the occupant of the wheelchair was a woman whose belly resembled a huge barrel. Carefully, he and the young woman dislodged the occupant into the wagon. "There's a special seat belt," said the young woman. Then he helped her put the wheelchair into the vehicle. "You're an angel," she said.

Leo was nearing the house—the house that soon would be sold. The eyes of the barrel woman stayed with him. "Cancer," her daughter had said. "But she's got a good heart."

Inside the house, he went up to his room. The turret room. Another problem. Edith couldn't die here. There would be too many questions. It would have to be in her own room. It would have to be a time when both Sidonia and Quigley were away. And Edith wanted

187

the night. Sidonia and Quigley were never away at night. How...? There were too many questions.

*　*　*

Fern splashed soda into the glass. "Make it a double," her husband said, plunking himself onto the sofa. She turned quickly. "What's wrong, Saul?" Just a light drink. That's what he'd always had before dinner for as long as she'd known him. "Saul?"

He reached for the tumbler she held out to him, took a deep swallow, then another. "Things," he said.

She put on the Brandenburg Concerto and sat down next to him. "What things?" He didn't answer. He took another gulp.

She was silent. He was overworked and not getting any younger. "You need a vacation, Saul. We have to get away. Tibet. You always wanted to go there."

Saul watched his wife watching him and was inclined to unburden his soul. But he couldn't. He mustn't. For her sake as well as his. At any rate, he might be wrong. Edith might indeed have used those pills for sleeping. It was so long ago. The diagnosis had not been made. She was having sleepless nights and why not give her something to help her sleep. Suddenly he said, "You never question, honey, do you?"

"Question what?"

"Anything."

"Saul, that's just a wee bit too vague for me."

"Okay then, the meaning of life. You never question why we're here at all."

Fern stopped the CD. Saul's eyes were focused inward. "What's wrong?" she asked.

He raised his eyes to meet hers. "Nothing's wrong. It's just that I go along, day after day, immersed in my work and you and the family. We give to certain charities. We're responsible citizens. But is there something more to life? Some deeper meaning?"

"I can only talk about myself, darling. You're right, I don't question. I fight for the causes I believe in. I do the best I can for my family. I try to live each day with a sense of purpose. There's so much that needs to be done." Not for the world would she have said this, but it seemed to her that philosophical pondering on life's meaning was, in a way, a kind of psychic masturbation. It seemed to her that each person had their own reason for living.

He leaned over and kissed her. "Let's put on the Brandenburg again, okay?"

She nodded, glad to see him smiling. "But have I answered your question?"

"Absolutely." As he listened to the lively variations on the theme, he felt himself a lucky man. Absolutely, he had told her. And for Fern, he had spoken the truth. It had been a while since he had been in one of his introspective moods. Perhaps it was Edith's state that had triggered this. And seeing Leo.

26

It was one week after the birth of their baby girl that Quigley and Sidonia received an email from Beau, up in the Yukon, inviting them–urging them–to come up north: *Hi you two. My Express Delivery is going like crazy. I need to expand. Pack up and come.*

"Just like that," Quigley said. He almost laughed, but laughing was becoming a thing of the past.

"How much money is there?" The words slipped out. Leo hadn't thought of asking. But Quigley didn't mind. "If Edith goes to a nursing home, there's enough for maybe a couple of years. The thing is it's more costly for Alzheimer's people; eventually, you've got to have two people lifting them–or more."

"But Edith is–not better, but she seems more clear these days," Leo said.

"It's only a reprieve." Sidonia sighed. "It can go as quickly as it came. Dr. Helperin says there's no way of knowing how long she can go on. I'm sick of hearing that, I really am." Then, stricken by her words, "I don't mean that; I don't know what I mean anymore," she said. "I hear the baby."

"Where is she now?" Quigley asked.

"She's in the garden. It's all right, she's in the big lawn chair, the one she can't get out of." Leo paused, then, "Is that what's going to happen? Is Edith going to a nursing home?"

"We don't want it. You've got to know how hard Sid and I have tried to keep her here, in her home. But Sid and I have finally decided. We're going up north. How can we possibly take Edith when she needs so much help? And you can't take care of her yourself, Leo—there's no way."

"Let me be the judge of that. But this house, will it have to be sold?"

Quigley was quiet.

* * *

Mountain Side Home was a long low structure with a magnificent view of Elephant Mountain. Quigley drove into the parking lot. He and Leo got out of the car. "I wasn't sure you would want to come," Quigley said. "But I'm glad you're here. This is a nice place; one of the best."

Leo followed him into the entrance. He felt sluggish, as though his body had vanished and all that remained of him was his heavy head. Sleep had evaded him; mechanically, wound up to go, he went about his work. As Quigley punched in the code to enter the building, he was once again having an interior dialogue with God: "I have not paid attention to You, God. I have not honored the Sabbath; I have not kept it holy. As for taking Your Name in vain, to tell the truth I have not thought about You at all."

Quigley looked left and right. "I think the Extended Care is to the right. Leo, are you coming?"

Leo made an effort to move more quickly. He put one foot after the other, but it seemed he had conjured up God just by his silent dialogue, for God was keeping in step: "You have not followed My Commandments, and now..."

Quigley had stopped at one of the little tables along the hallway, and was helping himself to some cookies. "I must say they do things nice." He turned to a man in a wheelchair talking to a bird in a cage. "Good morning." The man looked fearfully away, then turned back to the bird. "Tweet," he said, "tweet, tweet, tweet."

"The Alzheimer unit is at the end of the hall," Quigley said. "Are you sick or something?"

Leo pulled a hanky from his pant pocket and mopped his forehead. "It's hot," he said. "It's hotter in hell," said God, who had not lost a step and was now ticking off the Sixth Commandment. I'll just wash my hands of the whole affair, Leo told himself. Let Edith go into the nursing home. "That would suit You, wouldn't it?" he said to God. "That would be the right thing. All those 'Shalt Not's. Leaving me to figure out the 'Shall's."

But Quigley was tugging at him. "I don't know what's got into you, Leo. Heat stroke, maybe. Here we are—Forest Grove." Strapped into four wheelchairs were four inert bodies, heads

191

dropped, hands collapsed in their laps. "Everything looks real clean," Quigley remarked. "Beautiful view, isn't it."

"Don't look at the view," Leo silently told God. "Look at them." And his eyes directed God to the bodies strapped in wheelchairs facing the green and gold mountains. Sightless eyes in dropped heads. "Is this what you want for Edith?"

Two nurses came over to examine the occupants of the wheelchairs. "We'll have to get this one cleaned up right now," one said. "Damn, fourth time this morning," groaned the other. "Just let's get him to his room."

"They take good care of people here." Quigley watched the nurses wheel away the chair. "Sidonia didn't want to come. She still can't stand the idea of Edith in a nursing home. Neither can I, but what can we do?" He turned toward Leo. "Seen enough?" Leo nodded and followed him back down the long corridor to the exit.

* * *

Edith couldn't sleep. Night shadows played along the wall. Fantastic shapes and figures merged, fell apart, merged again. Then, the wall was dark. Outside, a bird cried forlornly. A ray of moonlight shot through the curtain. She stared at the bright wall. The brightness was love. The word swam in her marshy brain. There was the love of God. There was the love of a mother for her child. There was romantic love. What was the word for how she felt about the man who changed her diapers?

* * *

When Leo came into the living room, Sidonia was shifting her baby so that her head rested more easily in the crook of her arm. "I know it may sound crazy at first, but so did the idea of Quigley and me having a baby at middle age." She smiled at the baby. "And here you are, Sunshine."

"Where's Edith?" Quigley looked up from the map he had spread out on his lap.

"She says she knows what you're going to say."

"I don't know." Sidonia shook her head. "It's strange about Edith; she's better than she was but there's something–" and she said

192

again, "I don't know." She was cradling the baby now, rocking her gently. Leo watched the baby's eyes flutter. Was she smiling? And was that a dimple in her left cheek? He thought, This is what Edith will be giving up–the chance to hold new life in her arms. But new life was leaving. And in a month, or week, would it mean anything to her? came another voice within.

"And what about you? Are you all right?" Sidonia's eyes had left her sleeping baby and were scanning his face. "You look kind of peaked–as my mother used to say." There was a rustling as Quigley refolded the map. "That's what I've been telling him. Nelson's getting too citified. Up north–the pioneer life–that's what you need, Leo."

"I'm all right," he said, and thought, I'm all wrong. Date set or not—he felt like a prisoner waiting for his execution. Outside the birds were singing, but he was aware of their music only as background to the non-stop chatter in his head. Edith said something about a bottle of whiskey—did she stash it somewhere? I'd better get another bottle, just in case. Perhaps it would be better to mix the pills with some other drink. There was so much to find out and so little time. Most important: once started, nothing must go wrong. It would be monstrous if the pills left her worse. They must do the job. And he thought, *When it is done, then 'tis done...* "I can't come to the Yukon with you," Leo said, watching hope fly out the window, "since I'll be here with Edith."

"It's a big responsibility." Sidonia was smiling at the baby, who was coming out of sleep. Opening her eyes, seeing her mother, the baby smiled back.

"It sets our minds at ease to know you're the one who'll be caring for Edith," Quigley said.

"You're a good man, Leo. Quigley and I want you to know we feel real lucky to know you." Sidonia reached the baby's hand out to touch Leo's arm. "Sunshine thinks so too."

Outside, the birds were scattering. Then they flew off, taking their music with them. In the quiet room, Leo could hear his mother singing a favorite song–*I'll bear thee off, my dearest, off on the wings of my song...* It was how the Just Men survived, she told him, flying high above their suffering on the wings of their songs. How fanciful my mother was, Leo thought. Surely, it was not the wings of their songs that sustained them in their suffering but their homage to God–their obedience to His Laws and Commandments, so that at all times they knew for Whom they suffered and why.

Quigley and Sidonia were looking at him, puzzled. "Are you sure you're okay?" Sidonia said. "We don't want you getting sick."

"I'm not a good man."

"You're just modest, Leo."

He put his hands on his knees to hide his trembling. God was gone. The Voice that had followed him around was silent. At last he understood: all I have is myself. A feeling of awe and terror came over him. He pressed still harder on his knees and finally, they stopped shaking. I am not a Just Man—I am just a man, he thought.

Even now he was smiling as he lied. "Edith will have whatever she wants." Not needs. How cunningly he had put it—with just enough truth to make the statement valid. For didn't Edith want Death? Had she not so clearly, so urgently, made her case for easeful Death? And was he not, in charity, in compassion, honoring her wish? He heard her voice: 'Promise me!'

How good and trusting these two people are. Here was still another chance to do the right thing—to tell them the truth. They had always met difficulty with spunk and optimism. "You're a good friend to Edith," Quigley said. In the way that certain words trigger others, Leo heard in that moment, "We're friends to the end," and saw Edith's joyless weary face.

"Well, we've got a million things to do." Sidonia was getting up slowly, carefully gathering the baby to her as she rose from the chair. Quigley got up too. "Someone like you," he told Leo, "it makes me believe there's good in this crazy world."

* * *

In the liquor shop, Leo walked up to the clerk mumbling, *"Oh, what a tangled web we weave, when first we practice to deceive."*

"Excuse me, I didn't hear you." No matter, Leo thought; is it so obvious this state I'm in? Has my torment become a living thing? "Every time a shipment comes in, everything goes up. Look at this." The clerk held up a sheet with prices ticked off. "French Rabbit—fourteen dollars two months ago and now it's seventeen. What can I get you?"

"A good whiskey." What exactly would work best with the pills? "Something smooth," he finally managed.

The clerk went to a shelf, pulled off a bottle. "Nothing like Canadian—smooth's the word if you take it straight, but you can mix it with anything you like. A liter do you?"

"Fine. I'll just put it in my pack."

"Having a little celebration, are you? Well, enjoy life while you can. You're dead a long time. That's what I always say."

When he left the store, Leo sat in the car, trying to keep his mind clear. There was still so much to do and so little time. It was the details. It seemed that each step taken gave birth to something else that must be done.

He stopped at Save On Foods and got a big jar of applesauce. The internet printouts said applesauce was good for mixing medications when the patient couldn't swallow a pill. He wanted to be certain, to cover all possibilities. He bought some muffins—for Edith. His eyes filled with tears as he thought these could be the last muffins she would eat.

There was a weariness about Edith's face. Since their fateful talk, she had declined. Perhaps she had forgotten, he hoped. But whatever else had deteriorated—and much had—somewhere within, her engagement with Death stayed strong.

"Soon," she said, when they were in the house.

He nodded.

"And you'll be with me to the end."

He nodded again.

"I'm happy," she said.

27

Quigley, Sidonia and their baby were to leave for the Yukon at the end of August. The magnitude of this move from a small mountain town to a fabled land up north stirred and quickened their imagination. The stories of the Klondike Gold Rush–the thousands of prospectors risking their lives to get to the icy isolated territory– began to take on new meaning. They were going to be pioneers. Not, of course, as those early settlers of Whitehorse had been, but still, life would be harsher, more demanding. "A challenge," said Sidonia. Quigley agreed. "Sunshine will grow up strong and self-reliant," he said. Sometimes, it seemed to both, whose lives had been so difficult, that God was guiding them to this new beginning. And in a burst of gratitude, and for the baby, they joined the New Baptist Church.

They were going over some documents that Sidonia had discovered in the back of a desk in the computer room. "Look at these," she said. He took the paper she handed him. "It's a Living Will," he said, surprised, "dated September 5, 2006. It's signed: Edith Martin. She must have made it around the time when we came to live here, before she got this Alzheimer's." He lifted a troubled face to Sidonia. "Now what the heck did she do that for?"

She frowned. "Give it to me." She read: "*I do not want any life-support machines or feeding tubes if I'm in a terminal state.* Now why would she write something like that? Well, some people don't want to be hooked up to life-support systems. I guess they feel like it's fate—you die when you die."

"Edith always was a secret kind of person." He stopped, uncomfortable; he was talking about Edith as though she was dead. "Anyway, Edith's not in a terminal state, so what do we do with this?"

"Give it to Leo, I guess. We'll be leaving soon and he's going to be taking care of her. Quiggy, do you think God knows about all those machines–respirators and ventilators and all that?"

"God knows about everything. He's got the whole world in His hands, remember? Look, let's put it back in the drawer and we'll tell Leo it's there. Sunshine's up. Sorry, but I can't feed her."

Sidonia gave him a gentle poke as she left. "Real funny, you are."

* * *

Sidonia opened the front door. "Betty, Harry!" she exclaimed to the couple standing on the threshold. "I thought you were in Blewett, escaping the heat. Come in." Sidonia was really pleased to see them. Not that they had known each other a long time, but since meeting at the church, they had become rather close.

"We had to come to town, get a few things," Betty said. "So we thought, why not drop in at Sid and Quigley's. Harry, show them the cute rattle we got for Sunshine."

When they were in the house, Sidonia said, "I'll just go get Quigley; he's discussing something with Leo. There's so much to work out and they have to do it when Edith's resting." She was back in a few minutes. "Help yourselves to the cookies. I'll get some cold drinks." She left the living room, went into the kitchen.

Betty and Harry looked at each other from their armchairs. There were boxes all around. "The church should really be having some kind of going-away celebration," Betty said. Harry took a cookie. "They don't want anything big. Besides, they only joined a couple of months ago. Let's have them over–just the four of us–they'd like that—and they could bring Sunshine," Harry said.

"Great idea. They could even sleep over. We've got the guest room all set up and Bobby will be crazy to see the baby."

Sidonia and Quigley came into the room. She set a tray of drinks on the coffee table. He held out a computer printout of a van, emblazoned on its side with electric letters: EXPRESS DELIVERY. "This is how it's going to look," he said. "I just love those ice daggers dripping down," said Betty. "Awesome!" "We have a great idea," Harry said. "Why don't you and Sidonia come to Blewett for a sleepover. Don't laugh. Why not? With Sunshine, of course. We'll have dinner and sit around and you can see what we're doing with the garden. It'll be good for you–all the hurrying around and getting ready for the move."

"Thanks, but I don't know, we still have a lot to do. What do you think?" Sidonia turned to Quigley. He meant to say they couldn't but he found himself saying, "Let's, Sid, it'll be fun." And to Betty and Harry, "Thanks, you've been real friends to us. And just think, only a couple of months ago we didn't even know each other."

"The church does that, you know." Betty tucked her blouse more securely into her skirt. Thin and energetic, she got up and did a few twirls. "I feel real good. You know, like I'm truly spreading God's love. In my own little way, of course. I've gone on every one of those 'Walk For Life' marches. Harry couldn't, of course, what with needing to be at the store. All those banners. And you should have seen the young people. I know you've got your hands full but I sure would've loved to have you walking with me. How is the old lady? My mom says she knew her mom when they were riding horses to school in Blewett."

Sidonia felt uncomfortable. Betty's zeal for making others believe as she did troubled her. Still, she'd been a wonderful friend. Better not to discuss certain subjects. "Edith's got Alzheimer's, you know."

"We think it's truly Christian, the way you've been caring for her," said Harry.

"It's Leo who should get the credit." Quigley's voice, usually even, rose in admiration, "The man's practically a saint. He's just plain good. He doesn't even have to try to be; he just is. The way he takes care of Edith, you'd think she was his own kin."

"Why not have him join the church?" said Betty.

"He doesn't go to any church," Sidonia told her. There was a small tentative cry. "That's Sunshine, up from her nap. Gotta go."

As though this were a prompt, Harry looked at his watch. "We should get going. I've got to pick up a package at Greyhound. Listen, it's a date then. August tenth, and you're staying over. Plenty of room. Our send-off. By the way, how's this for a catchy slogan for your business: Yu kon count on Express Delivery." His wife shook her curly head. "Harry and his corny jokes," she laughed.

* * *

In all his life Leo had never felt lonelier, and yet, he had never been busier. It was the very nature of this busyness–the constant mental energy needed to maintain his usual calm demeanor, to be the Leo that Sidonia and Quigley knew–that created his terrible soul-searing loneliness. If only he were able to talk to someone. If only he could be free from this quicksand of deceit.

But who? Surely not Sidonia and Quigley, these two good people who were so soon going on their great adventure. Surely not Dr. Helperin who would...Leo had no idea what he might think or do. Many months of medical school had taught him that doctors were trained to keep life going at any cost, surely not to even suggest any other option. He could not confide in Jake either. As for talking to Edith...her sudden relapse, the accelerated progression of the Alzheimer's presented a new and horrifying reality: he would not merely be holding her hand as she took the fatal drink—he would have to help her drink it.

Helping Sidonia and Quigley pack, searching for the gear and clothing they would need for the Yukon, Leo had to remind himself to keep silent, to not, by some accidental weakness, divulge what fully occupied his head and heart. They must not know what was going to happen at midnight on the night of August tenth. If they found out, they would call upon God to forgive them both; they would ask gentle Jesus to take their hands, his and Edith's. They would talk about God's Will and Jesus on the cross.

* * *

Leo ducked as a diaper came flying across the room. He felt thankful it was only urine—it could have been worse. Edith sat on the bed glaring at the white soggy cloth, which now hung on the light fixture dripping urine. "No," she commanded. "Go away." The acrid odor in the room grew stronger. Suspiciously, as though this were something separate, detached from the rest of her, she regarded her right arm, which lay heavily beside her, the wrist encased in plaster.

Leo retrieved the diaper, put it into the pail. "It's all right," he told her. How many times had he said those words. But they served, for he said them soothingly, trying not to sound as though he were talking to a small child. He wished still another time that he might enter her diminishing world.

Gently, carefully, Leo rearranged her on the bed to clean her.

At first, she had cried, tears rolling down her face soundlessly. But now, she lay quiet. "Wh–?" she mouthed. Was she asking why, was she asking what? He could only guess. She seemed to be in some bardo of the disease's journey through her. Whatever rage had given her working arm–if it could be called that–the power to throw the diaper, had distilled into helpless acceptance. He supposed a prisoner must feel this way after a time: certain things will be done to me and it's not worth the struggle to object.

He put a fresh gown over her head. That she trusted him, had come to see him as kindness made the care-giving possible, endowed her endless needs with a kind of grace, evoking from him a reservoir of patience he did not know he possessed.

He helped her under the coverlet. She had to lie on her back because of the fractured wrist whose cast staked her to one position. He sat down at the window, where he could have a good view of the bed but still enjoy the lovely day. She would probably fall asleep. Usually, dramatic episodes of frustration exhausted her.

The window was open. Robins and cardinals were clustering around the feeders. The usual assembly of sparrows were chattering on the lawn. Leo looked toward the bed. Edith was still awake— rather, she seemed in that state between sleep and wakefulness. Her breathing was somewhat labored but steady. Her good hand scratched at her thigh. So much of her skin was paper-thin, brittle, covered with bruises, cuts and various abrasions, bumps and moles, which had to be carefully checked.

He left the window and went over to the bed. There was a rising and falling where the coverlet lay on her feet, as though some insect were burrowing within. He would have to find another anti-fungal. This one didn't seem to be doing much good.

He sat down on the chair, head bowed, elbows on his lap, and cupped his head in his hands. Like the downward plunge of a roller coaster, the disease had worsened in the past week. "Still, her heart is fairly strong," Dr. Helperin had said. Can I talk to him? Leo wondered again. There was something about the man—perhaps because he, too, was in his seventies—that projected something more than medical knowledge. Still, one couldn't be sure. What if I was to tell him what Edith wants? It was too risky.

He had things to do. But he couldn't move from the chair. He felt himself drowning in her suffering—her pride and dignity violated, her body falling away, as the disease munched lazily at her defenseless brain.

A noise from the bed. He took it to be a sigh but then, it seemed something else–a noise he hadn't heard before, an offspring of the disease. He sat in the chair in the darkening room. Dante's lines came into his ears: *I did not die, but nothing of life remained.* For a few minutes he allowed himself to get lost in that other purgatory, then reality confronted him. The broken wrist put a stamp on what he already knew. He found himself repeating what he did not want to—I will have to do it—knowing, but unable to voice even in thought that which he had to do. Jake had come back from Mexico with some Pentobarbital. He was going to have coffee with him in a couple of days.

PART FIVE

28

"We'll be at Betty and Harry's place in Blewett," Sidonia said, shifting the bundled-up baby to her other arm. "Their phone number is in the address book on top of the directories. There's some chocolate gelato in the freezer." She turned to go. "Oh, Beau is going to phone from Whitehorse. Just tell him we've decided 'Sunshine's Express' will be great for the second vehicle. Some icy stuff around the block letters. A feeling of the Yukon."

Quigley was pulling at her arm. "For the love of Pete, Sid, you've told Leo all that." Leo said quickly, "You have a good time and don't worry, I'll give Beau the info."

Quigley had one foot out the door, "There they are, coming up the drive. Let's go, Sid."

Leo stood at the door and waved. He waited until the SUV rounded the drive and disappeared down the road. Then he closed the door.

The grandfather clock in the hall chimed eight times and each tolled Leo back to himself. At his right was a long mirror. He didn't want to look into it. Would it show the Leo Sidonia and Quigley knew—clear-eyed, face weathered but firmly-textured, head erect—a strong lean sixty-nine year old man—the Leo you could count on for reliability and truth? Or would it show the Leo who lurked beneath—a face marked with pinpoints of concealment, lines etched by a secret, a body shaken by the nature of that secret?

In four hours he would release Edith from her suffering. Midnight. The time between now and midnight seemed a vast and perilous ocean, full of unforeseen currents and storms, that he must cross alone, carrying the secret to an infinitely distant shore. In one corner of his closet shelf was the Pentobarbital along with an anti-emetic, the bottle of whiskey, the plastic bag—waiting. If they were not there, he might say it had all been a dream, a fantastic plot in some book he had read. But he could not will them away—the apparatus for death existed.

No one must know. He must at all costs answer the phone in his usual calm and friendly manner. His voice must not waver. He must not give himself away. He owed that to Edith—to his promise to her.

He went into the living room. Edith was seated in her wheelchair, looking out the window. "Sidonia and Quigley won't be back until tomorrow," he said, coming up to her. At the sound of his voice, she turned her head from the window to him. Does she see me? he wondered. What does she see? "Do you know what day this is, Edith?" he had to ask, hoping for one of her greatly decreased moments of understanding.

Her bland eyes wandered trying to put him in focus. A corner of her mouth twitched faintly. Was this an attempt to smile? Another tic? At the last meeting of the Alzheimer's support group, caregivers had discussed the frustrations they experienced at this stage of their loved ones —somewhere after the midpoint of the disease, when forgetting–a name, a book, an event–changed to not remembering forgetting. "You have to guess at so much," one of the caregivers had said.

Edith turned back to the window. Was she seeing the delicately muted shades of falling night? Undefined space? Nothing at all? Glaucoma and macular degeneration had joined forces with the Alzheimer's. "She can go on like this for a long time," Dr. Helperin had said. "One never knows."

Time knows, Leo thought. Time sets its own agenda and waits for no one. Time had caught up with Edith and now she was incapable of taking the Pentobarbital herself. She could swallow. She could still do that. She could drink and eat. But for how much longer?

He touched her arm, gently. "It's August tenth," he said. "The tenth of August." Her head had drooped again. He bent to look at her. How could he access some part of her that would tell him whether she wanted to go on like this or not? Leo remembered his time in medical school. Vascular dementia, senile dementia, it had been called in those days. Would he have learned more if he had not left medical school?

He put his hand around hers. Her forefinger closed around his, as a baby grabs hold of a finger. The phone rang.

He made sure the safety belt was in place and went to answer the phone. He prepared himself for the role he must play.

"Leo here."

"How you doing, Leo?"

"Fine. And you?"

"Couldn't be better. I won't keep you; I know you're alone there with the old lady. How is she?" Leo murmured she was doing as well as expected, which seemed to cover everything. "Sidonia and Quigley said to tell you they'd like 'Sunshine's Express' on their vehicle. Maybe a snow and ice design–nothing complicated–around it."

"Okay, but I've gotten real friendly with an Inuit family here. There's this carving of a mother seal and her baby I bought from them that I've been using for my Express Delivery van. Well, I'll get to them by email. Take care, Leo."

When he hung up, Leo considered the question of food. He had no appetite but Edith must have something. Something light–tea and crackers. The stomach should not be entirely empty nor should it be full; how many times had he gone over what had to be done.

"We'll get you something to eat," he said. Her eyes were on him, hesitant, the eyes of a frightened child. She squirmed and Leo realized he would have to change her diapers again. She lay on the bed, allowed him to wash her, to put fresh diapers on, without making a sound. He had to hold his nose; he could never get used to it–the debris the body threw off. But all the while his heart felt for her–for indignities the disease had inflicted, the theft of modesty. When he put a fresh gown over her, it took all his attention to maneuver the gown without disturbing her encased arm. She made a sound he couldn't understand. Her thumb brushed his.

Was she in a world of her own or drifting in a wide Sargasso Sea? Or—was there nothing at all? There was no way to know. A half-million mice had been injected with a human gene to render them fitting for research on Alzheimer's, and still, Leo thought, there are questions that have no answer. "Poor Edith," Fern Helperin had said to him. "Life pulled her along and she followed in its footsteps." Private–hard to know—and now, thought Leo, we will never know who she really was. Or wasn't.

Just as they entered the kitchen, the grandfather clock began to chime. Edith seemed to be hearing some kind of noise, for she looked up from her wheelchair. At the ninth chime, her head sank again. Three hours till midnight. How would he get through those hours? Leo wondered.

He set the brake of the wheelchair and made sure she was comfortable. He put some crackers in a bowl, crumbled one, put a bit in her mouth. Her mouth closed but did not move, as though she didn't know what to do. He put his finger to her lips gently and now they began to move slowly. He waited. After a few seconds, she swallowed. "You can still swallow," he told her, and he waited for the twitch at the corner of her mouth, which he had come to see as an attempt at a smile. But it didn't come. He managed to feed her two crackers and a small cup of tea. It took a long time.

The phone rang. He went to the counter, grateful for all the extensions. It was a neighbor down the road, a good-hearted woman whose husband had recently died. "I saw Sidonia and Quigley leaving," she said, "and I wondered if you needed someone to sit with Edith—what with the Alzheimer group meeting tonight."

He told himself to remain calm, to act naturally. "I'm not going to the meeting," he managed, "but thank you anyway." He wondered what he would say if she pursued her offer—she must be lonely. He held his breath. Would she offer to bring over a pie she had baked? But she only said, "I just wanted you to know."

He helped Edith into the big easy chair in the living room. Sunken back she could be comfortable—if comfortable was the word—but still secure from falling. She looked at him as though to say, Is this where I'm supposed to be? Like a child. But this was no child. This was an eighty-one year old woman, grey-faced, head drooped, diapered, the Edith Martin that Alzheimer's had created, who was going backward in time to infancy. But are you suffering, Edith?

Edith lay deep in the armchair, eyes adrift. He had arranged the encased arm on her lap and the other, as though to keep it company, beside it. Seeing her so, Leo felt stirred by poignant memories of their friendship. Outside the dark windows, rain fell softly on rustling oaks and aspens. As darkness deepened into night, the round moon leaned down over the sleeping town. Inside the living room, the air was still and quivering. Leo fell into a trance. He began to talk, as he had never talked. Words poured from his heart. "Edith, remember those days when you told me about your

Expeditions? You climbed the staircase–Duck was with you. How hard it must have been. You thought you couldn't get all the way up, but you did. And the other Expedition, when you drove to town in the pouring rain? And your keys locked inside when you parked your car. How your hands must have trembled, how frightened you must have been. I've been frightened too." Deep within the trance, he began to chant:

> *Darkling I listen; and for many a time*
> *I have been half in love with easeful Death,*
> *Called him soft names in many a mused rhyme,*
> *To take into the air my quiet breath;*
> *Now more than ever seems it rich to die,*
> *To cease upon the midnight with no pain…*

Leo stopped. "Oh, Edith, I look at you–your slumped body and blank eyes—and I see, behind this exterior, a hidden Edith. And wasn't I hiding too—a handyman on the outside, a poetry lover within?" And he heard the voice of his father: "Poetry is for women–a diversion from children and home."

"We were sorcerers," Leo said, "creating an island all to ourselves. You're not the same Edith now, I know, but that other Edith–she's got to be there–some place where the plaques and tangles can't reach. Oh, Edith, release me from my promise. I'm begging you." Leo's voice was low, low and distraught. The only other sound in the room was Edith's steady breathing as she slept, her encased arm outside the cover.

"You would say to me," he went on, "in those early days, 'Choose for me, Leo.' It would be some fixture needing replacement, the kind of thing you knew nothing about. So I chose. But you are not a fixture." Leo's voice broke. He began to sob. "I don't want to take your life. You say it is not a life but while you breathe it is. Oh, Edith, I know you want easeful Death but I can't do it." Tormented, he repeated, "I can't, I can't." Suddenly, the sound of his voice pulled him out of his trance. She would have to sip the whiskey first. He would have to mix the Pentobarbital with applesauce and feed it to her slowly. And then, if need be, the plastic bag. But even as he shuddered, he knew the apparatus of death waited on the shelf in his closet.

The rain intensified to a downpour. The sheets, like rods, knocked against the window.

The grandfather clock tolled ten. There was nothing more to do but wait. Silence between him and Edith had been serene in their relationship; no words were necessary to affirm their friendship. Now, silence was heavy with dread.

The phone jangled. Leo let it ring three times. Then he picked up the receiver. "Leo here," he said, as calmly as he could. No one answered; in the background, he thought he heard computers running, foreign voices. He replaced the receiver. Another outsourced telemarketer gone amuck.

He tried to read; the words meant nothing. He put on a CD; the music only increased his wracking uncertainty. The shelf in his closet, the deadly contents, kept drifting before his eyes.

He moved a chair close to her bed. How she slept. How evenly her breathing came, as though her heart and lungs had been set to go on forever. And looking at her, "I can't," he told her. He touched her cheek. Her eyelids fluttered. Tears overflowed his eyes, rolled down his cheeks, fell on her face. Beneath the dim wall sconce, her wet gray face took on a crystalline light.

He got off the bed and sank into the easy chair. He felt wiped out, as though he were navigating treacherous currents in a boat meant for smooth waters. He could not keep his eyes from closing and he slept. He dreamed he was watching a parade. Thousands of mice marched, amidst banners held high: HONOUR THOSE WHO DIED SO YOU CAN LIVE. There were many contingents. The placard that read: BETA-AMYLOID, was followed by mice with four ears and moody eyes. He wanted to talk to one of them, to ask how it felt to have a human gene implanted, but these were only later generations; the first had died in the service of humanity.

The grandfather clock chimed eleven times but Leo, deep in his dream, watched a parade that seemed endless. The mice were followed by thousands of monkeys. After them came rats, guinea pigs and finally, strange-looking creatures he couldn't recognize. Music played: a requiem. Demonstrators–a motley assortment of crippled and maimed animals–jeered and shouted. Helmeted mice kept them in check. Leo wanted to leave but the scene was too dense. He couldn't get through.

The last chime of twelve was tolling as he opened his eyes. How could he have slept right through to midnight?

Leo rose stiffly, intensely aware of a peculiar stillness. He went over to the bed. Edith lay motionless, eyes staring emptily at the ceiling. He knew at once she was dead. He had seen death many times and this was death. She had heard him and her soul had answered. There is no such thing as a soul, he told himself, but how else could he explain this sudden death when the disease had been going on so slowly? Gratitude overwhelmed him. She had rescued him from committing an unpardonable act. She had given him a gift. He spoke to the utterly still body. "Thank you, Edith."

Now, he could only think to take all the implements of, yes, murder, and do away with them as though they never existed. He moved quickly, poured the whiskey down the sink, flushed the Pentobarbital and anti-emetic down the toilet, put the plastic bag in the garbage. But he was not satisfied. A stink still clung to him—the stench of what he had almost done. He needed fresh air to wash over him, cleanse him. He ran out of the house and into the garden.

The fog beckoned him, as though, behind its swirling mist, it too held a fearful secret. He glanced all around; behind a tree, a bush, a rooftop, someone might be watching. The leaves of the aspens trembled–or perhaps it was his heart–as his feet slipped through the damp earth. He leaned against a tree out of breath. He had to get back. He must call Dr. Helperin. Overwhelmed by sadness, he was unable to move.

It was the rain that set him in motion. He ran back to the house in the clearing fog. The room and Edith seemed different. It took a few moments for Leo to realize the difference was in himself. If the rain had washed away the fog outside, it had as well cleared the mists within him. It seemed to Leo that he had been in some virtual reality. Now he had come back to himself. He did what he should have done before—took her pulse, put his ear to her chest and examined her eyes. There were no signs of life. Edith was dead. He realized he had been outside for surely twenty minutes. It was possible she had been alive when he ran out. If he had stayed, he could have done something to keep her life going.

The clock chimed one. He phoned Dr. Helperin: "Edith died in her sleep." There seemed nothing more to say.

29

It was three days since Edith had been cremated. Sidonia and Quigley sat around the kitchen table, still in bathrobes and slippers, although it was ten in the morning. Mugs of coffee and a basket of muffins before them were untouched. Sidonia gently smoothed the fuzzy head of the baby in her lap.

"I can't believe Edith's gone," she said. "I go through the house and there are all those beaded curtains Leo put up so she would know one room from another, and plugs covered, and all the other stuff we had to do."

Quigley reached for his coffee. He sipped it slowly. "Yeah, it seemed she'd go on forever. I can't understand Leo not calling us right away when it happened."

"He said there was nothing we could do. He did the right thing–calling Dr. Helperin. It must have been awful for him, being alone with her when she died; they were friends." Sidonia looked around the kitchen. "Well, the labels are off all the cabinets, and we don't have to worry about stockings in the frig."

"Or other things," Quigley reminded her. They both made an attempt at a smile but couldn't. "I guess she liked the house more than she liked people. Strange how many came to the Service; I didn't think Edith had that many friends."

"They came because of Leo." Sidonia kissed the baby's hand reaching up for the muffin. "Look, Sunshine thinks she can eat a muffin." Then she grew serious. "You know that Betty and Harry have been tweeting that Leo's a Divine Messenger."

Quigley frowned. "I just wish Betty and Harry would get off the internet. Why can't they keep their preaching in the church where it belongs?" He growled. "Anyway, Leo's just a real good human being. You know what he did? He tweeted them back: 'Shut up!' Not a tweet, more like a crow's caw."

Sidonia dipped a finger in her coffee and put it to the baby's mouth. Sunshine sucked energetically. "Their problem is," Sidonia stated, "they can't wait for the Second Coming, the world being so messed up with all the earthquakes and tornados and tsunamis and all the killing and violence..." she stopped, out of breath. "So they want to make our Leo into a Messiah."

"Still," Quigley said, reflectively, "remember how we used to call Leo a Godsend–the way he came in when we were going nuts trying to figure out how to deal with Edith when the Alzheimer's started acting up. And it seemed he was sent to help us, we used to say that: taking over, never complaining, even when Edith was impossible–not that she could help it. He just hung in there right to the end."

"Funny, it's not as though it was a romantic kind of love. I guess Harry and Betty would say Leo *is* Love. She says all his denials are because he is truly humble, reluctant to reveal his true self."

"Well, one thing is for sure: Leo's devotion to Edith was not for money. He would've cared for her even if he didn't get the little we could pay him. No, he never did anything for the money. Being a handyman wasn't going to make him rich and Edith was too far-gone to change her will for him even if she'd wanted to. Not for money."

They sat silently. The last few words hovered in the air, flew from the cabinets, lighted on the ceiling, came down to flutter in their ears like a trio of moths. It was Sidonia who broke the stillness. "It doesn't seem right to talk about it with Edith dead less than a week, but, Quiggy, where is the rest of her money?

He shrugged. "Looks like we'll never know. We have the house. We've got a buyer. And we still have a good bit of the money Edith gave us. Who knows if there's more? What's it to us? Edith was good to us–real good." He paused. "Though not exactly a saint..."

30

Fern said to her husband, "If I were a flaky lady, I'd say it's a bit queer–Edith dying the night of August tenth."

Saul stirred his martini and grinned. "Be a flaky lady and tell me why it's so strange. After all, she could have died at any time. She was eighty-one and in a rapidly advancing stage of Alzheimer's."

"Oh, nothing." Fern sat back in the chair and took up her knitting.

"I hate it when you do that."

"Okay, I'll tell you: Because August tenth was the night James had the police out looking for her all those years ago. Remember? They'd been married ten years; I know the date because Sally turned four that day. Anyway, James came home from some business trip–or wherever he went on all those trips–and she was gone. And the day care where Tim was couldn't locate her. He had the whole police force out looking. Do you want another olive?"

"Two, please, and a couple of those little onions." Saul sipped the martini she handed him. "And then she came back all by herself," he said. "Turned out she'd gotten lost somewhere or other. She did tend to daydream."

"We never saw much of them after that. James was always away and Edith was always not available." Fern lingered on the last two words. She said them again, "Not available." She frowned. "Well, she's certainly not available now, so we'll never know, but I think there's something strange about her dying on the one night that— darn, I dropped a stitch."

Saul watched his wife pick up the stitch, quickly but carefully, the way she did most things. Cooking, she followed the recipe, measuring ingredients, adhering to times, and came up with a perfect dish. And even when the recipe was in her head, she went through the steps, wasting no energy, producing what she had meant to produce. Where had Fern gotten such certainty? he wondered. She had put her newborns to breast with a no-nonsense directness. He could imagine her licking them clean after birth.

He was not that certain about anything. And he was tired now. The last few days had been filled with even more forms than usual. Cuts affected not only social services but necessitated ever more paring down of the patient's time with him. He had to be vigilant in his documentation of each appointment.

He was suddenly aware that Fern was regarding him attentively. "Sorry," he said. "What were you saying? And don't tell me, nothing," for she made a dismissing motion with her hand.

She put down her knitting. They had never had secrets from each other. Why, she wondered, is this so hard to say? Because, she silently answered herself, it's only conjecture. To voice it would give it form, make it real. "Saul," she finally said, "isn't it strange–Edith dying on the very night when Sidonia and Quigley were away and Leo is left alone with her?"

"That again! I've told you—she died naturally. Her heart gave out. It could have been pneumonia or a stroke. Alzheimer's patients usually die before the disease finally takes them. As for an autopsy, there was no reason for one. She wanted to be cremated; it's in her will and she was clear about that." Suddenly, he sat bolt upright. "Are you saying Leo had something to do with her death?"

"I'm not saying anything. You know how Leo is, though, remember when we hired him? —forever plucking lice off a field mouse or patching up a wounded bird, and the way he's been caring for Edith... Suppose he couldn't bear her suffering–losing her dignity along with everything else..."

"Fern, they were friends. Good friends. He'd never think of hurting her."

She shook her head. "It's hard to think of them as friends; he's so open and easy and Edith–"

"Look at me!" He leaned forward. He put his martini on the table so abruptly, some spilled. "Just put that crazy idea out of your head. It's only that, you know–your romantic idea–left over from college days and reading *A Tale of Two Cities*. *It's a far better thing I do...* And how could it happen, anyway? The sleeping pills I gave her were all there; she hadn't even used most of them. Forget it, Fern."

"I know, I know, everyone thinks Leo's a saint—but, really,

we know very little about him."

Saul got up and started to pace. "I said, forget it. What's come over you? You used to be his biggest booster." He turned to face her. "I'll tell you again, I examined her. Her heart gave out. There was no reason for a post-mortem. She's dead and gone and at peace."

"She's ashes."

"I think I'll turn in early."

She looked at him, puzzled. "It's not even ten."

He sat down. "What's the matter?"

"It's all the tweets I've been getting. Not only me but lots of people in town. Little bits and snippits–'God's messenger–Divine Leo–sweet man of love...' They began from that couple at the church, but now Leo's all over the Net–Facebook, emails. Saul, there's even a group that calls itself *The Second Coming*. They claim Leo Mann may be the new Messiah." She added, quickly, "Not that Leo has anything to do with all this. Half the time he doesn't answer and when he does, it's either funny or nasty. It seems they think Leo took on Edith's suffering and is being readied to take on the whole world's suffering." She heaved a huge sigh. "Where did all this nonsense come from?"

She was looking at him. Saul fought off his fatigue. "Strange that it's a fundamentalist church saying Leo is a Lamed-Vov; I would have thought it might be coming from a synagogue or some Cabalistic group."

"Lamed-Vov?"

"An ancient Hebraic Legend says that the world could not exist in times of great peril if there were not thirty-six Just Men to take on its suffering. If even one of these men did not exist, the world would not survive."

"God said he would save Sodom if Abraham could find only ten Righteous Men," Fern said. "He couldn't," she sighed. They were both silent. "It will all go away," Saul said after a few minutes. "Sidonia and Quigley will be going to the Yukon; the house is sold. Leo will have to go his own way."

"He might succumb—" said Fern, "become another false Messiah. People are so desperate these days; the internet has become the modern–what's the name of the mythical Goddess that answered every question put to her? When will people learn to look to themselves for answers? Oh Saul, don't mind me, I'm being arrogant and judgmental."

"You're being human," he said.

"Go to bed, darling," she said. "I'll just read for a bit."

Tired as he was, he couldn't sleep. Why had Leo not phoned him sooner rather than waiting some forty minutes after her death? He had not thought of this before; the time delay seemed reasonable enough–the shock, the getting to the phone... And what did it matter, after all, if he had helped her die. It was through compassion.

He began to twist and turn. The bed seemed too large. His thoughts took off. This Civilization would vanish too. It happened periodically–a civilization was born, flourished, and, for one reason or another, perished. Sometimes it was a natural disaster; other times it was a powerful enemy. This time, Saul ruminated glumly, the world would perish, not by fire or flood or violent predator, but by sheer exhaustion–the earth ravaged relentlessly, the peoples slaughtering each other fanatically until, with a whimper and a sigh, it expired.

He wanted to be enclosed, held, comforted. He thought of calling down to Fern but didn't. Fern was a night person. If he called her, she would be concerned. Suddenly the lawyer popped into his head. Against his will, he felt sorry for the man. He had been disbarred and incarcerated.

Like fruit flies around decaying apple, his thoughts came: Where was the money Seaman had embezzled? Surely, some must remain. And where the devil could Tim be out there in Africa? And could a youth just vanish?—for there seemed no way to make contact with Edith's grandson. "In a vanishing world," the air sighed back, "people vanish all the time."

He heard Fern's footsteps with gratitude. She came into the room, thought him asleep, undressed quietly and got into bed. He welcomed her familiar body, turned to her. She enclosed him. He kissed her hair, her lips, her breast. Questions melted away.

31

In an old rundown Tabernacle in Vancouver, two ancient Rabbis in frock coats and sidelocks greeted each other: "Shalom Aleichem."

The elder, Reb Levy, took a large portfolio from a tattered leather briefcase as ancient as himself. With great seriousness, he placed it on the rotting wood table. "These are the printouts." He shook his weighty head and looked down a moment.

"And all this from the blog," the other Rabbi said, shifting his thin body. From outside the sooty broken windows came the sounds of street dealers, mumbled exchanges, then silence. "But will he come, this Leo Mann?" he asked finally.

"He said it was all a mistake, that he was an ordinary man. But he said he would come–in respect."

"Listen," the thin Rabbi stood at attention, his eyes large behind their spectacles. "There are footsteps."

"Let us prepare to welcome him." There was a discreet knock on the door. "Please to enter," Reb Levy said.

Leo walked in. "Shalom Aleichem," he said.

"Please to sit down, Mr. Mann."

Leo sat down carefully on one of the rickety chairs, facing them.

Reb Levy picked up the sheaf lying on the table. "These are all printouts from the various chatrooms." He held up one sheet after another. He stroked his beard, looked at the other Rabbi who nodded back, then he cleared his throat and spoke: "These remarks, which have been flooding various spiritual chatrooms, upon careful examination, all come to one irrefutable conclusion…" With a glance at Leo, as if to prepare him for what was to follow, he went on, "…that your steadfast devotion and care for Mrs. Edith Martin— who was not linked to you by family nor ordinary attachment of man and woman, nor by promise of pecuniary reward—was given with the rare pure compassion of a Just Man." The Rabbi paused. "And that you took to yourself her suffering in order to offer it up to the Almighty."

Leo felt as he had when he was a small child, desperate to respond to something his teacher had said. He had even begun to raise his hand. He sprang to his feet. "These people are wrong!" he exclaimed, passionately. "I am not a Divine Messenger! I have not come into the world to redeem it—but have hidden from the world in order to escape it. I do not want to do anything for the world."

He sat down heavily. "This is craziness," he muttered. They were drawing a computerized picture of him. He remembered his agonizing struggle with himself on the night of Edith's death.

Reb Levy said, "It is rumored your mother named you as one of the Just."

"I was a child," Leo exclaimed, a shade too forcefully. "My mother told me tales, legends, that her parents had told her. I was sensitive, an only child. My mother's life was hard. It made her happy to think of her son as a more than ordinary little boy."

Reb Levy nodded but went on: "And so you say it is only coincidence that so many think of you today as more than an ordinary man."

"And why not?" Leo parried. "Coincidences happen all the time. And what better place than on the internet with millions browsing here and there, on this and that site, chatting here and there, in this and that chatroom. And so, why not one person happening to say to another, 'There is a certain Leo Mann who is pure goodness,' and then another taking it and magnifying it." And even as he spoke, Leo thought, God is up to His old tricks. He lost me when I began to doubt and now, when I see His work as random happenings, He has gone on the internet to get me back. There was silence as Leo considered: It was not with this innocent old Rabbi he wanted to debate—it was with God Himself. He told the Almighty: You think You've caught another doubter and You want to set me straight. And why not? Why not get on Your surfboard and surf the e-trail, a spirit guide for the world wide web. Preposterous. Vapid. Without substance or character. A tunemaker finds an offbeat that strikes the yearning note in weary surfers, and ends up with a number one hit; a cook dribbles a secret South American herb into a chicken dish and becomes renowned as a master chef.

Well, why not a Just Man? Leo asked himself. He could join

forces with God. Banish his doubts and ride the waves to messianic fame, perhaps fortune.

The innocent trusting eyes of the Rabbis were on him. "I do not believe it is possible for anyone–" Leo said, "and that includes a just man and a righteous man–to redeem this world." The bearded men were scanning his face. It was impossible to tell what they were thinking. He decided to tell his truth. "I also believe that the idea of God is a worn-out superstition, just another myth. I for one do not believe in His Existence." Surely this was blasphemy. He waited for some register of anger, scorn, something, but their faces remained what could only be called patiently attentive.

The scream of a siren pierced the air. Another poor kid OD'ed, Leo thought. He would be fixed up and sent out to OD again. Leo rose from his chair. "So you see, it is all a mistake. Perhaps one of those viruses..."

"If a Just Man knows he has been chosen and refuses to accept," the elder said, "then it is not a good thing."

When Leo came outside, he saw someone with a sandwich board walking down East Hastings: REPENT. ARMAGEDDON IS UPON US.

We all live within the fables we have invented, Leo thought. And this was part of the legend too–that suffering must be accepted– no, welcomed–and borne. That endless weeping was a given. Another fable–that the bleeding, mutilated Christ would take onto himself the sins of all mankind. He had seen the High Mass–the wafer taken into the waiting mouth, the wine. The body and blood of Christ. If he had enclosed himself in a mythical world with Edith, a paper world of great people, noble actions and thoughts, were they not legends as well? And God–the Master of all legends?

The ancient pickup was where he had left it–parked on a side street. It was intact, no tires removed, no graffiti; it had not even merited recognition. But the vehicle still ran. Driving through the night back to Nelson, Leo thought, what a fool I've been. The years went by in his head: the handyman days, doing the best job, receiving so little, the endless hours helping Sidonia and Quigley, and then, the long wracking relationship with Edith. And where had it all landed him? The house was sold. He would have to move. He would be without a home and without money.

* * *

Sidonia was feeding the baby when he came in at dawn. "There's some porridge on the stove," she said.

"I'm not hungry." Leo let it out then: "It's those friends of yours, Betty and Harry, that started this whole charade, isn't it?"

Sidonia put a tiny spoonful of pablum in the baby's mouth. "I can see you're upset. But it's not what you think—some careless Jesus freaks. Betty and Harry had this chatroom on their blog. They call it *Goodness Chats*. The idea was that you logged on just to say something good about someone. So Betty started to talk about you, Leo, and somehow she couldn't stop. And then she started to talk about Edith and her Alzheimer's. And then somehow the Goodness Chatroom—and I swear I don't know how it happened—became God's Chatroom..."

Leo had heard enough. "I'd better go up to my room and get it cleared out."

Going up the long winding staircase, Leo was aware—with a shock—that he was having trouble climbing; not exactly trouble but a slowness that had not been there before. He found himself catching his breath. Several times he stopped. He couldn't be sure, but it seemed to him his heart beat faster.

He lay down on his bed, too tired to undress or to think. He wanted only to get back to normalcy. A clear understanding between God and himself. He would leave God alone and God would return the favor. But how was it possible to maintain this relationship when God had a chatroom of His own, inviting in eager seekers in a troubled world?

He let his eyes wander about the room aimlessly. Where would he go? A cabin? The word had changed; without the bounce and carefree embellishments of youth and vigor, it became as bare and cold as what it described.

"You've got to do something about it." He sprang off the bed and looked around the room. There was only himself. He admonished himself not to be spooked. He had simply spoken aloud. It was not his habit to do so but now he had. The Rabbis had gotten to him. He resolved to be sensible, and sensible meant that revelations were merely emotional states gone haywire, not too different from the apparitions brought on by hysterical excesses. He composed himself; he had been trembling. He must be sensible. Voices, strange coincidences–miracles–these desperate fancies were for the uninformed. Surely, his mother, an immigrant to an unknown country and culture had sought refuge in her Legends of Just Men and a powerful God.

"But what are you going to do?" This time Leo looked about more carefully. He listened at the door. He went to the window. There was no one about. He remembered his mother telling him of certain Jews, poor and unseen, charged, by accident, with the fearsome burden of a Just Man. "God had chosen them," she had said, and he thought, as the Old Testament God chose the people of His Book to be in His Image of perfection, for which they have been persecuted for centuries. And wanted him—and here Leo scowled in frustration—to be some kind of Savior.

"Well, what are you going to do?" This voice didn't sound like that other voice. Edith had heard voices at one stage of the Alzheimer's. Leo remembered sitting with her as she called him by one name, then another. Perhaps he had caught the disease–not by a cough or a sneeze but by sheer exposure to a disintegrating mind.

His eyes roved the room again. There wasn't much to see–the old trunk, the table and chairs, the narrow bed, the dormer. Then his eyes fell upon the sewing machine. It had been there for a long time; there was always something else that needed doing. He went over to the machine. He looked at it. It evoked images of Edith in her youth, sewing a dress. He would have to repair it…if indeed it needed repairing. Then he remembered the jammed compartment in the base. For accessories. Perhaps a manual? He gave it a tug then a wrench. Nothing. Finally, he wrenched it violently. It sprang open. But no manual inside. Only an envelope. A large thick manila envelope. He undid the clasp and, with his penknife, carefully cut the tape sealing it. He peered into the envelope. It was filled with bundles of hundred-dollar bills. Stunned, he had to sit down. Then he spread them out on the table and counted. A hundred thousand dollars. And a small envelope. A letter, hand-written, lay within.

Dear Leo, he read, *I'm doing this now while I can. I have given Sidonia and Quigley my money and my gratitude for all they have done for me.*

This is for you. I seem to have had a habit of hiding money. I hope you will be content and that God will bless you, as He has blessed me to have so good and true a friend.

Edith.

Leo went down the stairs more quickly; his tiredness had vanished. Quigley was up and having breakfast with Sidonia. Sunshine was in her highchair. "It's kind of hard to say goodbye," Sidonia said. "We don't know how to thank you." She brushed some crumbs from Sunshine's face.

Leo started walking toward the door, a duffel bag in tow. "You have a great new life, you and your baby. 'Sunshine's Express'– I think that's a great name for your business." They were walking him to the door. "You got everything you need in that duffel bag of yours?" Quigley asked. Leo smiled, "Sure do," and waved to Sunshine.

"Well, Edith's off to a new life if you want to think of things that way," Quigley said, "and Sid and I are off to a new life, although it's really a new place. After all, we're just taking the Express Delivery up north. Funny, isn't it? When I was a kid, I used to play a game with myself–suppose I was God and could do anything at all, what would I do? Of course, all the things I wanted to do were for myself. Just think, Leo, all those people looking to you for help."

They hugged each other. Sidonia seemed about to cry. "We're going to miss you, Leo."

Leo carefully put the duffel bag on the seat of his pickup. He felt moved by Quigley's speech. Quigley was not given to talking about himself. Leo felt affection for the two of them. He had taken them rather for granted–good people, decent, uncomplicated.

He waved to them. He blew a kiss to Sunshine. "God bless you," they called.

But as he turned on the ignition and engaged the clutch, Leo smiled. As a child he had been a good player in the game of hide-and-seek, adept at secreting himself in obscure doorways, a twist of alley, a recessed hallway. He stepped on the accelerator. His smile deepened. God would have a hard time finding him.

Leo, wide awake, leaned on his pillow and watched the pure rays of sunrise. There was no need to hurry. Everything was peaceful and quiet. He was far removed from the world outside. He would not say where exactly he was—even to himself. The last leaves were falling. Winter was coming. He thought, long winter nights, and again, no need to hurry. Edith had made possible this serenity.

The morning was bright when he finally rose from the cot, changed his pants and T-shirt for loose slacks and a sweatshirt. He put the kettle on the hearth, assessed the bundle of firewood. More wood would be needed. He had only to split the logs that waited outside. He poured from the blackened kettle into his earthenware mug, put rice in the steamer.

He went outside. The air was brisk, clean, fresh. Next to his cabin, a tall cedar spread its green fingers. On the horizon, a flock of birds flew south in V-formation. He examined the patch that had been his garden. He had stored under the cabin onions, potatoes, carrots. He went down to the stream, took the pure clear water into his pot and went inside for breakfast.

Later Leo took down the earthen jar from the windowsill. He sat at the window, remembering her words: "In the time between autumn and winter–scatter my ashes." Finally, he took the jar outside and went up the bumpy narrow mountain path. He passed pines, elms, oaks, cedars. Before a mountain ash, he halted. The red-yellow berries danced in the slight breeze. He watched the last of her ashes disappear into a rivulet that ran amidst some bushes. Then Edith was gone.

He sat on a large flat rock, watching the day wind down–the colors mutate, become dimmer, fall into shadows.

It was near dusk when he went back to his cabin. He took a few vegetables from the storage bin, put them back. He had no appetite. He went inside. The windowsill was bare, the jar empty.

Leo sat in the dark, beside the empty jar. His thoughts drifted. "In the old country I had a garden," his mother had told him, when he was young. "Only a patch. Some potatoes, cabbage…" He'd asked if the garden made her happy. "Another thing to worry about—storms, sly animals in the night, hungry insects." She was silent. The lines in her face deepened. "You weep what you sow," she finally said. He had corrected her: "You reap what you sow," but she had shaken her head. Leo shifted in the chair. At the time, he had thought he was correcting a word but now, remembering a certain look on her face, he realized she was talking about her life.

Darkness was turning to night. The wind crept through the windows and sighed. Rain began to fall, drearily at first, then pounding the roof. Edith had died on a night like this. He didn't want to think about that night but there was no stopping the questions. Had she been truly dead when he ran from the room? What if he had stayed at her bedside?

He wanted those minutes back—those fateful minutes he'd spent outside. He should have stayed there with her. He needed to tell her. "Forgive me, Edith," he started to mumble, "I should have waited. I should not have left you and run out. Perhaps you were not—" Leo hesitated, "gone—perhaps those fifteen minutes of life still existed." He was talking low and earnestly as he had so many times in his childhood to an imaginary friend.

And then, like that friend, Edith was sitting there beside him. "Fifteen minutes, an hour, a day, weeks—what does it matter—I wanted to go, but you wouldn't let me." Her voice was low and petulant.

"I wanted you to stay," he told her.

"I couldn't stay, not even for you."

I must be going mad—hearing voices, Leo thought, glancing at the urn emptied of Edith's ashes, but turning back, seeing Edith there, he felt reassured. "Edith—" he couldn't help himself — "I'm so lonely. Edith, please stay."

"Let me go, Leo. I'm begging you."

There were miracles, he knew. Why not a miracle, if you wanted something that much. He thought of Edith going to church and the promise of resurrection. He looked at her more closely. She might have been sculpted from some soft and vaporous substance, so filled with pleading were her melting eyes. "*Your* God can bring you back," he said.

"Let me go, Leo." Now, her words were a prayer, beseeching.

He must keep her there. "Do you want something to drink? I'll get a blanket, Edith; it's gotten chilly. How about some rice, it's nice and soft—I'll help you eat it. And a pillow for your head."

He heard the tenuous dreary timbre of her voice. "Please. Please." Her cries echoed in the stillness of the deep night, and every cry smote his heart.

He reached out to comfort her but his fingers closed on air.

ABOUT THE AUTHOR

Esther Popkin-Clurman has been writing all her life. She has also taught French and Spanish literature at university. She has written four novels, a memoir and a book of verse. Eighty-nine years of opportunities missed, sign-posts ignored, and, most of all, the unanticipated and painful challenges of old age have gone into the creation of *Express Delivery*.

www.ingramcontent.com/pod-product-compliance
Lightning Source LLC
Chambersburg PA
CBHW051644260626
47170CB00004B/1319